PRAISE FOR *The Layover*

"The perfect escape—a hilarious, compulsive, swoony rom-com from an exciting new voice. Waldon's witty banter and laugh out loud fresh take on enemies-to-lovers are sure to satisfy readers and keep them smiling to the very last page."

—Robin Reul, author of *Where the Road Leads Us*

"A breath of fresh air! Lacie Waldon's exceptional debut combines sharp, clever writing with crackling sexual tension for pure enemies-to-lovers gold. *The Layover* is the ultimate summer beach read and a new favorite."

—Devon Daniels, author of *Meet You in the Middle*

"A highly recommended read for fans of enemies-to-lovers and anyone who feels the pull of wanderlust."

—Sarah Hogle, author of *You Deserve Each Other* and *Twice Shy*

"*The Layover* is an ideal escape—from the intriguing insider's view of air travel to the picturesque setting on the shores of Belize. . . . A fun and irresistible romance that soars."

—Libby Hubscher, author of *Meet Me in Paradise*

"Once I started *The Layover*, I couldn't put it down! This is a lovely escape full of sun, swoons, and sexual tension."

—Kerry Winfrey, author of *Waiting for Tom Hanks*

"A jet fuel-powered rom-com that had me dreaming of sun-soaked beaches and a view from 35,000 feet.

—Angie Hockman, author of *Shipped*

The Layover

Lacie Waldon

G. P. Putnam's Sons
New York

PUTNAM
— EST. 1838 —
G. P. PUTNAM'S SONS
Publishers Since 1838
An imprint of Penguin Random House LLC
penguinrandomhouse.com

Library of Congress Cataloging-in-Publication Data

Names: Waldon, Lacie, author.
Title: The layover / Lacie Waldon.
Description: New York: G. P. Putnam's Sons, [2021] |
Summary: "An unexpected tropical layover with her nemesis turns a flight attendant's life upside down in this witty, breezy debut romantic comedy about life—and love—30,000 feet above the ground" —Provided by publisher.
Identifiers: LCCN 2021012463 (print) | LCCN 2021012464 (ebook) |
ISBN 9780593328255 (trade paperback) | ISBN 9780593328262 (ebook)
Subjects: GSAFD: Love stories.
Classification: LCC PS3623.A35688 L39 2021 (print) |
LCC PS3623.A35688 (ebook) | DDC 813/.6—dc23
LC record available at https://lccn.loc.gov/2021012463
LC ebook record available at https://lccn.loc.gov/2021012464

Printed in the United States of America
1st Printing

Book design by Ashley Tucker

This is a work of fiction. Names, characters, places, and incidents either are the product of the author's imagination or are used fictitiously, and any resemblance to actual persons, living or dead, businesses, companies, events, or locales is entirely coincidental.

For Carey Page, who taught me that everything is an adventure when you're with the right person.

The Layover

Chapter 1

I don't know what city I'm in. The alarm on my phone is blaring the *Rocky* song, lighting up the room just enough for me to see the shadowed outlines of walls and corners. I blink, trying to orient myself. There's no strip of hallway light coming from under the door. The sheets are silky, not worn-down cotton slept on by millions of bodies. They're probably not even white. This can't be a hotel.

Someone groans beside me, and my stomach sinks with realization. I'm at home, where I promised not to use my *Rocky* alarm anymore. Alexander says it gets into his dreams. I grab for the phone, but it's 3:30 in the morning—too early for coordination. It crashes to the floor, an electronic trumpet encouraging me to jab at the air with curled fists. Staying beneath the covers, I dip my head over the side of the bed and silence the noise before easing myself back up.

I should go, but instead I peek across the king-sized bed toward Alexander. I just want to see his face, to make sure I haven't managed to annoy him before I leave for three days. But the blackout curtains make it impossible. I can't even spot his outline through the darkness.

With a sigh, I slip my legs toward the edge of the bed. The chilled air outside the duvet hits one foot, and I steel myself for full-body contact with the icy conditions Alexander requires to sleep. An arm shoots around my waist, dragging me into a cocoon of hot skin and muscles. I exhale my relief and melt into him.

"I'm sorry about *Rocky*," I whisper.

"It's okay." Alexander's voice is husky with sleep. He presses a kiss against my bare shoulder. "In my dream, I ducked at exactly the right moment. Then I came back up with a right hook that sent the other guy flying. Knocked him clean out."

"Of course you did." A smile tugs at my mouth. Even in his dreams, Alexander triumphs. Some people might call this arrogance, but I recognize it as the confidence it is. There's a reason the other lawyers at his firm refer to him as the go-to guy. Alexander is reliable. He's unflappable. These are the qualities I appreciate most about him. "I wouldn't have expected anything less."

"His face was blurry," he says, "but I'm hoping it was a predictive dream about McMurphy. I'm up against him in court today, and to say I despise that man would be an understatement."

"It was definitely him. I'd recognize that stupid face anywhere."

"You were in my dream?"

"Oh, yes." I wriggle deeper into his embrace. "Right there on the sidelines, cheering you on."

"You're such an odd little duckling." Alexander laughs softly against the back of my head. His voice turns serious. "But he really does have a stupid face, doesn't he?"

"The stupidest."

He sighs and presses another kiss against the back of my neck. "I'll miss you while you're gone."

"It's only a few days." The reminder of work makes my leg twitch. It's probably been three minutes since my alarm went off. Maybe even four.

"Still."

"I know." I get it. I do. Nobody likes being left behind. It's only a few days, but it's the dinners we'll eat separately. The nights we'll go to bed without each other. Large bodies of water will separate us. "I'll miss you, too."

"It's the last time, though." There's no question in his words. It's a fact that's been decided, was agreed to this weekend, the moment I accepted his proposal. "We should celebrate when you get back. An engagement dinner. You land late on Thursday, right? Let's do it Friday. We can toast to the end of one chapter and the beginning of another."

"Yes." It's a lovely idea. Perfect, actually. What better thing to toast to than the ending of a nine-year career and the start of a marriage destined to last much longer? "Let's do it."

"I'll make a reservation," Alexander says, loosening his hold. "And you'd better go. You're way behind on the schedule."

I smile at his words. *Of course* Alexander would realize the value of the moments I've lost. He runs his entire life with the precision I reserve for work mornings. It's one of the things that most attracted me to him in the beginning. That and the set of his shoulders, so firm and self-assured. I can't believe he's going to be my husband. I, Ava Greene, am getting married. It's hands down the most permanent thing I've ever committed to.

"I love you." I press a kiss to his forearm and scramble out of the bed. "See you soon!"

I grab my phone and check it as I ease the door shut behind me: 3:34. Sure enough, I've already used four of my twenty-five minutes allotted to getting out of the house. On tiptoe, I sprint down the moonlit hallway. Chicago's December wind howls against the windowed walls of the tenth-story condo, making me feel like I'm at risk of being swept away. It's the perfect start to a trip, like I've already taken off and am coasting through the clouds.

Security lights outside provide the kitchen with enough light that I don't have to flip the switch on the wall. I beeline it toward the kettle I brought with me when I moved in. It looks ridiculously out of place next to Alexander's restaurant-grade espresso machine. No more so than me, though, racing past the black marble countertops in my bra and panties.

Alexander would be appalled if he could see me flitting around like a half-naked pixie in the moonlight. He's chastised me more than once about my tendency to go in search of coffee before putting on clothes. He has such concern about these nameless neighbors and their ability to spy on us. As if, out of all the people in our city, we are the show they want to see.

There's very little chance of being caught by him now, though. Even if he can't get back to sleep, I know he'll stay in bed and try. Alexander gets into bed at 10:30 and rises at 5:30, because Alexander believes in consistency. He's never said it aloud, but I know my moving in has been much harder on him than he expected. It's difficult to adapt to someone's presence when every time you start to get used to them, they disappear.

With a flick of my finger, I start the kettle. I filled it with water last night to save precious seconds this morning. My other hand reaches for my food bag. The movements happen without thought; this is a routine I've performed a thousand times.

The fridge is perfectly organized except for the little piles of food I've left. I set them up yesterday, balancing the baggies of cherries and grapes on rolling string cheeses in a way that would inform even the most casual of observers I'm not destined to be an architect. There's another pile of individually bagged meals in the freezer that I lay across the top of the bag. Since they're frozen, they can function as ice packs until I eat enough food to make room for a bag of ice from the plane. I zip up my large black mesh adult lunch box, grab the coffee, pour too much of it into the French press, and race to the guest bathroom.

It's the one place in this condo I've taken over as my own. The official reason is I don't want to wake Alexander up on mornings like today. Secretly, though, I like having a spot where I can leave things on the counter and don't have to worry about the hand towels hanging at exactly the same length. It's not that I don't appreciate Alexander's neatness. I do. In fact, I love how organized he is. His home—*our* home—is exactly the kind of perfectly ordered place I've spent my whole life dreaming of living in.

Yet for some reason, since being here, I seem to have discovered some tiny, deviant side of me that relishes this small area of relief from all the perfection. It's a disconcerting blip, contrary to who I want to be, and it embarrasses me enough that I've made every effort to hide it from Alexander. "Whatever you do," I told him early on, "don't open this door. I keep all my lady tools in there. You don't want to see how the sausage is made, do you?" He cringed and has left a wide berth since.

The bathroom fills with light, and my gaze is drawn to the sparkle of my new engagement ring. For a moment, I allow myself a break in routine to study this thing that is suddenly mine. It's massive, likely several carats. When Alexander got down on one knee Saturday night and opened the small velvet box, I had a terrible temptation to laugh at the glittering disco ball inside; it's such a departure from the small turquoise stone I asked for. Now that I've had a few days to get used to it, though, I can see that it's right. It's exactly what I need: a sharp, heavy rock to weigh me to the ground. After a lifetime of floating, I'm grateful to have found an anchor.

Alexander has always been clear about the fact that he didn't want his future partner to travel for a living, just like I've told him from the beginning I'm ready to move on from flying. Everyone knows you don't confess to a man you've just met—an attractive man whose lips you can't stop staring at, no less—that you want to get married, but I did. I broke all the rules, gazing up at him and earnestly confessing my desire to settle down. Life on the road was what I grew up with, my parents' ideal. My dream has always been to stay still.

In the corner of one of the drawers Alexander allotted me, I have a list I wrote when I was thirteen. Written across the top are the words *Ava's Adult Aspirations* (the latter word triumphantly discovered through a thesaurus search of *goals*). It's only two things, and I've long since memorized it, but I still pull it out sometimes to read it aloud, just to remind myself. It says:

1. Stay in one place.

2. Have real friends. Friends who don't travel. (They won't give up on you if you don't give them a reason

to. Just show up to the things that are important to them. *Be dependable.*)

If I had to give myself a progress report on achieving those goals, it wouldn't look good. I work a different three-day trip every week. The fact that those days change from month to month makes people feel like I'm constantly disappearing on them. I did have two good, perfectly sedentary friends until Meredith, the more sensitive of two, started referring to me as "Houdini" in a passive-aggressive way I've chosen to interpret as amusing. Now, due to too many magic acts on my part, I'm probably down to one.

That will all be behind me soon, though. It's time to trade the life I never aspired to for the one I've always wanted. Reluctantly, I slip the ring off my finger and place it reverentially in the corner of the counter. I've heard married women complain about chipping their diamonds in the cramped, metal galleys where we pour the passengers' drinks. I don't want to have to explain to Alexander that I've allowed that to happen to this horrifyingly expensive symbol of our future.

The moment the drawer closes, I jerk back into action. It's 3:47, only eight minutes before I need to hear the door click into place behind me. I wash my face and dab on mascara, noting the grayish hue to my hazel eyes. It's strange. They tend to turn green when I'm particularly happy or excited, and clearly I'm both. In addition to my new engagement, I've scored a much-coveted layover in Belize tomorrow night. International trips usually get snagged by the really senior flight attendants.

I braid my long dark hair down the side of my face like I do for every trip, but the strands slip out of place, costing me extra seconds I don't have. It's the water in Alexander's shower. He's put a filter on it that makes it and everything it touches feel like silk. It's considered a luxury, I know, but I can't seem to find it in myself to appreciate it. What, after all, is people's aversion to a bit of grit? Who doesn't want to feel the world on their skin?

I leave the braid loose, hoping the escaping wisps will look intentional, and secure it with a brown hair tie. It's time for my favorite part of my routine. In the guest room, my uniform is perfectly laid out: Dress spread across the bed. Each thigh-high stocking above its matching shoe. Earrings and mandatory watch next to the sleeve.

In less than a minute, I'm suited up. Every time I do this, I imagine I'm Superman in a phone booth. With the blink of an eye, I'm transformed from a civilian to a professional. *Ava Greene, SuperStewardess!*

Almost as quickly as it arrives, the feeling sinks into a pit in my stomach.

I can't believe this is the last trip I'll ever work.

Chapter 2

The sun is still buried in sleep, and Layla Day's call-in radio show, *In Love with Layla*, is playing through the car speakers. It's a rerun of her dedications from callers who want to send a song to their significant others, recycled for the listening pleasure of us misfits of the world who have gotten up too early or are coming home too late. I take a sip of coffee from my travel mug as I coast into the employee parking lot, my eyes narrowing at the two cars lurking near the front. Their engines are idling, headlights on in an aggressive show of intent.

They're determined to sit there until someone comes out and frees up a closer spot. If I were being uncharitable, I'd call them lazy. In fairness, though, a spot at the back will add an extra twenty-minute trudge through icy wind to the front of the lot before the even longer walk through the hourly parking garage to get inside the airport. It's not the worst strategy to invest a few minutes crossing your fingers. Normally I'd leave them to fight it out between themselves, but today I, too, want a good spot right up front. Every time I've ever scored one, I've ended up having an amazing trip.

I inch slowly forward, scanning for empty spaces the lurkers might've overlooked. On the radio, Layla Day cuts off a rambling ode to teen-dream Ashley from the self-proclaimed love of her life, a boy whose voice cracks at the end of his words as he claims to have held onto Ashley's heart for all of three weeks. "My Heart Will Go On" swells from the radio in honor of their grand romance.

Up ahead on my left, a parked car rumbles to life, its brake lights flaring red. Adrenaline hits my bloodstream like a shot. My fingers tighten against the padded steering wheel. This can't be happening, but it is. I, Ava Greene, am experiencing an airport miracle.

Since I didn't see anyone walk up to the parked car, I can only conclude some kindhearted employee has been just sitting there, braving the cold Chicago night while waiting for me to arrive so they could gift me with their primo parking spot. It's a going-away present. A sign. I whoop with glee and hit the gas, flicking on my blinker just as one of the lurkers rounds the corner.

The parked car begins to back out and, to my shock, the lurker inches closer, turning on a blinker of their own. I squint in disbelief. They saw my signaled claim. There's no way they could've missed it. It might still be dark out, but that would only make the light of my turn signal more prominent. This is Wild West behavior. The parking lot equivalent of a duel. Any other day, I wouldn't think twice. I'd duck my head and drive away. A parking space is hardly worth pistol play.

It's not any day, though. It's the last day I'll ever park in the airport's employee parking lot. It's the first day of the last trip I'll ever work. I need the luck this spot promises. If this trip isn't amazing, I'll end nine years of flying with a whimper.

There's something terribly depressing about the idea of entering such a significant era of my life with regret and leaving it the same way.

The lurker hits their gas again, sliding forward another few feet. It puts them in shining distance of one of the streetlights that line the lot. I lean forward, squinting through the windshield. My brow furrows in response to the face behind the wheel. It's Jack Stone, one of our own—not even, as I'd assumed, of TSA's evil ilk. I grunt my disgust.

He should be ashamed of himself. As a fellow flight attendant, he's meant to be one of the helpers of the airport. We're the ones who sneak sodas off the plane and pass them to the janitors. We save our DoubleTree cookies to give to the Ops agents. We do not rev our engines at other drivers like leather-clad hooligans playing a one-sided game of chicken.

I can only take this as further proof of what I've always known: Jack Stone might have given up his seat in the cockpit when he parted ways with the Air Force, but he's still a pilot at heart. In fact, he's probably not even here of his own volition. I bet they kicked him out for exactly this kind of lawless behavior.

Everyone else might think he's so charming, but Jack's superior officers must've seen beyond his perfect packaging, just like I have. I didn't give in the last time he tried to pull one over on me, and I won't this time either. This is *my* parking space. My grip on the steering wheel tightens.

The parked car inches farther into the streetlight's glow. My foot presses against the gas pedal, straining with impatience. Jack's eyes lock on mine. White teeth flash from his smile. Tumbleweeds skitter across the parking lot as the soundtrack from an old Western whistles through my head.

The parked car swings out, and I don't stop to consider how new my own car is, or that it's a gift from Alexander I've been trying to figure out how to return, or even that it's powerful beyond my experience and way too expensive for me to ever replace. I slam on the gas and rip the steering wheel to the left. I've lost my mind. My stomach drops as I veer toward the line of cars. They get larger as I get closer, looming like walls as I slide in between them. I exhale a lungful of breath I hadn't realized I've been holding.

I won!

My elation is brief. Sanity floods through, drowning it out, and my head drops to the steering wheel. Half the world hasn't even woken up yet, and I've already attempted to incur my own vehicular manslaughter charges. But at least I won't have to see Jack Stone ever again.

As if he instinctively understands my desire for him to disappear, Jack's car is idling behind mine as I get out. It's dirt brown, pleasantly old and oddly shaped, the kind of vehicle that looks like it's seen more than its share of the world. I feel a pang of loss for my cheerful old VW Bug that got replaced without my permission in Alexander's attempt to pamper me. There are people in the world who live by the adage that new is better. To me, it's the things that have lasted that are the most valuable. The things that have proven they can be counted on.

Ignoring Jack, I turn toward the trunk, sending my airline-issued trench coat flying up at the bottom so cold air bites at my stocking-clad legs. Rather than drive away, Jack rolls down his window. *Perfect.* Now, thanks to my deep-rooted need to restore order, I'll have to apologize for almost running him over. This innate need to smooth the waters is a quality I despise in myself.

"Nice driving, Danica Patrick. Practicing for Daytona?" Jack grins at me from the driver's seat. His eyes are startlingly light against his tanned skin and the darkness of his hair, which looks like he's been riding around with the window down. Maybe he has. Maybe when a person has no soul, they're incapable of feeling the cold.

"If you're asking for lessons, I'm going to have to turn you down. All potential driving students must have a basic understanding of turn signals." As far as apologies go, it probably doesn't rate as one of my best.

"Did I misunderstand?" Jack's effort at innocence is as convincing as a wolf playing puppy. "I assumed you were gesturing for me to take the spot."

"Right. Because I spotted a strong, able-bodied man and grew immediately concerned he might have to walk too far in his warm pants and comfortable shoes."

"Actually, you couldn't have spotted my body." His smile widens. "But it's flattering to discover you've noticed it before."

A flush of irritation heats my skin. The very idea that he'd think he could include me among the endless members of the Jack Stone fan club makes me want to get right back in my car and steal another parking spot from him.

"You should probably get going." I wave one hand toward the back of the lot. "It's going to be a long walk from your parking spot *back there*."

I spin on my heel, indicating the end of the conversation. Any warmth the trunk might have held has escaped, leaving me to paw around inside a chilly cavern. I listen for the sound of his car pulling away as I pull my roller bag out and hang the food bag on its hook before balancing a tote on top of the heap. Sadly, Jack's car continues to idle behind me.

"You're not really this mad about a parking space, are you?"

"What?" I tense before turning slowly back toward him.

Jack has his arm draped over the door of the car like it's a balmy eighty degrees outside. He's the wolf again, playing puppy. Or maybe he's not. Does he even remember me? Without knowing, I can't answer his question. There's no way I'm telling him our short conversation from two years ago has replayed in my mind a million times, the opening stanza to the song of my greatest heartbreak—not if his part in it ranked so low on his list of sins that he's already forgotten it happened. He'd think I was pathetic.

Still, what are the chances that, after all my efforts to avoid working with him and to dodge him in the lounge, Jack Stone would end up in front of me on my last trip? If I have something to say, the universe is clearly providing the opportunity. But there's really no point, is there? Jack is who he is, just like I am who I am—which, I'd do well to remember, is *not* someone who fights for parking spots and flings verbal barbs.

If this is an opportunity to get closure, maybe it's not supposed to come in the form of confrontation. Maybe it's better found in moving forward.

Unfortunately, that goal feels a little out of my benevolence range for such an early hour of the morning. Apathy might be a little more achievable. *I don't care because I'm over it. All of this is about to be in my rearview mirror anyway.*

"For the record," Jack says, alleviating my struggle to respond, "I was just joking. I never intended to take that spot."

"Yeah?" To my relief, I hit the note just right: casual, without an edge of accusation or disbelief.

"I hadn't even touched the gas pedal when you went full Mad Max on me."

The mental image almost makes me smile. "Whatever. You know what? Forget about it. I was probably overreacti—"

"Brake lights! And look at that: it's a way better spot than yours." Jack winks at me as he swings his car into a U-turn and races toward the front of the parking lot.

Just like that, apathy slips beyond my reach. I waste five scheduled seconds glaring after him.

THE PATH FROM the lot leads me underground through the lower level of a parking garage, which is somehow colder than outside. My heels make clicking noises that echo off the cement walls. They say, *Last time! Last time!* I veer toward the moving walkways. Each week, two of the three are broken. Not the same two, obviously. That would make too much sense. I like to play a little game called Which Will It Be? Today I guess incorrectly. In a surprise twist, all three are out of order.

Once I've checked in on the phone behind the ticket counter, I glance at my watch and allow my mind to downshift from the rigidity of my schedule. I've got forty-six minutes until I have to be at the gate. As long as I leave a good buffer to get there promptly, the rest of the time is mine to do with as I please. I force my back to loosen and shoulders to relax.

Taking the long way toward the special security entrance for crew, I let the brightness and bustle of my surroundings seep into me. The airport is the only place in the world where it isn't annoying when someone wanders into your path or bumps arms with you. Everyone has blinders on, homing in on the imaginary checklist in front of them. They're trying to figure out what needs to be done next. They're trying to remember anything they might've forgotten.

Every now and then, someone looks up, their eyes widening when they see me. Most are wondering if they have a question they might need to ask me; it's rare to spot an airport employee who doesn't have a line of people clamoring for their attention. Others scan the length of my body with appreciative eyes. It is an embarrassing but inarguable fact that I am more attractive when I'm in uniform.

It sounds ridiculous, I know; my dress is the color of a cartoon blueberry and is made of material so synthetic I suspect the real reason they've banned smoking on planes is from fear the crew would explode into blue fireballs if they ventured too close to anything lit. Facts are facts, though. Flight attendants fall into that category of careers TV and movies have decided to portray as sexy. Nurses. Cocktail waitresses. Lounge singers. In reality, I am a five-foot-tall twenty-eight-year-old who favors oversized T-shirts and often forgets to wash her face at night. But at work, I put on the issued heels and dress and suddenly have adult-length legs, pornographically large breasts, and the illusion of a waist.

In front of me, an old woman struggles with the bags that have been perched atop her roller. A businessman breaks free of his blinders and stops to adjust them for her. My heart swells. I'm thrilled to be finally settling down, but I can't help feeling the tiniest bit sad. I am going to miss this place and the people in it so much.

The feeling intensifies when the TSA agent makes small talk as he scans me through. Even the sight of the line snaking out from the McDonald's causes a hitch in my stomach. All of those people waiting for their frozen patties and spongy pancakes, with no idea the best breakfast in the world is ten feet away at LeeAnn Chin's. It's a secret I'm privy to because this is my domain. Only soon it won't be. I'll be eating my breakfast at a normal time, in a normal kitchen, with the man I love. A woman in line for McCoffee reluctantly shifts so I can get past her to go to LeeAnn's.

For the first time ever, there's someone already at the counter as I walk up. The secret's out. I'm not even gone yet, and someone's already taken my place.

I stand back, giving him space, but I can hear him asking what's in the spring rolls. His voice sounds familiar, but when you're in customer service, everyone begins to sound the same. No doubt See-Yun has heard these questions a thousand times. *Anything breakfasty? Bacon? Sausage?*

Behind the counter, she shakes her head and smiles. She doesn't point out that there are several pans of food between them that an American might consider "breakfasty." Nor does she state the very obvious fact that the spring rolls, egg rolls, and cream cheese wontons grouped together at the end will be fantastic, regardless of the time of day.

"Just order the Asian scramble," I say to the man's broad-shouldered back, referring to the scrambled eggs with the chunks of sausage, peppers, and onions mixed in. The words linger in the air, sharper than I've intended, likely still colored by my unfriendly encounter in the parking lot. I shake my head at myself and soften my tone, because I'm in uniform, and it's my job to be kind, and it's not this man's fault I feel weirdly proprietary over a pan of eggs I had no part in making. "You won't be disappointed."

"Good morning, Ava." See-Yun shifts her gaze toward me as the man turns around.

The smile I give her turns to a grimace as I register the strong jaw and ridiculously blue eyes. Is this man absolutely determined to ruin the first day of my last trip? Somehow Jack Stone has beaten me here. Probably because he didn't care enough to stroll through the airport, soaking it all in. He took it for granted because he knows he'll do this all again next week.

My back stiffens with annoyance. It's obvious why I didn't realize it was him standing in front of me. Jack is supposed to be wearing the male version of the blueberry trench coat I have on, not his own jacket. It's made of canvas or something (that probably provides no actual warmth) with random straps and pockets on it. It's one of those irritating articles of clothing that manages to look so *not* trendy that it's actually trendy. I dislike it intensely.

"Hello again." Jack's expression is friendly, like he's already forgotten our fight. "Aviana, right?"

"It's Ava." I mentally add *poor listener* below *wrong jacket* and *parking anarchist* on the list of things that annoy me about him. I mean, See-Yun *just* said my name, did she not?

"I'm Jack."

Despite the fact that we've now had two previous encounters, I realize this is the first time we've properly introduced ourselves. His smile, I can now see, is crooked. It's baffling. The guy is probably thirty years old. How is it possible he hasn't figured out how to correctly use his face by now?

"Hello, Jack." I tilt my head toward the pans of breakfast food behind the glass. "Time's ticking. You know what they say: order or get off the pot."

Jack looks unfazed, undoubtedly assuming this is just the way I interact with people. See-Yun, however—like any other person who knows me would—looks taken aback. To her, I've always been sunshine and early-morning chatter. But she's not a terrible person. She's given me no reason to dislike her.

"I've had the Asian scramble before," Jack says. "It's great, but so is the ham-and-cheese scramble. Have you tried that?"

I shake my head.

"You should," he says.

"I'm not the one trying to decide what I want." I say the words lightly, and he laughs like I'm joking, but I'm not. How hard is it to find something good and stick with it? Why do people like him always have to keep searching for something better? Maybe it's a pilot thing. That would explain why Jack was so willing to aid and abet his slimy pilot buddy. They're kindred souls, bonded in their quest to sample everything . . . and everyone.

I shake the thought away. This is not the moment for a trip through the thorns that line memory lane. It's the last time I'll ever go to LeeAnn's in my uniform. It's the last Asian scramble I'll eat before a work trip. Jack already ruined my parking victory. I will not allow him to spoil my breakfast, too. Still, something must show on my face because Jack's head tilts and his eyes scan my face.

"You okay?" He leans forward, voice low, and I notice the dark stubble indicating he hasn't shaved this morning. Just further proof of his blatant disregard for the uniform policy.

"Actually," I say, "I'm hungry. That would be the reason I'm standing in front of a counter full of food. And I do understand that this seems to be the most important decision you've ever made in your life, but maybe you can do us all a favor and just *choose something*."

To his credit, Jack doesn't flinch. He merely steps back and waves me forward.

"See-Yun," he says, "the lady would like to place an order."

My feet stay planted against the floor. “I can wait my turn.”

Jack’s head tilts. “Maybe it’s better for everyone if you just recognize your limitations?”

“There are only two egg options and a few sides. Surely even you can narrow it down, if you focus really hard.”

“But why limit myself?” Jack flashes another crooked smile at me before turning back to See-Yun. “Actually, I think I’m in the mood for a little of both. Can you give me half of the Asian scramble and half ham-and-cheese scramble?”

Unsurprisingly, See-Yun nods and loads more than a half portion of each into the Styrofoam container. Some women can’t ever seem to resist feeding handsome men.

“And I’ll add two of those spring rolls,” Jack says. “Maybe that’s exactly what breakfast has been missing.”

I roll my eyes and sigh. The need for variety? A desire for excess? Jack Stone is exactly as advertised. *Once a pilot, always a pilot.*

Chapter 3

There's a time-honored game the plane likes to play with its crew. Rather than commit to a moderate temperature, it prefers to pump hot air into the cabin until it feels like a sauna. Then, once we've shed our sweaters, pulled our hair up, and stuffed our pockets with tissues to dab at the sweat slipping down our necks, it overcompensates with aircon until every passenger on board is waving at me with blanket requests. It's great fun for everyone, and the reason I end most trips with a stopped-up nose and a sore throat.

I've clearly arrived during Arctic Phase. As I drag my bags toward the back galley, even the pleather seats are cold to the touch. I'm the first on board, but my tower of bags bashing against the metal armrests as I pass makes enough noise that I glance back more than once, wondering if anyone has joined me.

By the time I've put my stuff up and done the security checks, the front of the plane is showing signs of life. At least two of our crew has arrived, one of whom I recognize. The bleached blonde with roots like charcoal is Gen Hefner. She has matching lines of soot etched around her eyes, legs like a

Rockette, and a uniform that's clearly been altered to show them off.

I rarely end up flying with the same person twice. When I do, it's usually been long enough between trips that it's like meeting them for the first time all over again. Gen is different, though. I've only worked with her twice over the last nine years, but she's the kind of person who's impossible to forget. Mainly because she won't let you. Last year, I ran into her in the employee lounge and she launched right into a story about a fight she'd just had with her boyfriend like we were friends who spoke daily instead of two people who last saw each other when a different president was in office. I hurry to the front to say hi.

"Ava!" Her voice is raspy. It's possible she has the airplane-inflicted Temperature-Swing Typhoid, but her voice might also be gone because (assuming nothing has changed) she spends most of her days off at clubs, drinking and smoking and conducting conversations at about fifteen decibels above normal volume. "Have you met Pilot Paul?"

A thick-set pilot with ruddy skin and a shy smile holds out his hand. He looks like he's been flown in from the cornfields of Nebraska. It's totally possible he has. Although we're all based in Chicago, only about 40 percent of us live there. Some were lucky enough to already be there, and others, like me, were willing and able to move. The rest, like Gen, commute from all around the country. She's originally from Pennsylvania but lives in Vegas, last I heard.

"Nice to meet you, Ava," Pilot Paul says.

"Isn't he gorgeous?" Gen's smile turns devilish when the poor man's cheeks flush.

My heart goes out to him. I've spent my entire life studying people, and I can already predict how this will go. For the next three days, Gen will flirt with him outrageously. If Paul is really lucky, he'll be amused by her efforts to charm him. It is, however, far more likely he'll develop an enormous crush, only to discover Gen has absolutely zero real interest in a nice man who's unfortunate enough to be gainfully employed.

"Can someone please take me to Belize?" A new person strolls on board, sparing me the need to attempt a professional response. I smile instinctively before my mind catalogues the lazy saunter and chiseled jaw. "I need to escape this winter weather."

"Jack!" Gen almost knocks Pilot Paul over in her rush to fling her arms around this barnacle plaguing my morning.

Paul watches them forlornly as I scowl.

As much as I'd love to pretend Jack is a stowaway begging for a ride, tonight's layover is in Portland, Oregon. We don't end up in Belize until tomorrow. Only another person on our crew would know tomorrow's destination, which means I can't toss his bag into the jetway and order him to hitchhike elsewhere. Because this must actually be happening. Jack Stone is working my last trip with me.

It's the worst possible way to end things. And not just for me. Poor Paul's whipped-puppy-dog expression is totally justified. If his chance with Gen was small ten seconds ago, it's just become minuscule. It's not only the eyes and fancy jacket Paul is up against. It's the confidence Jack's casual stance projects. It's the easy smile that says he might be trouble, but you'll enjoy finding out for yourself. This is a man who got See-Yun to give him extra eggs, for heaven's sake. Someone like Gen will gladly offer him all of hers.

If cabin crew assignments were a little fairer, Paul and I

could form an alliance and vote Jack off the plane. Since we can't, and I'm forced to spend the next three days with him, I suppose Jack Stone warrants an introduction. Obviously I've done everything in my power to avoid him since our chance encounter in a hotel bar. But good gossip does tend to get around, and I'm not above listening to it if it's about someone I despise.

These are the facts I've picked up:

1. Until three years ago, Jack was a pilot in the Air Force. Then, for some unknown but much-speculated-on reason, he decided to give up flying so he could serve sodas and pass out tiny bags of pretzels.

2. He was in a serious relationship with Hannah Robertson, a sweet flight attendant I've never flown with, but who seems to be adored by everyone.

3. He ended things with her because, like with his breakfast foods, he needed variety (and lots of it).

4. He exhibited his sympathy over her broken heart by finding said variety with all of her coworkers.

5. Yes, that means Hannah gets the pleasure of working with all of the women he's slept with.

6. He deserves to be pummeled with raw steaks and tossed into a pit of rabid dogs.

7. So does He Who Should Be Forgotten, his loathsome pilot friend, who shares his need for variety,

> and who I hate with a passion (that I've likely—but deservingly, I'm certain—allowed to spill over to Jack Stone).

"Aviana." Jack peers at me over Gen's shoulder. "I was just looking at the paperwork. I knew I had it right."

"Like I already told you, I go by Ava." Now that we're working together, I know I'll have to find a way to be friendlier. Still, the words come out in my frostiest voice, the one I've been practicing for when telemarketers call.

"*Aviana* is beautiful, though. Doesn't it mean 'bird'? It's the perfect name for a flight attendant. I don't know why you don't like it."

"I didn't say I don't like it." I shouldn't have to say it. It's none of Jack Stone's business how I feel about a name I've chosen not to use. It should be enough that I've *chosen not to use it*. It's not like I'm about to randomly start referring to him as Jackson. Granted, that might not be his given name like Aviana is mine. But still. I bet he wouldn't appreciate it if I did.

If Jackson Pebble was my friend, I might choose to share that it bothers me that my name coordinates so perfectly with my job. I might admit that it makes my whole life feel like destiny, which sounds lovely but is really just a dreamy term for having to endure something that's been forced on you. Aviana is the name of a girl who was yanked out of school so many times for "adventures" that she almost didn't graduate and had no hope of getting into college. A girl who was forced to feel grateful when her parents met the CEO of Northeast Air at a craps table in Reno and he offered to set their teenage daughter up with an interview. If my name were something sensible like Jane, I might be a doctor or an accountant right now, instead of a woman who's spent the last nine years failing in her goal to settle down.

Jackson is not my friend, though. A fact that he seems to pick up on, if the dismissiveness in his expression is any indication.

"Ava it is." He winks at Gen and slips out of her grasp before she can climb his body and wrap both legs around his waist. "And you must be our captain."

"First officer, actually," Paul says. "The name's Paul."

"Is everyone present?" A man with ramrod stiff posture exits the cockpit, his eyes scanning each of us, clearly trusting only himself to answer his question. A sharp nod indicates his satisfaction. He has salt-and-pepper hair, a thick, furrowed brow, and a stern expression. "I am Captain Ballinger. You may address me as Captain Ballinger."

It's such an unexpectedly formal greeting it leaves all of us momentarily speechless. Crews usually have the feel of a group of kids in detention, mismatched but bonded by the fact that nobody's leaving the metal tube until Scheduling releases us. Sure, technically there's a hierarchy. But it's rarely acknowledged.

Gen breaks the silence by laughing. "Is that what you make your wife call you?"

"My wife is none of your concern." His eyes run the length of Gen, no doubt taking in her numerous dress code violations: Feather earrings that almost touch her shoulders, significantly larger than the quarter-sized guideline. Twin bracelets so thick they give the impression she was handcuffed until she unearthed a saw powerful enough to cut through metal. Eye shadow that looks like she's dabbed a glue stick over her eyes and dumped glitter on top. "And you're lucky I don't consider the back of the aircraft my concern."

I stifle a giggle of my own. *Noted.* We are the waitstaff. If there were two entrances to this plane, we'd be relegated to the back one. I wonder if a curtsy is expected every time Captain Ballinger speaks, or if he prefers a salute. Gen's eyes spark like she's wondering the same thing and is ready to offer him one of the middle-finger variety.

"Thank you, Captain Ballinger." I grab Gen's arm and tug her toward the aisle. "We've still got equipment to check in the back, so Jackson can update us on the weather and stuff after you've briefed him."

"Actually," Jackson says, "it's Jack. And Gen is working A. I'm C, so I'll be in the back with you."

My eyes widen as Jack swaps places with Gen, stepping into the aisle. His shoulder brushes against mine, and I shrink back.

"No." The word escapes from my mouth. *It's not possible.*

There are three positions in each crew, uncreatively dubbed A, B, and C. I always work B because it allows me to hide in the back the entire trip. C takes off and lands up front but spends the rest of the time in the back, and A flight attendants spend all their time up front.

The A position is for control freaks who are willing to do extra work just so they can ensure it's done correctly. The last time I flew with Gen, she made a plane-wide announcement, lying about being out of apple juice. She didn't want to serve any, she told me, because it "smells like babies." I might not know her overly well, but I'm 100 percent certain Gen Hefner is not A material.

"It's true," Gen says. "Elena Rodriguez was scheduled for this trip and offered to trade with me. I had twelve hours in Philly tomorrow night, and now I've got twenty-four hours in Belize. I would've agreed to fly the plane for a trade like that."

Captain Ballinger's eyebrows crush together at the idea that someone like her could ever take his place. Gen looks delighted to have accidentally offended him. Jack takes another step forward, sending me skittering backward.

"Come on, sunshine," he says. "Let's go check that equipment."

Because I don't have any other options, I lead the way. When we get to the back, Jack slings his roller bag into one of the bins.

"So," he says.

This is the moment. No more sniping. We're part of a team now. Today alone, we've got to get from here to Atlanta to Boise to San Francisco to Portland. To survive it, we'll have to work together. I brace myself for the routine.

Where are you from? Do you commute? Married? Kids? There's a whole list of questions we, as a crew, tend to follow like a script. As strangers who are about to spend the next three days with our thighs and shoulders pressed together on jump seats, it makes things more comfortable to have a basic understanding of who the other person is. I'll answer politely because I am a professional. I can do this.

"Are you going to be able to close the bins, or am I going to have to do that for you?" Jack lifts an eyebrow at me before tucking his tote next to his bag.

"Excuse me?" My hands curl into fists, even as I exhale a tiny sigh of relief that we're not on one of the 700s with the modified bins. I actually *am* too short to close those. They were an unsuccessful experiment, and there are only a few in rotation, but it's always a nightmare when I discover myself flying on one. There is nothing more humiliating than having to pull a fellow flight attendant aside and confess your need for them to do one of your duties for you.

"It's fine if you're too vertically challenged." Jackson's smile says it would be more than fine; that, in fact, he'd take a significant amount of joy in my inability to perform such a simple duty. "Just let me know so I can step in before you embarrass yourself."

"I'm perfectly capable of reaching the bins, thank you very much."

"You're welcome."

"I wasn't—" I stop myself. Jackson *knows* I wasn't actually thanking him.

"Wasn't what?" The corner of his lips flicks up as he attempts to lure me into his trap.

"Nothing."

He shrugs and reaches into his food bag. "I'm just glad the airlines dropped all those requirements they used to have. You're a good stretch south of five feet six, aren't you? How often do you think about the fact that, if you'd been born thirty years earlier, you wouldn't have been allowed to have this job?"

Heat rises to my cheeks. "Probably about as often as you. Thank goodness they finally opened up the position to men, right? What else would you have fallen back on when you realized you couldn't hack it as a pilot?"

Our eyes lock, and my hand strains toward the imaginary gun in the holster on my hip. A ding cuts through the plane, breaking the spell. Two things occur to me simultaneously: boarding is beginning, and I've just swung a viciously low blow. I don't have to know why Jack is no longer a pilot to be certain it wasn't his choice. Nobody would invest hundreds of hours into learning to fly a plane only to decide they'd rather brew coffee in back. The pay cut is too great, not to mention the fall in status. I brace myself for retaliation, but Jack surprises me with a slow smile.

"Interesting," he says.

"What?"

"I didn't tell you I used to be a pilot." He starts back down the aisle, his smile widening even further, eyes still locked on mine. "Did your research also inform you I always eat at LeeAnn Chin's before a trip? Is that why you showed up behind me in line?"

My mouth drops, and before I can form a single word of defense, Jack turns his back on me, whistling as his long stride carries him off to the safety of the exit row. I glare after him, my mind scrambling for a cutting response I could've made. So much for playing nice.

With that clearly unrealistic goal abandoned, I endeavor to take joy instead in the fact that I get to stay half a plane away from Jack while he's stuck spending the next thirty minutes playing goalie against the FAA-declared undesirables who will attempt to sneak into those seats. Still, I can't stop thinking about the implication of his parting shot. It's the arrogance that gets me. The absolute obliviousness to how much I dislike him. Never in my life have I been so cold to someone, combative even, and *still* Jack assumes I must be another sucker for his good looks and easy charm. The thought makes my nails dig into my palms.

I break my own rules and attempt to distract myself by brewing a pot of coffee. It's an amateur move. I'll have to sip at it in secret, but the aroma will fill the cabin anyway, and at least one person will come back and ask for a cup. Explaining that I'm not allowed to give out anything below ten thousand feet will only make me look worse when they inevitably catch me topping up my own cup.

If I'd known you'd be at LeeAnn's, I would've choked down a smoothie just to avoid you. That's what I should've said. I take a sip of black coffee. The preboarders are trickling on like zombies. They haven't even breached the second row of the plane yet, which makes my wait feel even more endless. If only I could use my phone.

During boarding, however, phones are strictly forbidden, as are books or magazines or anything else that might commit the cardinal sin of making time pass faster. It's just me and my thoughts, so I stare down a line of people heading toward me, too engaged in the strategic task of picking a seat to notice my existence. If you think about it, thirty minutes is a really long time to exist entirely within your own head. It's the length of an entire sitcom *with* commercials.

I'll just send one quick text to Alexander to let him know I got to the airport safely. I pull the phone out of my pocket and discover he's already texted me. Let's get married in the spring. I know it's soon, but I can't wait for you to be my wife.

It's the sweetest thing he could've said, and I love the idea. Spring is a perfect time for a wedding. I can see it now: just us and the people we love, in a small park or garden, surrounded by the heady fragrance of freshly blooming flowers, the trill of birds accompanying our vows. It's perfect, I type covertly. I'll be there.

A ring *and* a wedding date. It's all becoming real. The last two days, I've lived in a bubble of disbelief and joy, but it's actually happening. Soon. I should tell someone.

With a smile, I click over to a group text between me, Meredith, and Ro. My smile fades. The last message is dated August 6. I can't believe it's been almost four months since we've communicated. Meredith should've forgiven me by now. I only missed a day at the pool. It's not like it was her birthday or anything. And it's not like I skipped it so I could do something better. I got called in to work. In retrospect, I probably should've told Meredith when she invited me that I was sitting reserve and would only have a two-hour window to report to the airport if Scheduling contacted me. But she'd gotten so critical of my job by that point that I didn't want to do anything to rock the boat before a wave had even arrived.

At least Ro and I are still okay. I click on her name, but my last couple of texts to her have gone unanswered. She's not mad. She's probably just hedging her bets. I can't blame her for that. Our schedules are so out of sync. I'm gone a couple of nights a week, and I'm always at some work function of Alexander's on the weekends. During the weekdays when I'm available, Ro is at work. It's no wonder she sees Meredith more often than she sees me, and as such, I can see why she might have ever-so-slightly taken her side.

Still, my engagement could be the perfect opportunity to smooth the waters. Doesn't everyone love love? It feels odd to just announce I'm getting married, though; the last thing I want to do is come across like I'm bragging. I hesitate for a moment before typing, Hi! Can we get together for drinks soon? I have some news!

I glance up and freeze when I catch Jack's eyes on me. He lifts his eyebrows and tilts his head at the passengers who are pushing down the aisle. I shove the phone into my pocket. *Tell on me*, I dare him silently through narrowing eyes. *What are they going to do? Fire me?* It's all bluster, though. It doesn't matter if this is my last trip. I'm not a rule-breaker, and the thought of getting busted doing something wrong makes my stomach tighten with unease.

I press my phone deeper into my pocket to stop myself

from checking if Ro has magically responded in the three seconds since I texted her. I'll be so hurt if she ignores me. At times like this, I wish I could break my policy about befriending my coworkers. A flight attendant would never get mad at me for leaving town for a few days. But that's the problem, isn't it? I don't want to attempt to form real friendships with travelers. I grew up with the wanderers of the world. I've met more of them over my lifetime than I can count. And I know from extensive experience that you're better off having no friends at all than having the kind of friends who flit in and out of your life at their own whim. Unfortunately, it's a lesson I'm worried I might've also taught Meredith.

"We have a spinner!" Gen projects the words over the intercom like a sports announcer.

I cringe at her lack of tact and peer down the aisle. Sure enough, there's a woman in heels and a pencil skirt hovering in the aisle. The whole open-seating thing has thrown her for a loop. She doesn't know where she wants to put her bag. She doesn't know where she wants to sit. This two-hour flight to Atlanta will set the tone of her entire life, and she's petrified in the midst of options. She's stopping at every open spot, sniffing like a dog searching for a place to relieve itself, and the people behind are too polite to go around her. (Their patience might be admirable if it weren't guaranteed to disappear the moment it's time to deplane.)

I hurry toward her as Jack comes from the opposite direction. It only takes one spinner to delay the flight and throw off every departure time for the rest of the day.

"That looks heavy," I say, coaxing the bag out of her grip. "Let me help you put it up."

She gapes at me as I heave it in the overhead bin. She can't decide if she owes me thanks for the assistance or if she's just been politely robbed. Both are true.

"Thank you," she says finally.

"You're welcome." I smile encouragingly and gesture toward an open seat beneath her bag.

She glances toward the opposite side of the aisle, and I shrug as if to say, *That's fine, too.* It doesn't matter to me where she sits. I just need her to make a choice. I know where she'll end up, though. It's Pavlovian. People sit as close to their bag as possible. They can't help themselves.

I head back to the galley, expecting Jack to follow me. When I turn around, he's not there. He's in the cabin, closing all the bins by himself. I try to help, but before I can get anywhere, someone tugs on my arm with the request for a seat belt extension. By the time I retrieve it, the bins are all taken care of. I stare after Jack, expecting him to turn back and smirk at me, but he doesn't.

I don't see him again before the Ops agent closes the airplane doors. I can feel his eyes on me during taxi, though. I'm at the emergency row, demonstrating the safety equipment while he does the same from the front. The plane is full. At least ninety faces are pointed my way. A teenage girl is recording my movements with her phone in case she ever needs a visual reminder on how to buckle a seat belt. Still, it's the back of me that feels most exposed.

Gen begins the announcement about the oxygen masks, sounding bored: "Should the cabin lose pressure, four yellow oxygen masks will drop from the compartment overhead."

I bend carefully to retrieve mine from the floor. I'm strangely terrified Jack's view from the front will give him a glimpse of my panties.

"Pull down on the mask until the plastic tubes are fully extended."

It's not like I have anything to be embarrassed of. They're basic cotton briefs, providing full coverage. I'm pretty sure the bluebirds on them are too small to be seen from fifteen rows behind me. Still, it's the principle. Jack has already been up close and personal with everyone else's panties. If I can prevent him from spotting mine, I'll end this job with one accomplishment under my belt. Literally.

"Place the mask over your mouth and breathe normally."

Without permission, my hand swipes at my butt, ensuring my dress is still covering it.

"If you're traveling with a child or anyone needing special assistance, put on your mask first."

I breathe a sigh of relief at the final cue and start a slow, careful squat to collect my demo equipment.

"If you're traveling with more than one child, choose the one with the most potential and save them."

Gen has given her inappropriate suggestion so seriously I almost miss the words. The lady in front of me on the aisle clearly catches them, though. She gasps and twists toward me, the child on her lap turning with her. His leg swings out and smashes against my nose. I tilt backward on my heels, teetering for one hopeful moment before I tip over like a felled tree. My head hits the floor and stars explode above my eyes.

The cabin fills with gasps, but the only movement comes from a set of footsteps pounding down the aisle toward me. I feel the shudder of the floor as a set of knees drop behind me. Strong hands slide under my head. The smell of leather and cedar drifts from the uniformed chest that leans over me. I squeeze my eyes shut so I don't have to see Jack this close. I can't handle his amusement in high-def.

I hear the woman's voice above me, defensive and unapologetic.

"It's not like he knew she was going to put her face right in front of his foot. He's been practicing his kicks for Little League soccer." Her voice hardens. "I guess you could say he has the most *potential* of anyone on the team."

I groan and sit up, pulling myself from Jack's grip.

"No pretzels for that kid," Gen says over the speaker.

Before I can reassure the mother that Gen is joking, Jack laughs and says, "You heard the woman." Then he slips his hands under my armpits and lifts me to my feet in one effortless swoop, sending me tottering down the aisle like a toddler. A smattering of applause greets me, and my cheeks flush with embarrassment.

This is going to be the longest trip ever.

Chapter 4

The lights are turned down for takeoff, and everyone is buckled in. That includes us flight attendants. Outside the windows, the sun is just beginning to crest through the clouds. A strip of orange streaks through the sky. The plane roars as it rises to meet it. My head is throbbing, but it's just as likely it's from the conversation as the kick in the face. Gen is pressed against me on the jump seat, legs spread like she's never been introduced to the concept of personal space or decorum.

My brow furrows as I realize I've been tricked. Jack played the role of concern so well: "You can't sit in the back by yourself. What if you have a concussion? You could fall asleep and nobody would know. Let's swap. Just for this leg." I was such a sucker I'm pretty sure I even thanked him. Now he's back there on my jump seat enjoying the blissful silence of an empty galley, while I'm the one who will be included in the complaint letters written by passengers close enough to hear Gen's diatribe against whining children on planes.

"I just don't understand why we're not allowed to slip a little bit of Benadryl into their juice," she says, too loudly.

"Please stop talking about it." My words come out in a hiss.

"What?" Somehow Gen manages to look innocent.

"You can't say things like that. It's terrifying. And very, very illegal."

"I didn't say I was *going to.* I'm saying it would be a nice service we could offer. You don't think the parents would appreciate it?"

"I'm certain they would not."

"But—"

I hold up my hand to stop her. "Can we talk about something else, please? Something that isn't guaranteed to get us both investigated by the FBI?"

"Sure." Gen pulls a strand of hair into her mouth and sucks it while she thinks.

I study her, wondering if this is the secret to her personality. Could there be enough alcohol in her hair spray that she's always a little drunk?

"Ooh." Her eyes gleam in the dim lighting. "Let's talk about that hot hunk of bratwurst we're flying with."

My mind flashes to Jack's stupid windswept hair, and I resist the urge to demonstrate vomiting. Instead I feign cluelessness. "Paul?"

"Paul looks like he goes to church on Sundays and takes his golden retriever to the dog park after." If there's a way to say those words like they equate to assault and battery, Gen manages.

"How deviant."

"You know what I mean," she says. "He's friend material, not, like, the stuff of fantasies."

"I don't know. I can think of quite a few friends who dream of a Sunday afternoon stroll at the dog park with an attractive, attentive man."

"Really?" Gen lifts her legs in the air and props her feet against the bulkhead. If any passengers walk up here, they are guaranteed a show. Fingers crossed she's wearing panties. "You need more interesting friends."

I shake my head but can't tamp down my grin. Gen's comment might feel more offensive if (a) I was talking about real people and not just people on TV who feel like my friends, and (b) Gen thought anything through before she said it aloud. She doesn't, though. She reminds me of one of those broken faucets that sends water shooting everywhere the moment it's touched.

"Probably," I admit.

"Back to the stuff of fantasies, though. What do you think?"

"I think . . ." I stall, trying to figure out how to not disparage one coworker to another when the one coworker has the appeal of a particularly irritating rash. "I think he's attractive. I mean, obviously he's attractive. But he's a little bit rude, isn't he? I don't know. I guess I expected him to be more charming. You'd think to sleep with so many flight attendants, he'd be a flirt. But he's done nothing but try to pick fights with me today."

Gen's face lights up. "Captain Ballinger has slept with a lot of flight attendants?"

"What?" Embarrassment burns a trail up my stomach into my cheeks. "Captain Ballinger? No. I don't know."

"But who were you—"

"Gen!" I cut her off, my eyes going wide. "Captain Ballinger? Seriously?"

"He's so stern. It makes me want a spanking."

This time, I don't hold back my gag. "But he's married!"

"We don't know that. He doesn't wear a ring, and he never

actually said he was married. He just said it wasn't my concern."

"But he's old!"

"Mid- to late fifties, probably. Don't forget I'm older than you. My scale swings wider."

"You're twenty-nine, which is all of one year older than me. And your scale swings like a ride at an amusement park. What ever happened to that felon you were dating? Is he still in the picture?"

"Ryan isn't a felon. He hasn't been officially convicted yet."

"Ryan?" I squint at her. "I thought he had a more unusual name. Like Spike. Stab?"

"Oh." Gen's face goes slack. Without one of her ever-present theatrical expressions, she looks bare. Vulnerable. It makes me want to reach into the air and grab my words back. "Stake. Yeah. We broke up."

I don't know what to say. The last time Gen and I flew together, she told me men were like fish: "You try to hold onto them and they'll start to stink." Only she doesn't look like someone who wanted to toss that particular bass back into the dating pool.

"It's his loss, Gen." I mean it. I still would, even if I didn't believe she's too good for him, which I do, firmly.

"He dumped me," she says. "I think I freaked him out when I asked him to marry me."

"You *wanted to marry him*?" The moment the words are out, I find myself, once again, wishing to yank them back out of the air. They've come out too loud. Too incredulous. But there's so much in that tiny statement that's shocking. Gen wanted to get married? Granted, I don't know her well, but I can't imagine her embracing something so rigid as a marriage.

It's like a professional dancer voluntarily taking a desk job. And marrying someone named Stake? It's like the desk job comes with rats in the drawers.

"Well, yeah." Thankfully, Gen looks more confused than offended. "Doesn't everyone want to marry the person they're in love with?"

"No."

My answer seems so obvious, I don't stop to consider the fact that I myself have just said yes to the proposition. I know I'm right, though. Tons of people don't want to get married. Marriages end every day. Or couples eschew the institution entirely. My parents have been together for almost thirty years, and they've never tied the knot.

Marriage is a choice, which is why I want to do it. It *means* something when someone decides to get married. It's an opt-in to stability. Normalcy. It's a choice to join civilized society.

"Well," Gen says, "I wanted to marry him, and have a wedding filled with glitter and magic, and ride off into the sunset together. I bought a ring and everything. It wasn't that expensive or anything. It was made out of a guitar string. But it was awesome. It fit him, you know? And I had it all planned out. I got tickets to Slick Weezle when they came in town, and I gave one of the security guards a buddy pass to let us sneak up to one of the balconies. We had it all to ourselves. I waited until the end of the last song when the whole place was screaming before I got down on one knee."

"So, what did he say?"

She shrugs, but her face has tightened in a very un-Gen-like way. "Nothing really. He kissed me, and he said he liked the ring. It didn't really bother me that he didn't answer, I swear it didn't. I figured he was thinking about it. But he didn't call the next day. And then he didn't call the next. He wasn't home when I showed up. And you know how it goes . . ."

"That's it?" My voice catches in my throat. "He just disappeared?"

"I mean, he called to yell at me after I keyed his bike. But yeah, he pretty much vanished after that. I saw him out with a girl a couple of weeks ago."

I flinch. Partly because I've experienced that pain before, but also because that couldn't have gone well for either Stake or the girl. "Please tell me you didn't hurt her."

"I wish." Gen scoffs, but her eyes fall to the floor. "I couldn't move. I felt like I'd been hit by a baseball bat. I swear, it literally felt like a big wooden stick had knocked the wind out of me."

Without warning, my mind flashes back to a hotel room two years ago. Two figures on the bed. Patterned rain against the window. Clothes scattered across the floor. A flight attendant's dress, just like mine, only mine was still on my body. Gen is right. A baseball bat is exactly what it felt like. A Louisville Slugger straight to the gut.

"I'm so sorry." I wouldn't wish that feeling on anyone.

"I'm fine." Gen straightens up and tosses her hair over her shoulder, but her smile is a watered-down version of itself. "You're lucky, though, not wanting to get married. That means it will happen for you. They say love always comes to the people who want it the least."

My thumb reaches for the bare skin of my finger, and I feel a surge of relief that I decided not to wear Alexander's ring. Gen has misunderstood me, but maybe that's for the best. The last thing I want to do right now is tell her exactly how lucky I am.

Gen doesn't even know Alexander and I are dating. Nobody I work with does. Details of my love life are reserved for friends—however few they may be—not coworkers. When you're trapped on a jump seat like we are, it's too easy to find yourself giving parts of yourself away to someone you might not run into again for another several years, if ever. Before you know it, too much of you is floating out in the world, carried by people who don't care about you. It's better to keep the personal details to myself.

Anyway, even if I weren't being sensitive toward Gen's feelings, there's something pathetic about telling her before I've told anyone else in the world. It's like the lonely cat lady who tells the gas station cashier about her promotion because nobody else sticks around long enough for her to get the words out.

Gen is still looking at me, seemingly waiting for some kind of answer, so I lift my lips into a smile I hope looks reassuring and say, "I'm sure it will happen for both of us one day."

Chapter 5

I jump up the moment the bell dings for ten thousand feet, not because I'm scared my omission will turn into an outright lie if Gen and I continue this conversation, but because I am an excellent flight attendant who is eager to please. Also, Gen has grabbed the interphone to make her announcements, and it's probably smartest to be in the cabin in front of the passengers so if she says anything crazy, they'll know it wasn't me speaking. I grab a drink-order pad and toss on my apron before leaving her to it.

There's a perfect amount of light in the cabin, enough to see comfortably without waking every person on board. It's not quite 6:30 and every third person is sleeping. A man on the aisle clutches a Starbucks coffee to his belly as he snores above it. I turn to my side to slide past his knee, which has sunk into the aisle.

As B, I am responsible for the back eight rows. During the day, these will often be the most laid-back passengers on the plane. They're the ones who didn't bother to check in early and don't care about getting off the plane quickly. At night, those same people will become the party animals who keep us running to and from the liquor kit.

I get more soda orders than I expect. Only a few coffees, despite the early hour. People aren't interested in our tired old brew anymore. They want lattes. They want iced drinks with soy milk and pumps of artificial flavor. What they don't want is coffee the color of tea with unrefrigerated thimbles of "creamer."

Two people already have their noise-canceling headphones on, faces tilted toward screens. I'm unable to get their attention, but it doesn't matter. They'll manage to look up once I'm serving their neighbors, at which point they'll inform me (with the slightest edge to their tone at the injustice of it all) that I neglected to offer them anything.

Jack is still sitting on the jump seat when I get to the back. The lights are off, and his face is lit by the glow of his phone. It's colder back here than it was in front, as is always the case. He looks up in surprise at my footsteps.

"You got started fast," he says.

My back stiffens at the implication I've somehow cut his break short. Jackson has clearly enjoyed his time alone, in my galley, on my jump seat.

"I take my duties seriously," I say primly. I am such a professional.

He stands up and squeezes by me to get into the cubby where we keep the drink-order pads. His arm brushes against mine, firm and warm. My skin tingles, and my stomach sinks. I knew I didn't want to spend three days in a tiny galley with him, but I didn't think through how big he actually is.

I step to the side and peek at him from the corner of my eye. He must be at least six foot, but it's his shoulders that are the real problem. They're too broad. Standing side by side, pouring our drinks, we won't be able to avoid brushing up against each other. And sitting on the jump seat? I'd have to amputate a butt cheek just to keep mine from pressing against his.

"How's the head?"

I jump at his question, ripping my gaze away from him just as he's turning toward me. The same drink pad that looks normal-sized in my hand looks tiny in his.

"If that's your way of asking if I need you to steal my seat again," I say, "I do not."

He lifts an eyebrow. "Your command of the English language is incredible."

"Well, I do spend a lot of time thinking about words. For example, I was just trying to think of adjectives for undesirable coworkers. So far, I've come up with *disagreeable*, *obnoxious*, and *jack . . . asses*."

"Don't forget *clumsy*."

My hand goes to my hip. "I was kicked in the face!"

"Oh, we were talking about you? I guess I hadn't noticed your obnoxious side yet." He slides past me, disappearing into the cabin.

I glare after him, trying to determine which of us just insulted me more. What's worse is I'm pretty sure I *am* being disagreeable. Maybe even a jackass. Something about Jack Stone brings out my terrible side. I wonder if it's possible to be allergic to people. Like, proximity to them can make your personality begin to sneeze and hack.

But maybe this is exactly what I needed. The truth is, I didn't have to work this trip. In my industry, there's no such thing as two weeks' notice. Flight attendants bid for monthly schedules, and the computer program assigns trips to the monthly calendar known as our "board." One call to Scheduling, and my board would've been erased, all remaining trips easily given away to some low-seniority flight attendant sitting reserve. But I didn't make the call. If I'm being perfectly honest, I wasn't ready to quit.

I needed to work one last trip. I wanted the one last goodbye, and the fact that this trip included a layover in Belize was just the icing on the cake. But how much harder would it have been to let go if everything went idyllically? An unpleasant coworker. An unlikeable version of myself. A kick to the face. These might be the best possible ways to finish off the career I'm walking away from.

I nod at the realization, somewhat appeased, and turn on the work lights. They fill the space with a bluish light that resembles something you'd find in a mortuary. It sounds depressing, but it's actually quite soothing. This is *my* space.

My favorite part of flying B is that I'm the one who gets to set up the galley for service. Flipping open the cabinets, I take a moment to appreciate the sight of rows and rows of organized cans. I hated traveling as a child because it was a life of chaos and disorder. What I've discovered in this job is that, when done right, travel is one of the most ordered existences possible.

On the road, everything is compacted into a small space, so you always know exactly what you're working with. There are sixteen cans of Coke in this cubby. Eight cans of Dr Pepper. It doesn't matter where I'm going, this compartment will always start with sixteen cans of Coke, eight Sprites, sixteen Diet Cokes, and so on, and so on. I pull out one of each and set them in the middle of the counter, using an old hotel key card I keep in my apron to pop them open.

I grab the trays and set one on each side of the cans before retrieving a sleeve of cups from a cubby behind me. A few years ago, I discovered I have a knack for pulling exactly twelve cups out of the sleeve without having to count. There just happens to be twelve slots in each tray. It's a useless skill, but one that brings me a hefty amount of satisfaction every time I work.

By the time Jack returns, I've filled the cups with ice and am pulling the rest of the compartments open. I have to stand on my tiptoes to reach the latch to the napkin cubby. The little door swings up, and a stack of napkins that had clearly been shoved in fall out and cascade over my head.

"What was that about not being clumsy?" Jack says mildly.

I choose to ignore him because he's already bending down to scoop the napkins off the ground and throw them in the trash. I stick my drink sheet on the cabinet in front of me and start pouring. Jack finishes with the napkins and does the same. He's fast, though. Maybe even faster than me. He grabs cans with a military precision that gives me visions of a soldier assembling a gun.

Once again, I find myself wondering how he ended up in this job. How does someone who once chose to wear the uniform of an organization with the motto "Fly-Fight-Win" end up handling carry-on luggage? It's a bit of a comedown for someone who previously manned a 155,000-pound vehicle. If he didn't like the Air Force, he could've gone commercial. He could've become a bush pilot in Alaska. He must've had loads of options.

Maybe he really is so dedicated to his pursuit of feminine variety that he couldn't resist putting himself in a job made up mostly of women. Straight males probably make up 20 percent of the flight attendants at Northeast Air, and most of them were retired cops before they were hired. As a handsome, fit, heterosexual man, Jack is basically our unicorn, with a penis as the horn atop his head. It's a disgusting realization, and there's no way I can allow him to be better at this job than me when he's only here to play the field.

Taking a peek at his tray, I speed up. I pour a row of Diet Cokes too fast, and the fizz burbles and merges into one long bubbly line before sinking over the sides of the cups. This never happens to me. I'm a master at pouring drinks. I pour them to the perfect height and always divide one can into exactly three cups.

I glance at Jack as I turn to get some napkins, noting the way his lip curls at my mess. He's not doing much better, though. There's a puddle of brown at the top of a cup of orange juice that has to be spilled coffee. The moment my back is completely turned, I hear the plop of a cup getting thrown into the trash. I hold in a laugh.

We finish at the same time, much to my disappointment. I tilt my chin at him to go, because his section is past mine. I serve my drinks, managing to beat him back, and rush to get started. For the first time in years, I end up with two extras when I pull out the cups. I curse Jack for his sabotage on my own grip. Imagine having the ability to mess me up when he's not even back here. He's like some kind of evil magician.

"What was that?" Jack appears from behind me, and I realize my mental curses were audible.

"Nothing."

He lifts an eyebrow but doesn't press me. Instead he starts pouring. To my infinite fury, he manages to finish first, despite starting after me. It's a double win, and he knows it.

"Did you need help with anything?" He asks the question sweetly, his voice like honey.

"I'm done, thanks." I pour the Sprite I'm holding into the last cup. It's not what they ordered, but I can deal with that later.

Jack nods and heads up the aisle. This time, I'm desperate to beat him back. I shove drinks into the flaccid hands of half-sleeping passengers. One lady is so unnerved, she jerks her hand back just as I'm letting go. The cup plummets, and Diet Coke explodes into her lap. She gives a shriek Jack is certain to hear.

"I'm so sorry." I give her a few napkins before relenting and handing her the rest of my stack. "But Diet Coke doesn't stain. It's all chemicals. There's nothing real to stick to the material."

Her mouth pinches, and she grabs the napkins from my hand, her grip suddenly and magically strengthened. I'm too busy glancing behind me at Jack's progress to feel shame. Normally I'd go to the back and resupply myself with napkins before continuing to pass out drinks. Now I just give the cups by themselves, cold and naked. People take them from me with trembling hands, their eyes wide with fear. Mine are probably wild with the frenzy of my own speed.

I'm able to get to the back and dump the cup of Sprite into the trash before Jack arrives. We both start icing new cups without speaking. But he still has two-thirds of a tray left, and I only have four more orders. My reliable section in the back of the plane. They really are the best. I swan out with my air-light tray and step back in just as Jack's finishing up pouring.

"Did you need help with anything?" My voice is angelic.

"I'm good. I just had a few more orders than you."

"Mm-hmm."

I grab a book the moment he's gone and make a point to

be lounging on the jump seat, deep into the story by the time he returns. In case he doesn't get the picture, I give a start of surprise at some imaginary scene I'm pretending to read. *Look at me. I am so into my book that I actually feel like I'm inside it.* That's *how long I've been reading.* Jack remains silent, and I can't look up to see if he's noticed, even though I want to. I make an effort to read a full sentence, but it's impossible with him hulking over me.

"Did you forget something?" His voice is quiet, but I jump in my seat anyway.

"Me?"

"Well, me, too." Jack's mouth curves into a sheepish smile. "Pretzels."

I jerk upright. "Pretzels!"

According to Northeast Air standards, we're meant to do service in a specific order. First, we pour our first tray of drinks. Then, we deliver the snacks. Then, we serve the drinks. I never, ever deviate from the order. It's a good thing this is my last trip because I wouldn't be able to stand working a job I'm clearly getting worse at. I scowl at Jack as I drop the book and jerk to my feet. The jump seat folds up with a bang.

A small, irritatingly rational section of my brain tells me that my ridiculous need to race through service caused me to forget the pretzels. Another more compelling and infinitely larger section of my brain insists it's Jackson's fault; he's destroying all sense of the order that makes me love this job. He's a problem. Still, it feels like wanting to rip open the emergency exit and shove him out might be an overreaction on my part.

I reach for the basket as Jack grabs several sacks of pretzels. He rips one open with a savagery that's impressive. He's probably imagining it's my skull. I pull one of the bags from his grip and tear it open. Pretzels scatter across the galley floor. For the second time in less than an hour, Jack bends to the ground to gather up my mess. Last time wasn't my fault, but this time clearly is. As thoroughly as I search my mind, I can't come up with a justification for staying silent.

"Thank you," I say coolly, squatting to join him in collecting pretzel bags.

"Don't mention it." His voice lacks my frost, but it contains that dismissiveness I find so infuriating. *I'm just doing my job*, it insinuates. *Someone has to clean up your messes.*

When the basket is full, we stand and each take one side. Jack backs into the aisle, pulling me along. I'm forced to walk face-to-face with him over our trough of shiny red packets. Through the windows, the sky is now blue and cloudless. Jack's eyes are the exact same color. I focus on the little packs of pretzels and offering a smile at each passenger I hand one to.

For several rows, we move at the same pace. He covers the left side of the plane while I cover the right. We're at row twenty-two when progress stalls. A woman's hand hovers beside Jack's. There's always someone who can't decide if they're willing to accept a free offering of approximately nine mini-pretzels. This is that woman. She's got long, elegant limbs and shoulder-length hair that looks like it's been professionally blown out. It shines with expensive highlights.

"What is it?" Her tone is suspicious, like she believes it's possible that we're passing out yogurt-covered rat droppings.

"Pretzels," Jack says.

"I don't know." She leans closer to his hand, studying the package.

"Don't leave me hanging." Jack offers her a flirtatious smile. "You don't want to hurt my feelings, do you?"

She laughs in a way that makes me hate her almost as much as I hate him. To cover my snort, I lean over the basket and start shoving pretzels into the hands of people in the next row. Jack looks at me in confusion, and I lift my watch in the air. I'm being ridiculous; we have nothing but time. Still, he's clearly holding us up. His eyes narrow.

"Put them in your purse for later." He winks at the woman, and she slips the pretzels from his hand, one manicured finger stroking the length of his thumb.

I subtly pretend to vomit. Jack rolls his eyes at me and resumes his progress down the aisle. I start to pass them out faster. He speeds up, and by the time we reach the exit row, shiny red bags are flying like shrapnel.

Chapter 6

I'm exhausted when we get to the hotel in Portland. I've spent the entire day in a silent race with Jack. The majority of the words I've spoken have been directed toward Gen. Instead of staying up front and guarding the cockpit like a good A, she kept coming back and camping out in the back galley. Her braying laughter is still ringing in my ears. Apparently Jack is capable of being funny. It's just not a facet of his personality he chooses to share with me.

The first thing I do when I enter the room is find the box on the wall that controls the temperature. It's set to sixty-three. I exhale from deep in my lungs and am surprised I can't see my breath in the air. Rebelliously, I notch it up to seventy-eight.

If Alexander were here and didn't actually dissolve into a puddle at the heat, he'd certainly lecture me about wasting electricity. But one of the greatest things about hotels is the godlike ability they offer to control my environment. Before long, this room will be as inviting as a warm bath.

Another thing I love about hotel rooms is their lack of

clutter. This one is painted in chocolate hues with a fluffy white duvet on the king-sized bed. It has one large white painting with black strokes creating the silhouette of a tree. Another framed photograph shows a path through a park in autumn, leaves red and golden, shining beneath the glow of the sun. There are four pillows, all of them bulging at the seams.

It's a beautiful room, but I have a secret preference for cheaper hotels. Motels, even. They always have flat, worn pillows that don't leave a crick in my neck. They have thin blankets with tacky, multicolored designs that tend to slip off the bed like they're trying to escape. But I never sweat beneath those blankets like I do the feather-down duvets in fancier hotels.

I slide the bag rack out of the closet and set it up along the wall. Unzipping it, I only pull out a change of clothes. The trick to leaving a hotel room with everything you entered with is to keep everything exactly where it belongs. If you use a charger, you return it to its assigned pocket the moment your phone hits 100 percent. Nothing is allowed to linger out of place. If something is left on any available surface, it is almost guaranteed to still be there when you check out.

I've pulled on a thick-knit maroon sweater and am slipping on a pair of faded jeans with a hole in the knee when my phone rings. For a moment, I'm certain it must be Ro. This is why she hasn't returned my text. She missed me like I missed her and wanted to hear my voice.

It's not her, though.

I stare at the name on the screen. I haven't heard from my mom in months. Not after I left a message telling her Alexander and I said we loved each other for the first time. Not even when I told her voicemail Alexander and I were moving in together. No congratulations. No parental words of wisdom. Just a gaping cavern of silence.

Alexander was disgusted on my behalf, despite my repeated reassurances it's not personal. This is just how it goes with my parents. Once, they called every day for thirteen days in a row. On the fourteenth, I didn't hear from them. Something about the regularity made me feel nervous. I left voicemails. I begged them to return my call. Two months later, they finally did. They'd been at a meditation retreat in Thailand. They were happy.

My finger sways back and forth between the red icon and the green. It must mean something that my mom is finally calling today of all days, the very week I get engaged. Some kind of latent motherly instinct has caused her to reach out. Hesitantly I click the green icon.

"Hi!" I speak in a bright and peppy tone. Even to my own ears, it sounds fake.

"Where are you?" My mom's voice sounds the same as ever: breathless, excited, and a little distracted.

"Portland. Why?" My heart rate picks up speed. "Is everything okay?"

"Of course, sweetie." There's a muffled sound on the phone like she's covered it with her hand. She parrots the word *Portland*, most likely to my dad. "We were just hoping you were in Colorado Springs. Sterling is about to take us on the most amazing hike, and I thought you'd love it."

Irritation tags in to run the race with my nerves. "Why would I be in Colorado Springs? Northeast Air doesn't even fly there."

"They fly to Denver."

"Okay." The two places are hours apart, but reminding my mom of that fact is pointless. She'd just say she's willing to drive to get me, like she's the kind of mother who would do anything for her daughter. Then I'd have to bite my tongue to keep from arguing that (a) I'm *not there*, and (b) the last time I was stupid enough to let her pick me up while I was working, she made me miss my flight. I almost lost my job, and the next few months were the first time in my life the silence between us was my choice instead of theirs.

"But I guess we'll just have to go without you." Mom's voice dips like she's disappointed. Like, despite not seeing each other in almost a year, she'd managed to convince herself today was the day. "It's too bad. I really do think you would've loved it."

"I'm sure I would've." Despite my annoyance, I can't help feeling touched to have been thought of at all. My mom is right; I probably would have loved that hike. The mountains in Colorado are amazing.

I used to fly standby there on my days off, before those were committed to being Alexander's date to business dinners. With just a small pack on my back, I'd trek higher and higher until my legs shrieked with life. The sky felt so close I could almost touch it.

I even considered moving to Denver once. I had my phone in my hand, ready to call my landlord and tell him to start the search for new renters. Northeast Air has a base there. It would've been the easiest thing in the world to transfer. In the end, I couldn't do it, though. I'd spent too many years promising myself I'd live life differently once I was the one making the choices. To stay true to that promise, I needed to stay in one place.

Thank goodness I kept myself in line. A few weeks later, I met Alexander.

"Mom?" I take a deep breath. "I have news."

"News?" She sounds interested, if a little distracted.

"Yes, exciting news. I'm getting married."

"Sweetheart! Married? I'm so delighted for you!"

"You are?" I don't know why I feel so relieved. I guess, since she and Dad never got married, I thought she might consider such a decision silly.

"Of course I am. Finding your life partner is a beautiful thing." Her voice lowers confidingly. "And I had a feeling about you two, you know."

"You did?" The relief swells back up in another wave so strong I can hear it in my voice.

"I'm sure everyone did. It's just too perfect, isn't it? A pilot and a flight attendant. It's like you were made for each other."

My stomach sinks like the ground beneath a cannonball. "No, Mom. Not R—" My throat closes over his name. I can't even say it. It's such a stupid, *stupid* name. "I'm marrying Alexander."

"Oh, Ava." To her credit, she sounds genuinely horrified. "I'm such an airhead. Alexander. Obviously Alexander. I don't know what I was thinking."

"It's fine. We haven't been together that long." *Nine months.* Before that, I was single for well over a year. It would almost be better if this were some kind of passive-aggressive move on my mother's part, indicating a dislike of Alexander. But I know it's not. Somehow, my own mother has managed to blank out two years of my life. "And you've only met him once. It's an understandable mistake."

"It's an incredibly rude mistake. And it's proof that I

should skip my turn hitting Sterling's bong, at least while the sun is still up."

I laugh in spite of myself. "Sure. And I'll stop drinking coffee in the mornings."

She giggles in a childlike way. It makes me feel like the adult.

"Well," she says, clearing her throat, "it sounds like your dad and I need to plan a little road trip. What do you think? Are you up for a visit? I'd love to get to know my future son-in-law better."

"Really?" I push down the hope that rises at her words. It's a nice offer, but it doesn't necessarily mean anything. She's likely to get off the phone, go hiking, and forget all about this conversation.

"Sure," she says. "Today is what, Wednesday?"

"Tuesday."

"Right. Tuesday. If we got in the car now, we could take back roads all the way there—you know they're always prettier than the highways—and get to Chicago by the weekend. Wouldn't that be fun?"

"It would be." I lower myself into the rolling chair in front of the desk. It faces a mirror, and I can see the hopefulness in my expression, despite my effort to manage my expectations. My lips have curved. The hazel eyes I've gotten from my mom—never able to pick a color and just stick with it—are sparkling at the idea of seeing my parents. It *would* be fun. My parents might not be the most dependable people in the world, but if you're lucky enough to end up where they are, they're guaranteed to be a good time. It was the only thing that made the endless moving bearable when I was a child. I lost so many friends, but even when I didn't know another living soul in town, I couldn't be truly lonely, not when I lived with two presences as large as my parents.

"That's what we'll do then," she says decisively.

"I'd love that." I wonder if Alexander expects our engagement dinner to be an intimate, romantic affair. I hope not. I'd love it if my parents could join us. A celebration with family would be the perfect thing to make this next step in our relationship feel real.

"Oh," she says, "but there's a festival in town on Saturday. I wouldn't want to miss it. They're putting up a Ferris wheel!"

"Of course not." My sentiment is devoid of sarcasm. In the mirror, my smile wavers for only a moment before widening. As comforting as it might be to have the kind of parents who prioritize a visit to see their only child, there's an undeniable charm to the ones I've been given instead. Back roads or a festival. My mom makes them sound like once-in-a-lifetime opportunities. To her, that's what they are.

For a moment, in the stillness of the hotel room, a whiff of funnel cakes and corn dogs tickles at my nose. I remember the three of us, years ago, the weight of my dad's hand in my own as my mom danced to the pop song accompanying the ride that swung from side to side, spinning its screaming passengers. The neon lights flashed across my face as it passed, and my stomach sank when we moved forward in line and I saw the sign. I wasn't tall enough. They weren't going to let me ride. I licked my lips, still sticky from cotton candy, and looked up at my mom, but she grabbed my free hand before I could say anything.

"Look over there," she said, lifting her long, slender arm to point. "It's a fun house!" She bounced with excitement. "Don't you want to see if they have those crazy mirrors?"

Without waiting for an answer, she tugged me out of line, the three of us a chain that jolted forward as she ran. I giggled as I stumbled between them, pulled along by the tide that was my parents. The ride behind us was instantly forgotten. There was no way it could be as exciting as whatever we were running toward.

"Maybe next weekend," she says.

"That would be nice." There's a hitch in my voice.

"I hate that it's been so long since we've seen each other. I'm being thoughtless, though. Poor Sterling is probably waiting for us. We'll come soon, okay?"

"Okay," I say, pretending to believe her.

"I miss you, sweetheart."

"I miss you, too."

After I hang up, I swivel the chair toward the window and stare out at the emptied parking lot. It's so strange how sometimes a conversation can make you feel lonelier than silence ever did. A brittle brown leaf skitters across the faded tar beneath my window. I pull up Alexander's smiling face on my phone. I don't like to call him while he's working, but my finger is not quite as considerate as my mind. It presses the green icon.

"Hello, future Mrs. Raphael." His words come out sweet but rushed.

"I've caught you at a bad time," I say.

"No." He sighs. "Well, yes. But I'm glad you called. It's always nice to hear your voice."

"I'm sorry. I just wanted to tell you that I talked to my mom. She was thrilled to hear that we're getting married. I was hoping they'd be able to come for the engagement dinner, but it doesn't look like they'll be able to make it."

"Oh, we're inviting other people to that?" His voice muffles, and he says something to someone else before returning to the phone. "Perfect. My mother wanted to talk to you about booking the Starlight for our wedding. She's pulling some strings to get us in. Friday night will be a perfect time to discuss it. Although, if you ask me, you should hire a wedding planner before then. Otherwise, Mother is likely to steamroll you on all the decisions. You know how she is."

My grip on the phone tightens. As immature as it might be, it doesn't feel fair of Alexander to take the news that my parents can't make it as an excuse to have his come. Plus, I *do* know how his mother is. I also know the Starlight. It's ornate to the point of gaudy, and any event held there is guaranteed to be fancier than anything I'd want to attend, much less plan.

"It's very sweet of her to want to help us out," I say, "but I was actually envisioning something smaller and more intimate. I'm not sure pulled strings or a wedding planner will be necessary."

"Of course. Whatever you want, my love. But this will be an important day with a lot of important people in attendance. Having a wedding planner will ensure they walk away with the best possible impression."

Best possible impression? Of what? Of us?

"But—"

Alexander cuts me off. "Let's talk about this tonight, shall we? Things are a little crazy here at the moment."

I nod as if he can see me and find myself apologizing before hanging up. The entire conversation has left a bad taste in my mouth. I tell myself it's because, despite Alexander saying "Whatever you want," it's clear our wedding is going to end up being something I don't, in fact, want. The truth, however, is that I'm most annoyed that I inadvertently opened the door to Alexander's parents coming to our special night.

They don't like me. They never have. They're not openly hostile, but their disdain of me is evident. His father is merely dismissive, but his mother likes to make snide comments when Alexander isn't paying attention. *That's such a brave outfit, dear. Not everyone has the courage to mix patterns with such abandon.*

It's my fault, though. If I didn't want them at the dinner, I shouldn't have admitted to inviting my own parents. Obviously Alexander would take that as a prompt to invite his. How could he be expected to realize his casual assuredness that they'd come might feel like salt in my wounds? I can't expect him to be a mind reader. If I wanted sympathy from him, I should've shared that it made me sad my parents couldn't make it.

On the desk, the hotel phone rings. I close my eyes, not wanting to talk anymore. It's probably Gen, trying to lock down dinner plans. I was deliberately distracted in the lobby while she and Paul were discussing what time to meet. I may not be skilled at saying no, but I have a lifetime of experience at being noncommittal. I'm not proud of that particular personality trait, but it is built into who I am.

Sighing, I let the phone ring until it fades to voicemail. Gen will just assume I've already unplugged it. It's part of the routine we all follow, along with muting our phones once it's time to sleep. Scheduling only has one way of catching you once you're in the room. If, in a groggy, unaware state, you're foolish enough to answer a call, you're likely to find yourself with an updated trip complete with earlier report time, four extra legs of flight, and a shortened overnight for the next day.

If they can't reach you, however, that misery will pass to some other flight attendant foolish enough to allow themselves to be contacted.

When the phone goes silent, I unplug it. As much as I love Gen, I've had enough of her today. It goes without saying I've had enough of Jack Stone. Still, I feel guilty about ditching them. I bet even Captain Ballinger will show for dinner. It's a crew thing. It's just what you do. People who don't are called Slam-Clickers. Nobody wants to be the kind of person who beelines it to their room and locks the door behind them. It's just unfriendly.

I feel too unsettled to make any more polite conversation today, though. I've got that familiar buzz in my veins, a restlessness I know exactly how to appease. I should fight it. Put on pajamas. Settle in. Order room service and fire up Netflix. Instead I put on my uniform trench coat and head out.

I close the door with a gentle tug, hoping Gen won't hear it and pop out of the room across from me. Thankfully, the hallway stays still and empty. Unwanted anticipation builds in me as I near the end of the long stretch of worn carpet. I take the stairs instead of the elevator. My footsteps tap an echoing tune that fills me with joy. The door at the bottom swings into the sunlit lobby, a portal to a new adventure.

I stroll out the glass double doors, the frigid air hitting my cheeks. It's invigorating. I have no idea where I'm going, but it doesn't matter. I'm not looking for fun. I just want to feel it. Portland. The world. The rush I get every time I'm somewhere different, alone and untethered.

I hate it as much as I love it.

I hate that this desire to wander has been knit into my DNA. A part of me. *Inflicted*. Nonetheless, it's as inescapable as my mom's indecisive eyes that stare back at me every time I look into a mirror, or the too-large upper lip I tend to tug between my teeth, just like Dad does whenever he's stressed.

I'd run from it if I could, but that's not possible. Even if it were, it's not the answer. My parents are the runners. I have to stop. And I will. I have tonight and tomorrow, and then it's over. This trip. This job. Over.

No more excuses.

Chapter 7

There's a park behind our hotel filled with tall, bushy trees and winding paths. I pick one and follow it. Mothers with matching strollers and yoga pants pass by, gossiping without fear of being overheard. Children shriek and scatter beneath the trees in a game of tag. The twangy strum of a guitar drifts through the air. A mismatched group of people lounge on the grass in a patch of sunlight. Some have dreadlocks. Others wear tattered baseball caps. The guitarist begins to sing in a weathered voice that tells of whiskey-soaked days and nights that don't end until the sun rises. I stop to listen for a while before the lure of adventure makes my feet twitch with anticipation.

I'm at the edge of the park when I spot the brown-bricked buildings down a hill, lined like a little downtown area. I skirt around a chain-link fence and cross a field. Ten minutes later I'm surrounded by restaurants and shops. I stop inside a bookstore and breathe in the smell of old leather and fresh paper. The brightly colored covers promise entrance into fictional worlds filled with witty banter and passionate kisses. I flirt back with them, caressing their pages and peeking beneath their covers, but I don't buy one. I've traveled long enough to know you should never pick up anything that might weigh you down.

It's a lesson I repeat to myself when I spot the dress in the window of a thrift shop on the corner. Still, I can't resist going inside to see it up close. It would make a perfect wedding dress. A bell chimes over my head as the door opens. A young woman with spiked blue hair and hot-pink lips leans back in a chair behind the checkout desk, chunky black boots propped in front of her on a stack of papers. She looks over her book and flashes a smile.

"Let me know if you need anything." Her voice is high-pitched like that of a cartoon mouse.

"Thanks," I say. But her eyes have already returned to the open pages in front of her.

Aside from her, the shop is empty. Well, not at all empty, actually. There are no other people, but it's plenty cramped, full of racks bursting with clothes. Even the walls are covered in colorful posters and whimsical hats. It smells like cinnamon, like there's a big pot of apple cider brewing in back. I inhale deeply as I wind my way to the dress in the window.

Up close, I can see the fabric is more yellow than cream. I've always thought of yellow as the color of happiness. When I was younger, wherever we lived, I would go out in search of yellow flowers and pick every one I could find. Sometimes I had my own room. Sometimes I just had a corner of someone else's room. It didn't matter. I would set a pile of flowers next to my pillow, and every morning I would wake up to little yellow petals of happiness.

"May I try this on, please?" I'm being silly. This dress is not even fancy enough to wear to one of Alexander's business events, much less in a wedding. It's knee-length, light, and wispy. It's for dancing in the sunlight, twirling in the breeze.

Still, I follow the shopkeeper to the small purple closet she claims is a dressing room, and I know the moment I zip it up that it was created specifically for me. I have to take my bra off because of the spaghetti straps, but even without it, the fit is flawless. The material is soft against my skin. The waist nips in. The skirt flutters out. It is exactly the kind of thing someone would wear in a sunlit garden, surrounded by flowers, exchanging vows with the person they're going to spend the rest of their life with.

It's also only thirty-five dollars. With a carefree laugh, I buy it. I can't even feel bad about breaking one of my travel rules. I love this dress, and there's something perfect about finding it on my last trip. I've been so determined to leave this life behind, but maybe it's okay to bring a tiny part of my past with me into my future. I've spent nine years wandering the world on my own. Why shouldn't I want that part of me represented when I start my next adventure?

To celebrate, I take my new wedding dress to dinner. We end up at the counter of a deli I've never heard of with exposed brick walls and black piping that winds across the ceiling. It's cute, but more importantly, it feels local, the kind of place that's unique to this area, this moment. My sandwich comes out piled high with roast beef and turkey, served with a mountain of chips and a pickle that makes my lips pucker. One bite in, and I'm already tempted to ask for a second one. An elderly man settles at the counter next to me. The wired back of the stool groans as he leans into it. He has weathered skin and deep lines around his eyes, but the build of someone who's retaining his grip on a lifetime of fitness.

"Thank you for your service," I say. When he looks at me in surprise, I motion to his Portland Fire & Rescue hat.

"Ah. Sorry to disappoint, but they were giving them out at some pancake fundraiser my wife dragged me along to." His voice is gruff. "I'm former military, though, so I'll take the gratitude. And a couple of those chips, if you're not planning on eating them all."

"Actually," I say, "I was planning to finish these and then see if they'd top them off with another round."

"Really?" His eyes widen. "You have my respect."

I laugh. "No, not really. I have to save room for one of those black-and-white cookies."

"Only a sucker would fall for that cookie trick. They look good, but this place makes them too sweet. It's the brownie you really want. They're the best in town."

"Sold." I look down at my plate, where I still have about three meals' worth of food. I'm already getting full. "Is it weird if I offer you half of this sandwich to go with the chips you already claimed?"

"It's only weird if you've added vegetables in there that I can't see."

"Nope. It's a Number Three, straight off the menu."

"A fellow purist." He requests an extra plate and introduces himself as Ronald but says I can call him R.J.

I ask what the *J* stands for, and he tells me about his amateur boxing days in the military where he had a right hook that came back so quickly it was like being on the wrong end of a jackhammer. There's an edge to his demeanor, a sharpness that makes me suspect dissatisfaction is something that's always tugging at him, shadowing everything he sees with gray strokes. He reminds me of a bulldog, reluctantly domesticated but surly at heart.

Through bites of roast beef, we swap stories. His are about

dangerous missions and fights he almost didn't—but, of course, did—win. Mine are of misbehaving passengers. At first, he shuts me down, telling me his kid is a flight attendant and he's heard it all before. But I reel him in with the one about a woman who brought a duck on board as her "emotional support animal." And when my tale of the drunk guy who peed in the back galley makes him bark with laughter, I flush with triumph. R.J. doesn't strike me as the kind of man who laughs easily.

"Sorry," he says before letting another chuckle escape. "It probably wasn't funny for you. I bet you were the one who ended up cleaning it."

"Yep. Plus, a substantial amount splattered onto my pantyhose."

R.J. snorts.

"But it's fine." My voice flattens with sarcasm. "He explained to me that pee is sterile."

"What an asshole." He shakes his head. "Brownies are on me. As a man who's gotten drunk and drained the pipe in a few inappropriate places myself, consider it an apology on behalf of all mankind."

"I'll take it. We could split, if you want? I'm pretty full."

The hard-earned smile disappears from R.J.'s face in answer. A minute later, two brownies the size of my hand are sitting in front of us. Like Costco shoppers vying for the last samples on the tray, we each snatch one up and shove it into our mouths. Mine is rich and fudgy and has thick pecans that crunch delightfully as I chew them.

"Mmm." The involuntary sound hums from my throat.

"Sounds like I missed out." A familiar, extremely unwelcome voice filters through my chocolatey haze.

I jerk around to discover my least favorite coworker standing behind us, one uninvited hand resting against the back of my stool. Strangely, his attention is directed not toward me but at R.J. I blink at him in confusion.

Without his uniform on, Jack looks like a completely different person. The gray Henley settles over a chest that boasts of years of military training. The well-worn jeans hug his legs in a way the khaki was too polite to do. I tug my gaze up before he can catch me ogling. When my eyes reach his face, I discover it's not just the clothes that are different. That trademark carefree expression of his has been replaced by a tight jaw and furrowed brow. It occurs to me that, despite all the animosity I've thrown his way today, this is the first time I've seen any emanating from him.

"So much for eating dinner together." Jack directs the words toward R.J. without acknowledging my presence.

My eyes flick back and forth between the two of them. Because of my surprise at Jack's appearance—in this restaurant, at my stool, in those *jeans*—it takes me longer than it probably should to fit the pieces together. Jack hasn't come in here because he spotted me at the counter. He's here because he's R.J.'s flight attendant kid. He's here to meet his dad. *I've been hanging out with Jack Stone's father.*

I don't know what the odds are of this kind of coincidence happening, but I'm guessing it's on par with running into your high school biology teacher in Morocco. I can only assume this is the universe's determination to reward me with the knowledge that my stories are better than Jack's. As petty as it might be, I'm delighted by the victory.

"You're late," R.J. says before unapologetically stuffing another bite of brownie in his mouth.

"Actually, I'm right on time."

"If you're not—"

"Early," Jack says over him, "you're late. Yeah. Between you and basic training, I've been fully indoctrinated. Which is why I showed up at your house an hour ago so we could walk over together." Finally he slants a glance toward me. "Hello, Ava. Strange seeing you here."

I smile, not because I'm happy to see him but because I appreciate the fact that he's said *strange* instead of *good*. I certainly didn't intend to hijack his dinner, but that doesn't make me any happier about the fact that he's now hijacked mine.

"Hello, Jack," I say curtly.

"You went to my house?" R.J. makes it sound more like an accusation than a question.

"I thought I could help out with that bum washing machine," Jack says.

"I told you I don't need your help."

"Really?" Jack lifts an eyebrow. "Because I barely got up the stairs to your front door before some guy came charging across the lawn waving a tire iron and threatening to burn the place down."

"You think I can't hold my own against some punk with a hunk of metal and a loud mouth?" R.J.'s face flushes red with anger, and I wonder if this is my cue to leave. What, exactly, is the etiquette for a dinner with a stranger that has turned into a family squabble with a coworker over the course of approximately fifteen seconds? Surprisingly, I've never seen an Emily Post article dedicated to this particular situation. I pick up my brownie and nibble silently at the edges.

"I *think* he has fifty pounds on you," Jack says, "and you have about that many years on him. What are you doing stealing car batteries anyway?"

"I warned him to put the muffler back on. What did he expect? I couldn't hear myself think through all that noise. I don't suppose you took that tire iron from him and put it to good use."

"You mean, did I bludgeon a man with a metal pipe and then come looking for a tasty sandwich?"

R.J. throws his hands out like he's waiting for an answer.

"No, Dad." Jack sighs. "I didn't."

"So, what? My house is on fire now?"

Jack shakes his head. "We came to an agreement. I gave his battery back, added fifty bucks for a new muffler, and explained to him that I used to work on cars and know at least five guys who could crush that metal trash heap into a cube that would fit in my trunk, no questions asked."

"Fifty bucks?" R.J. mutters. "Sucker."

"How did you know where his battery was?" I ask, licking a bit of chocolate off my thumb.

"Oh, good," Jack says flatly. "You're a part of this conversation."

"And yet you're not answering my question," I say.

R.J. smiles. "Yeah, answer my good friend Ava's question."

Jack's eyes narrow as he takes the two of us in. I'm not sure if he's only just realizing his dad and I have been talking for a while or if he's surprised to discover his dad likes me. Either way, I suspect he doesn't approve. But I can't be certain because he only shrugs and lifts a hand to R.J.'s shoulder. "Oh, Juan José Padilla here set it up in the front window. He had to wave that red cape. Taunt the bull."

"Who the hell is Juan Padilla?" R.J. asks.

"A famous matador," I say absently, my eyes narrowing on Jack's hand. "But if you resolved everything so peacefully, why are your knuckles scraped up?"

Jack stiffens and his hand drops back to his side. Something that looks like betrayal sweeps across his face. Before I can make sense of it, it's replaced by a studied nonchalance that's a little too tight at the edges to be believable.

"The guy didn't exactly show up looking for a conversation," Jack says.

"Now we're talking!" R.J.'s eyes light up. "There was a fight? How bad off did you leave him? Did you break his nose? Knock a couple of teeth out of that loud mouth of his? I told him he was in for a world of pain. I just wish I could've been the one to deliver it myself."

I ignore R.J., focused instead on the way Jack's lips press together. With every word R.J. says, they grow a little whiter at the edges, like Jack is focusing his entire being on keeping them shut.

"I didn't fight him," Jack says. "I just knocked him to the ground so I could hold him still long enough to work things out."

R.J. groans and drops his head into his hands.

"Poor Dad." Jack turns to me and winks, but it lacks the cheekiness he manages to infuse into everything else. "For a minute, he got to believe I was more like my brother. How lucky to have *two* sons who enjoy knocking a couple of teeth out of a stranger's mouth."

"You can't say that punk wasn't asking for it," R.J. says, lifting his head.

"Sorry, Sarge." Jack shrugs. "I'm going to get a sandwich. Need anything? Or are you too full from your meal with your good friend?"

"A coffee," R.J. says. "And don't let them put any of that flavored crap in it."

Jack nods, tilting his chin at me in question as he backs away.

"No." I hesitate for a moment before adding a begrudging "Thanks."

Jack must catch the reluctance in my gratitude because a smug grin stretches across his face before he turns and heads to the other end of the counter. It's such a reassuring contrast to the tension he's exhibited since he arrived, I don't even find myself longing to slap it off.

"So," R.J. says, "you know my son. Makes sense, I suppose. Most women seem to."

"We work together." I can't help saying it like an excuse. It's obvious that the moment of easy conversation we've shared has passed, spoiled by the invasion of the man who seems determined to ruin everything about my last trip.

"I should probably go." I slide off the stool and reach for the bag holding my dress. "I didn't mean to interrupt your dinner plans with Jack."

"You didn't interrupt anything. That boy tries to feed me every time he comes into town. Ever since his mother died, it's like he thinks I need him to buy me something to eat. But you know who was paying for that food his mother put on the table for the eighteen years he was living in my house? Me, that's who."

I freeze, half in response to the fist he's just slammed down on the counter, and half from the weightiness of his words. I've just met R.J., but I already know he's not looking for, nor would he appreciate, my sympathy. Still, the information has been shared, and I'm not capable of pretending I haven't heard it.

"I'm sorry for your loss," I say quietly.

"What? The wife? Yeah. She was a good egg. Looked damn fine in a skirt, too." A wistful smile flits across R.J.'s face before it's squashed out by the furrowing of his brow. "I'm doing fine on my own, though. Sure as hell am capable of keeping myself fed."

I hesitate again. Like with the sympathy, I'm confident R.J. wouldn't appreciate a stranger's perspective on his family's dynamic. And I don't even like his son, so there's no reason for me to defend him. Still . . .

"If it were just about the food, wouldn't Jack have been happier when he showed up and discovered you eating without him?" I glance over and see Jack talking to the woman at the cash register. Her head is thrown back with laughter, and the tightness has eased from his body, making him look much more like the self-satisfied ladies' man I find so easy to dislike. "Maybe he just wants to spend time with you."

"Yeah. Because we have so much to talk about. I can tell him about all the lives I saved in Iraq, and he can catch me up on what color apron he was wearing today when he served some old lady tea." R.J.'s head snaps up, and he meets my eyes before offering a beleaguered shrug. "No offense. I'm sure it's a great job for a girl."

"Yes," I say. "As a woman, I've been uniquely blessed with the ability to dunk a bag into a hot cup of water."

"Exactly." Apparently he has decided to ignore my sarcasm, or he's so out of touch it's simply lost on him.

"I bet Jack would look great in an apron, though. Hopefully, he'll start wearing one soon." I wag a finger. "That devil-may-care attitude of his is going to lead straight to stains."

R.J.'s eyes narrow, and his jaw juts out. "You joke, but I bet he didn't tell you he had a promising military career. Top of his class. They gave him the Airman's Medal for—"

"Ah, the What Could Have Been game," Jack interrupts, setting his plate on the counter next to R.J. "Always a fun one.

Well, it's been great running into you, Ava. We can move to a table if you'd like to stay. Or . . ."

He trails off, but the expression on his face says it all. He doesn't want me here. And who could blame him? I've made it clear I don't like him, we've done nothing but fight all day, and I've managed to serve as witness to an argument he'd clearly rather not have been a part of. If I didn't hate him so much, I'd be impressed that he managed to make the offer to move to a table instead of bodily ushering me out the door.

"I should go. I have a hot shower and tiny toiletries waiting for me." I cringe as I hear the words come out of my mouth. Nobody was asking for details.

"That's adorable," Jack says. "Do those tiny toiletries make you feel normal-sized?"

I ignore him, because my love for hotel shampoos and conditioners shouldn't need to be defended. Who wouldn't appreciate the way those little potions are always some absurd scent like ambrosia and cumulus clouds or toasted coconut and pine cones? I like to close my eyes and try to guess the smell before reading the label. The fact that I almost never get it right just makes them that much more delightful.

Instead of lowering myself to respond, I thank R.J. for the brownie. He tells me the sandwich was good but would've been better with a few more chips, while Jack takes a large, conveniently timed bite that allows him to wave goodbye without having to waste any more words on me. When I leave, I find myself feeling alone in a way that hadn't occurred to me before I walked into the deli.

The sun is setting, turning the sky a shade somewhere between gray and lavender. The temperature has dropped from cold to icy. Despite the way the air stings my skin, I don't hurry back to the hotel. I wander aimlessly, my mind racing with the glimpse I've just been granted into another family.

Even once I've showered and crawled into bed, the thoughts keep churning. All day long, I've demonstrated nothing but hostility toward Jack. There's no question that, in his son's position, R.J. would've declared war on me in return. Jack, on the other hand, has not once shown the slightest inclination of even becoming defensive, much less allowed me to push him to anything resembling anger. He's infuriated me by seeming to find amusement at my expense. He's certainly prodded back more than once. But in spite of being the product of a father like R.J., he hasn't exhibited any signs of aggression.

Did Jack Stone and I both grow up in one way of life, determined to live the opposite?

If so, why has he been more successful at it than me?

The questions loop through my head, keeping me tossing and turning long into the night.

THE NEXT MORNING, I blink in the darkness, struggling to figure out where I am. Hotel or home? The realization that it's the former doesn't click me into gear like it normally does. Last night's soul-searching has left me worn out and uncertain.

I drag myself out of bed, but the minutes of my perfectly coordinated schedule bleed into each other and disappear. I'm sweaty and discombobulated by the time the door of my room swings shut behind me. I reach for the key, but I've left it inside. It's a mistake I've never made before. Checking my watch, I gasp at the realization I have three minutes to get to the lobby. Four minutes before the van pulls out of the lot and leaves me behind. I run down the hall, my bag banging against my heels, and press the button to the elevator harder than necessary. Impatiently I press it again.

The elevator deposits me in an empty lobby, but I can see the van through the glass doors. The driver is standing behind it alone, waiting for me. I run for him, my bags skidding to a halt at his feet.

"I'm sorry I'm late." I gasp out the words, pulling my tote from the top and slinging it over my shoulder. It catches my hair and pulls painfully.

"You still had one minute." He smiles kindly like I was always safe, but we both know the hotel shuttles wait for no one. Sixty seconds more and he would've left me.

It's dark inside the van except for the lights from the dash. Gen and Paul say hello as Captain Ballinger offers a stern "How generous of you to join us."

"Good morning," I say. Thankfully my voice doesn't come out as anxious as I feel.

The van has two-seated rows on one side of the aisle and solo seats on the other. The front seats are occupied by civilians. I drag my tote bag to the only space left. It's in the two-seater in the back row. It just happens to be where Jack is sitting in his stupid, nonregulation jacket. I lower myself reluctantly beside him.

There are a million people I'd be happy to admire. Jack Stone is not one of them. I don't want to know where he came from. I refuse to compare myself to him. All I want to do is avoid him, but our thighs and shoulders press together, and I can feel the heat of his skin through the layers of clothing between us. I scrunch over in my seat, but it's too small. There's nowhere to go. The spicy smell of his cologne tickles at my nose, taunting me. He's inescapable. The engine starts up, and the van pulls away from the hotel, trapping us together.

"We missed you last night at dinner." Gen turns and leans into the aisle. Her hair is pulled into two high ponytails, one on each side of her head. She looks like a degenerate Spice Girl. It's strangely cute.

"Yes." Jack turns toward me. In the darkness, his eyes are no longer blue. They're dark and mysterious. "What did you do, Ava?"

I blink at his prompt. *So, that's how we're playing it.* Fine by me. I didn't want to see behind the curtain, and he clearly didn't want to be seen. For once, we're on exactly the same page.

"Nothing." I search his face, but it's all angular lines and shadow.

"You stood us up so you could do nothing?" Gen sounds insulted.

I drag my eyes away from Jack and turn toward her. "Sorry. I wanted to come, but I was too tired."

"What's with this crew? If Pilot Paul hadn't been up for a little fun, I would've been all alone. This one left before the appetizers arrived." She flicks her hand toward Jack. "And Captain Ballinger didn't show at all. Where were you, huh?"

Captain Ballinger doesn't respond to her question, so Gen taps him on the shoulder.

He turns slowly. "Did you need something?"

She nods. "Why didn't you show up last night? Were you scared we'd call you Marty?"

I can't see his expression, but I imagine it's one of bafflement.

"That's not my name," he says.

"Well, you haven't told us what your name is, have you? Until you do, I'm going to assume it's Marty."

I sneak another peek at Jack, but he's scrolling through his phone. I'm not sure if he's making a deliberate effort not to engage or genuinely has more interesting things going on in his life. Either option compels me to pull out my own phone.

I open an unread text and let out a little strangled cry.

"What's wrong?" Jack turns toward me.

"Nothing." I flip the phone over and press it to my lap.

He holds my gaze for a moment before shrugging and turning away. I stare at the dark side of the phone like it's a ticking bomb. I forgot to call Alexander last night. *Again.* He called while I was at the bookstore, but I waited to call him while I was at dinner. I thought it would be nice, having a meal together over the phone. Only Jack's dad and his stupid son ended up at the deli with me and managed to throw things so out of whack that I forgot all about Alexander. Gingerly I turn my phone back over and open his text.

I'm going to bed now. I'm telling myself you're safe. I'm telling myself you're in your pajamas, too caught up in a TV show to notice that I've called. I hope I'm right.

He's angry. It's there in the glaring absence of an *I love you.* Still, it's a kind message. Much kinder than I deserve.

Once again, I've been thoughtless. Unforgivably so. This is exactly the kind of thing my parents would do—the kind of thing they have done, often. I know how it affects other people. I know the feeling of worry that comes from loving someone who tends to disappear. I would never wish it on anyone, much less the man I love.

And I have no excuse.

If Jack can evade his father's anger, I can evade my parents' thoughtlessness. Because I am a better person than he is. I just need to stay in my hotel room instead of wandering around a strange city. Then I'd be available to answer Alexander's call. And I definitely wouldn't be spending my nights thinking about a guy I don't even like and his relationship with his father.

"Can you turn down the brightness on that thing?" Jack squints at my phone. "It's blinding me."

Even though I know it's not technically his fault I missed Alexander's call, I can't help noticing his name has popped up in my thoughts on the matter quite a bit, which must indicate he can't be entirely free of blame.

"No." I shoot him a glittering smile meant to sear his eyes even more than my phone does. "Just consider it practice for that bright Belizean sun."

Chapter 8

It's the kind of day every flight attendant dreams about. We'll only work two legs before we get to Belize City, where we'll then get to enjoy a twenty-four-hour layover. If that sounds long, it's because it is. But there's only one flight a day into and out of Belize, so we're working the plane in, handing it over to the overnighting crew, and then we'll work it back out tomorrow. Even better, our first flight, into Houston, isn't full.

We only have sixty-two passengers boarding a plane with 143 seats. Accounting for sleepers, we'll end up with about forty passengers to serve between the three of us. That gives me approximately two and a half hours of the three-hour flight to read my book and drink free coffee. If I weren't wearing a dress and currently engaged in a brutal mental flogging of myself, I'd be doing cartwheels down the aisle.

The Ops agent nods as Captain Ballinger finishes his briefing. "It won't take long to board sixty people," he says, "so I'm gonna hang out here for a minute."

"Boarding," Captain Ballinger says, "is supposed to begin thirty minutes prior to departure."

"Right." The Ops agent sinks into a seat in the front row of the plane and begins scrolling on his phone. "But I load the bus up, and you drive it. As long as we both get our jobs done on time, everyone's happy."

Captain Ballinger grimaces, and I leave before they can begin to fight it out, hurrying down the aisle to take advantage of the extra minutes. Before I even reach the galley, I'm on my phone, calling Alexander. I exhale with relief when he answers.

"I'm sorry!" The words burst out of me. "I should've called. I'm so sorry for worrying you."

"What happened?"

The coolness in his voice makes me flinch.

"Nothing." I wish I had a better excuse to offer. "I just lost track of time. I went on a walk, and by the time I got back, I was so tired I just crashed without checking my phone. It was thoughtless of me, and I really am sorry. I can't believe I did that."

I steel myself for his *Again*, but to my surprise, it doesn't come. Instead he says, "It's fine, Ava."

My eyes widen. "It is?"

"Well," he says, "I certainly don't enjoy worrying about you, but I understand that it goes hand in hand with your current lifestyle. It seems pointless to fight about something that is soon to be behind us."

"Exactly." Accepting my own responsibility doesn't change the fact that my career does, at least, *add* to my communication shortcomings. After tonight, Alexander will never have to wonder where I am again. I'll be in his house—*our* house, I mean—forever. I tug at the collar of my dress. It feels like it's pressing against my throat, but it's still cut in a V, dipping well below my neck.

A ding sounds through the plane, indicating the beginning of boarding. Captain Ballinger must've triumphed in the battle of regulation versus efficiency. Somehow I'm not surprised. He doesn't seem the type to back down.

"I got a wedding dress." I hadn't planned to say it, but it feels important Alexander know I was thinking about him last night. About us. About the next chapter of our lives together.

"You did?" Alexander's voice warms, sending a wave of relief through me.

"I did."

"Well, I got something, too. The Starlight." He sounds unbearably proud. "There was a cancellation in February, and my mother was able to snag the spot."

"But . . ." The tightening of my chest moves up to my throat, cutting off my words. I feel blindsided. Worse, I feel terribly, horribly disappointed. "But you said we could get married in the spring. I wanted to do it outside, in a park or a garden."

"It's soon, I know. But why wait? We want to be together. Surely sooner is better? And the next opening at the Starlight is over a year away."

"But . . ." I feel like we're having two entirely different conversations. "I'm saying we don't need to be on the Starlight's schedule. If we got married in the spring, we could do it outside."

Alexander laughs. "Can you imagine my partners slapping away mosquitos while we take our vows? I'd be the laughingstock of the firm."

"But my dress is too casual." In front of me, passengers are trickling down the aisle. I drop my voice to a whisper. "I could never wear it in the Starlight."

"You can bring it on the honeymoon," Alexander says. "The wedding planner will help you find something more appropriate for the ceremony. Brides don't find dresses on their own anyway. You should have your friends with you. You know Ro loves any excuse to drink champagne."

I flinch at the reminder. Ro still hasn't texted me back. It feels cruel of Alexander to so casually reference a painful subject, but it's not his fault he doesn't know she's ignoring my effort to reconnect. Maybe if I'd called him back last night, he would.

"You're right," I say. "I'd better go, though. The passengers are coming down the aisle." It's not a lie. They've reached the exit row. But it's the fact that Jack has left them to it and is headed my way that's making me more uncomfortable.

"Perfect," Alexander says. "I've just parked. I'll see you tomorrow."

"See you then." I hang up and shove the phone into the pocket of my dress.

It doesn't matter that I'm about to quit this job. I can't get caught on my phone during boarding a second time; my pride in my work ethic forbids it. Jack doesn't acknowledge me or my phone, though. He stops in front of the last bin and pulls down the snack boxes as easily as if they weigh nothing. With a carefree whistle, he drops them on the aisle seats, one across from the other. My head tilts as he tears one open, the muscles on his arms rippling hypnotically. He pulls down a basket and slowly begins transferring the snacks from the box into the basket.

My eyes narrow, but a smile tugs at my lips. A woman in a muumuu with a rat dog clutched to her chest wanders back. She stops at the sight of the boxes. Jack stretches, making himself even bigger, a living, breathing wall. The woman backs up and plops into a seat closer to the front. I stifle a laugh.

"I know what you're doing." I say the words quietly, but he hears me.

Jack turns toward me, his eyes wide with innocence, but he gives up the act when he sees my face. His crooked smile makes its appearance. We both know I'm going to let him get away with it. What he doesn't know is that I'm not being nice; I'm grateful he's managed to distract me from a conversation that felt like the equivalent of being punched in the face.

Plus, I want the back row, too.

Per Northeast Air standards, if a flight is not full and no passengers choose to sit in the back row, the flight attendants may sit there while not conducting duties. It might seem like a small luxury, but if you've ever sat on the jump seat—a paper-thin cushion beneath you, your back ramrod straight and your coworker's elbow jammed into your side—you'll understand why the back row is a flight attendant's version of flying first class. The catch is that we're not allowed to deny a passenger those seats. To be caught doing so is a fireable offense. But the rule book does *not* specifically prohibit a flight attendant from pretending to organize snacks and puffing himself up like a blowfish in an effort to deter a passenger's approach. Although, I suppose, such a prohibition is likely implied.

Thanks to Jack's effort, the last person sits, and we still have four empty rows in the back. Jack holds up his hand for a high five. I hesitate for a moment, and he lifts an eyebrow. I don't want to touch him, but I don't feel the urge to hit his hand with a hammer either.

"I just built us a four-row employee breakroom," he says. "That means we don't have to sit together on the jump seat."

"Well, that *is* high-five-worthy." I have to stand on my tiptoes to reach his hand. When our palms slap together, his is almost twice the size of mine.

"Is that an actual smile on your face?" He grins. "Quick, aim that headlight you call a phone at your mouth so we can see for sure."

I pull it out of my pocket and hold it out in front of me with my right hand while lifting the middle finger on my left to my lips. "Is this what you were looking for?"

"Has anyone ever told you you're a charmer?"

"Sadly, no. But I bet Hannah wishes *you* were less of one." The words just fly out, and I flinch at the sound of them. I hate this side of me Jack seems to have summoned into existence.

"Oh, bringing up the ex. I see we're pulling out the big guns now." Jack tilts his head. "Just out of curiosity, when you're digging up information about me, do you commit it to memory, or are you writing it down in your diary so you can go back later to reread the dirty details?"

My cheeks flush. "It's not my fault I hear things."

He doesn't respond because he doesn't need to. We both know I lost that round. I tug my eyes away and busy myself by reaching up to start closing the overhead bins. My hand hits air, and my stomach sinks as I realize they've been modified; I'm too short to reach them. At least the seats are empty. I can stand on them to close the bins. Still, how mortifying. My cheeks get hotter, and I know they must have gone red because I can see the moment Jack notices.

His eyes flick from my face to the bins and back to my face again. My jaw clenches. A smile tugs at his mouth, and I brace myself. *The twenty-eight-year-old little girl is so tiny! She can't even do her job. Look, everyone! How hilarious!*

"I forgot to make sure we have enough seat belts to do our demo," he says. "Would you mind checking them? I need to brief the exit rows."

Without waiting for my response, Jack turns and heads up the aisle, closing the bins as he goes. My mouth drops open a little as I stare after him. His reach is so wide he can do both sides at the same time. In a few moments, the back half of the cabin is taken care of. If I hadn't watched him check the seat belts already, I might've believed him. I might not have had to acknowledge to myself that he decided to help me out.

THE SUN IS newly risen, filling the quiet cabin with a soft yellow glow. Most of the passengers are sleeping. The air buzzes with the work the heater is doing to combat the cold snap we endured during takeoff. It gives off the slight smell of bonfire, making it feel like we're flying through a crisp fall morning instead of the dreary winter beneath us. In the back row, Jack occupies one aisle seat and I'm in the other. We've already served drinks and snacks, gone back through and offered seconds, and collected trash. There's still almost three hours left of flight time.

I peek at Jack. Maybe it's the fact that we have so long to sit here. Or maybe it's his kindness with closing the bins. Maybe it's the fact that, with so few passengers on this leg, it felt pointless to race each other. Maybe it's the unwanted glimpse into his family life. Whatever the reason, I'm finding myself tempted to talk to him. Not, like, *talk* talk. Just run through the list of polite questions we should've covered yesterday. Recalibrate. Offer a tiny wave of the white flag.

I sneak another peek. Jack is reading a fat, worn copy of *The Pillars of the Earth*. It's a book I love. His head is bent low with concentration. His hair is every bit as windswept as it was yesterday in the parking lot. Some of it falls over his forehead, dark against his tanned skin. I open my mouth, then shut it again. I get up, grab a trash bag, and do a sweep through the cabin. Jack doesn't look up as I pass by to toss it in the bin.

"So," I say, sinking into my seat. "Jackson."

"Yes, Aviana?" His eyes don't leave his book.

"Did you grow up in Portland?"

"I did." He flips a page.

"But you don't live there anymore?"

"Nope." He puts his finger to the page and traces a line beneath one of the sentences like he's demonstrating his effort to read.

"Did you want to tell me where you do live?" Irritation prickles at my skin.

"Not particularly." He sighs and drags his eyes away from his book. They're darker than they were yesterday, more sapphire than sky. Maybe they've changed colors because they're full of the story inside those pages. "I appreciate the sudden interest halfway through the trip, but this really isn't necessary."

"What's not necessary?"

"This forced politeness. The routine. 'Where do you live? How long have you been flying? Are you married? Kids?' We don't have to do it. We can skip it."

My back tightens as my face grows warm. Jack hasn't said anything unfair. It was silly of me to think a sudden display of civility would come across as a normal offering at this point. Still, his rebuff makes me feel like an overeager puppy that's just had its nose swatted with a newspaper. *Settle down* is what he's really trying to say. *I'm not interested in you.* The fact that this kind of apathy is coming from a notorious man-whore just makes it that much more humiliating.

It doesn't matter, though. It's not like I don't already know all I need to know about Jack Stone—and not, might I add, because I've sought the information out. The answers simply spell themselves out.—*Where do you live?—Just past Failed Pilot Lane, on the corner of Obnoxious and Self-Satisfied.—Do you have kids?—Probably several I don't know about, scattered across the country.—Are you married?—Seriously? Hannah still has thousands of coworkers I haven't slept with yet. Why would I tie myself down to just one?*

I pick up my own book and furiously pretend to read.

"Is this because I didn't want you to call me Aviana?" The words slip out of my mouth in spite of myself.

Jack laughs and presses his book against the tray table, turning in his seat to face me. "Why are you acting like I'm doling out some kind of punishment? I'm trying to let you off the hook. You don't want to talk to me."

"You don't know that."

"Come on, Ava. Maybe this trip got off on a bad foot because of what happened in the parking lot. But I've seen you several times in the lounge, and you always blow off any efforts at friendliness. We ordered breakfast at the same time, in the same place. Yet you walked straight past me and sat three tables away, all alone."

"I wasn't on the clock then."

This time, the laugh comes from deep inside him, and it's so startling, so *real*, it makes my own mouth curl up in response.

"Exactly," he says. "Has it occurred to you that maybe I

don't want to be talked to because it feels like some kind of work duty to you?"

"Has it occurred to you that maybe I want to talk to you for other reasons?"

"No." He says the word simply, his eyes locking on mine. It doesn't sound like a challenge, but it feels like one. Like a coward, I break free of his gaze.

"My book is boring." My hand reaches for my Kindle guiltily, covering up the title. I'm reading *One Flew Over the Cuckoo's Nest* for the fifth time. Calling it boring is a form of blasphemy that makes my stomach twist with discomfort. "I thought the time might go faster if we chatted a little."

Jack's eyes search my face. "Fine," he says finally. "If you could change one thing about your life, what would it be?"

This wouldn't be my last trip. The words crash through my mind, unbidden and unwanted. I tense beneath the weight of them. "What are you doing?"

"Chatting," he says.

"That's not one of the questions you're supposed to ask."

"I thought you said this wasn't about fulfilling some kind of work duty."

Our eyes lock again, and this time the challenge is real instead of imagined. The tilt of Jack's mouth says he expects me to tap out. A ding sounds in the cabin, and I break eye contact with him, stifling my sigh of relief. A flight attendant call light shines at mid-cabin.

"I'll get it," I say.

"It's emergency trash." Jack waves a dismissive hand. "Answer the question."

"It could be a real emergency."

"It's not. I can see his bald head from here. He's the guy

who tried to shove an empty coffee cup in my hand when I was doing the safety briefing. He tried to give me his McDonald's sack while I was passing out drinks. He's all about emergency trash. He's the grand sultan of it."

"I'll check for myself."

"See?" Jack's eyebrows flick with satisfaction. "You'd rather do anything than have an actual conversation with me."

I ignore him and rise purposefully from my seat. It's not about avoidance. It's about professionalism. If a call button rings, we answer. That's the job. I'm not surprised a former pilot like Jack considers some of our flight attendant duties beneath him, but I take them seriously.

I walk swiftly up the aisle, demonstrating what a responsible employee looks like. Silently I pray that the man who has dinged us will be mid-stroke. Or, at the very least, be experiencing the symptoms of a heart attack. I know the moment he looks up at me my prayers have not been answered. Sure enough, he tucks a cup in my hand so carefully it feels like he's relieving himself of a bomb.

"Did you need anything else?" I glance back toward Jack before leaning in. "We have aspirin back there. Or maybe you'd like a tissue?"

"I just needed to get rid of that." The man shudders before helpfully adding, "It's trash."

"I see that."

I trudge to the back, ignoring Jack's smirk. I re-create his ex-girlfriend's face in my mind, but I've used her too many times. I've never even met the girl. Her power is fading. Squeezing my eyes shut, I summon my trump card.

Rex Blackwell. Jack's buddy. The pilot who taught me to steer clear of his kind. The man who juiced my heart like an orange and threw what was left in a blender. Jack might think I don't know whose side he was on when it mattered most, but I do.

My eyes narrow as I chuck the cup into the trash can. I summon my imaginary white flag while I'm at it and toss that in as well.

Chapter 9

Thanks to my thoughtlessness last night, I already suspect I'm a terrible fiancée before Gen proves it. Still, I don't realize the myriad ways in which I've betrayed Alexander until mid-flight on the way to Belize, when Gen tries to give my phone number to a passenger. The guy has hair to his shoulders, smells faintly of weed, and just wants to use the lavatory.

"What are you doing?" I hiss the words at Gen after I've shown the poor guy how to lock the door and pushed it closed behind him.

Jack looks up with interest. He's on the jump seat. For the first time since we finished service, he sets his book down.

"What?" Gen pulls open the drawer we toss leftover snacks in and starts digging inside. "He's perfect for you."

"He's a grown man who doesn't know how to close a bathroom door!"

"To be fair," Jack says, as if anyone has asked for his input, "nobody seems to know how to use the bathroom door. A significant portion of this job is showing people how to push down on a handle."

"Exactly." Gen pulls a packet of Oreos out and points them at Jack like she's waving a wand of approval. "And that guy looks like an artist. His thoughts are probably caught up in something more ethereal. You should like that, Ava. You're all artsy."

My mouth falls open. There is *nothing* artsy about me. I don't play any instruments. I don't draw. In sixth grade, I attempted a gingerbread man for our holiday assignment. My rendering was so inaccurate, I ended up in the principal's office, accused of turning in a penis.

My parents are the artsy ones, managing to eke out an existence from whatever painting or sculpture they've been inspired to create. I'm the dutiful one who's spent nine years at the same job.

"Well, I don't," I say firmly. "Like that, I mean. Artsiness."

"How do you know?"

"Yes, Ava," Jack says. "How do you know?"

I glare at both of them. "I just do."

Gen shoves an entire Oreo in her mouth. "If you're still waiting to find the right person, you've clearly been dating the wrong ones."

Her words hit me like a slap. I am engaged to be married, and I actually said the words *It will happen for both of us one day* aloud. It was a bizarre thing to do. Shady. A betrayal. To Alexander, and to our relationship. And for what? To protect Gen's feelings? It's not as if the woman is some delicate flower. A spray of black cookie just exited her mouth as she was speaking. Gen doesn't need my protection. I'm sure she'd be thrilled to hear I'm getting married.

I take a deep breath. I'll sound weird for lying in the first place, but that's hardly reason enough to continue the charade.

"Trust me," Gen says before I can speak. "When you meet that person, you'd do anything you can to guarantee the rest of your life with them. I would've injected Stake into my bloodstream if I could." Her eyes go shiny. "I would've chained him to my radiator and dead-bolted the door. I would've sewn his heart into my jacket and—"

The chime of the interphone interrupts her, and still staring dreamily into her imaginary closet of love-inspired hostage-taking, Gen reaches past me and grabs it off the wall.

I turn to Jack and widen my eyes. "Can you get her back to her galley before she confesses to some crime we'll be obligated to report?"

I'm joking, but not entirely. I can't help it—I want Gen to go away because I don't want to tell her I'm getting married. Partly because I still have this silly, unwarranted, deep-seated need to protect her. But mostly because I don't have my own list of things to compare if she asks. What would I be willing to do to guarantee the rest of my life with Alexander? He'd prosecute me if I tried to chain him up. He's far too solid to inject into my bloodstream.

"Plausible deniability." Jack shrugs and picks his book back up. "Just don't write it in your diary with the rest of your crew findings."

I roll my eyes, but he's already gone back to reading.

"They need a bathroom break," Gen says, hanging up the phone.

"I'll go." The words fly out of my mouth.

"But your food is probably ready by now." Gen gestures toward the coffeepot where I've shoved a freezer bag full of Lean Cuisine inside and brewed hot water over it. It's been in there simmering for the last twenty minutes.

"I'll eat it after." It sounds like I'm being generous, but I know I'm running away—from this conversation. From the feelings Gen's passionate (and slightly disturbing) illustrations have elicited. From my inability to find anything comparable to offer as proof of my own love for Alexander. *Running away.* Like my thoughtlessness, this is another thing I'm not proud of.

Gen holds up her Oreos at Jack to illustrate she's too busy eating to come with me. It takes two flight attendants to assist in a bathroom break. One to sit in the cockpit and another to stand at the front of the aisle and make sure no one attacks the peeing pilot.

"I'll take care of those for you," he says, sweeping the package out of her hand and popping one in his mouth. "You've got work to do."

"But you're so strong." Gen sinks onto the seat beside him and wraps her fingers around his bicep. "Don't you want to stand guard?" Her eyes brighten as her hand slips down his forearm before coasting back up and sliding across his chest.

"In *your* galley?" Jack moves her hand to her lap. "No."

"Fine." Gen lets him keep the cookies, as payment, I assume, for the feel she's just copped.

I shake my head and start down the aisle. Unlike earlier, every seat is full and every passenger awake. People are talking loudly, competing with the conversations around them. Someone is eating fast food, and the smell of greasy fries permeates the air. Elbows and shoulders and shoes have migrated into the aisle. I step carefully around them, turning sideways in parts just to get through. Miraculously, no one stops either of us with requests.

"You go in," Gen says, opening the lav door to make sure

it's empty. "Pilot Paul is staying put, and Captain Sexy Scowl is coming out."

I nod, but she's already picking up the phone to call them. It clearly wasn't a request so much as an order. I flip the lights off and wait for the door to open. When it does, it fills the galley with light. Captain Ballinger comes out.

"Hurry," he says, ushering me in. "I'd like to keep the smell of a hundred and fifty pairs of feet out of the cockpit."

I tug the door closed behind me and blink against the brightness. There are only 143 passengers on board, so my feet must be included in the dirty category. I stifle the urge to slide my heels off and grind my stockings into the back of his seat.

Sunlight streams through the windshield, heating the small, enclosed space. It's at least ten degrees hotter in here than it is in the cabin. The sky spreads out before us, brilliantly blue. A smattering of cotton clouds stretches beneath the plane's path. It's a perfect, beautiful view. The traffic radio crackles.

Paul turns in his seat. He has an oxygen mask strapped to his face. It makes the same sound as Darth Vader's. It's a safety precaution that pilots use when there's only one of them in the cockpit, but I often wonder if it's more enjoyable than they let on. I bet it gives them a mini-high. Not fuzzy like you get from alcohol, but a special alertness like you're running on premium when your engine is more accustomed to 87. Paul lifts it and smiles at me.

"Hi," he says before putting it back in place.

I smile back at him. "Hi."

I don't know what it is about him that's so likeable. He just seems like the kind of guy who helps old ladies cross the street and offers to fix stuff in his neighbors' houses. I bet he's a good hugger.

There's a small seat behind the captain's chair that I perch on. "So, what's your story, Paul? Do you live in Chicago?"

He lifts the mask again. "Wisconsin. I keep saying I'll make the move so I don't have to commute, but honestly, I'm just not sure I can live around all those buildings. I like being able to see the sky."

"You don't get enough of that here?" This view is one of the things I'll miss the most. Just the thought of it makes my stomach tighten. It's one of the purest places on earth. And, yes, it does make me feel like a bird, in an undeniably great way.

Paul grins. "When it comes to the sky, there's no such thing as enough."

"Do you ever wonder if you'd miss it?" I don't intend to ask the question. It just comes out. "This view, I mean. If you realized one day you'd never see it like this again?"

"I don't have to wonder." He squints at me curiously before taking a hit off the mask. "I know I would. Wouldn't you?"

"Yeah." A memory flashes through my mind. Me, ten years old, on a beach on Anastasia Island. My parents and I had driven through the night to get to St. Augustine. They'd heard about an art fair happening at Flagler College and decided they needed to walk through the booths in person. We got there, though, and there was this bridge shooting past the city, out into the ocean. It shimmered with promise, the kind of thing I imagined you'd see in Oz.

My mom turned around in the front passenger seat and smiled at me in a way that made my blood fizz with anticipation. "What do you think, jelly bean? Should we keep going?"

Just a moment earlier, I'd been desperate to get out of the car and stretch my legs. Still, I didn't hesitate. "Let's go, let's go!"

I'd been to beaches before. I'd felt the sea breeze on my skin. I'd run through the surf. But as I spun in the soft sand that day, arms stretched above my head, face tilted toward the sky, it felt different. It felt like my parents and I had made it to the edge of the world. For a moment, I forgot about the math test I was missing. I forgot about Annabelle's sleepover, which I wouldn't make it home in time for. I felt wild and free and impossibly alive. And I loved it.

"Yeah," I repeat, my voice suddenly thin and shaky. "I would."

"Hey." Paul pulls his mask off and leans toward me. "Are you okay?"

I'm shocked to feel a tear slide down my cheek. I reach up and swipe it away, but there's another one trailing after it.

"I'm fine." I squeeze my eyes closed for a moment, holding the rest in. When the ache eases from my chest, I open them again. "This is my last trip," I confess. "I just got engaged, and my fiancé doesn't want me to fly anymore."

Something flickers across Paul's face, and for a moment, I could swear it's pity.

"It makes sense, you know," I say quickly. "There was a time when you *couldn't* keep this job once you got married. The airlines didn't allow it."

I steel myself for Paul to point out that sexism drove that standard; it was during a time of weigh-ins and age limits, when the airlines wanted stewardesses to be single and appealing to the men traveling for business. Instead he smiles.

"You just got engaged? Congratulations, Ava! You must be so excited."

"I am." An image of me in the Starlight fills my mind. I'm wearing an appropriate dress, something made of lace and itchy fabric, picked by a woman who cares more about pictures than actual memories. The thought makes my throat tighten.

I push it out of my mind, focusing on Alexander instead. Him, and his dependable schedule. How he might work too many hours, but I always know where he's going to be. How he makes me feel secure in a way I've never experienced before. My breath steadies and the cloud evaporates from my chest.

"I'm very excited," I say. "It's going to be a whole new life for me."

"And twenty-four hours in Belize to finish off your career." Paul lets out an appreciative whistle. "Not a bad way to go out. We should celebrate tonight."

I shrug. "I'm kind of keeping it a secret from Gen, actually. She went through a bad breakup recently."

"Gen?" His eyes drift up in thought as he takes a hit off the oxygen. "That's surprising."

"I know. She seems like she'd be impervious to heartbreak, doesn't she?"

"I guess," he says, "but that's not what I meant. She's just so exciting, you know? Like a firework, all explosive but all bright and colorful at the same time. I can't imagine any man letting someone like her go."

My heart swells as I study his sweet, flushed face.

"Exactly," I say. "The right man wouldn't."

Suddenly, the fact that this is my last trip ever doesn't feel so terrible. I just have to make it matter. And I know exactly how I'm going to do that.

I'm going to make Genevieve Hefner give Pilot Paul a chance.

....

"SO," I SAY when I arrive in the galley with an overflowing bag of trash I've collected on the way back from the cockpit, "we've established that you used to be a pilot, right?"

"We've established that you've added that fact to the fan page you're running about me." Jack doesn't bother looking up from his book. "Along with my former girlfriends, and who knows what else in my past. Is that why you managed to track down my dad? Were you hoping to get some juicy new details from him?"

"Yes. I was curious if there was any age when you were less annoying." It's a half-hearted insult, and I regret being goaded into it when he still doesn't look up from his book. "Can you just give me a second, Jack? I'm trying to ask you something."

I'm not sure if it's the use of his real name or something in my tone, but he finally deigns to tear his eyes away from the page.

"By all means," he says, waving one regal hand at me. "Proceed."

"You must've known a lot of other pilots then, right?"

"Yep."

"And were they all womanizing dirtbags?"

Jack sighs and returns to reading.

"I'm not picking a fight," I say. "I'm really asking."

"You're genuinely asking me to confirm or deny whether a love of flying is intrinsically linked to one's ability to point their . . . joystick in a singular direction?"

"I am."

"And I'm supposed to ignore the fact that there are women pilots as well?"

"This question is specifically in reference to the male variety."

"Fine." He looks up. "No, Ava. Not every male pilot is a womanizing dirtbag."

Just the ones you choose to hang out with? The question zings through my mind, but I smother it before it can dampen my enthusiasm. This isn't about He Who Should Be Forgotten. It's not even about me. It's about Gen and Paul and their potential future together.

"Then it's actually possible," I say excitedly, "that Pilot Paul is as nice as he seems?"

Jack's expression turns guarded. "Maybe even likely."

"Then I could help." My gaze drifts toward the little porthole to the sky as my hands rub together. "*We* could help."

"We? As in, you and Paul?"

"It's only one night, but it's a night in *Belize*. We couldn't ask for a more romantic setting than that."

"Who is *we*, Ava?" The irritation in Jack's voice is enough to jerk me out of my haze of strategizing.

"You and I." I hear the wrongness in the words the moment I say them aloud.

Jack clearly hears it, too, because he grins in a way that makes me wish I could rewind time. "And what exactly are *we* helping with?"

"I'm not asking for much," I say quickly. "I just need someone to assist me in steering Gen and Paul toward each other."

"You need someone? Or you need me?" Jack's obvious amusement makes me yearn to stomp on his foot.

"Well, Captain Ballinger would be my first choice, but I just don't think he's going to be up for it."

Jack doesn't acknowledge the intended slight. "And you think I would be?"

"I know you like Gen. And we've just established that Paul is nice. So, it stands to reason you'd be willing to lend a hand in any plan that might make them happy." My enthusiasm about the prospect of playing Cupid, coupled with the unconvinced look on Jack's face, turns me into a strange cross between a cheerleader and a saleswoman. "Plus, it will be fun, don't you think? Gen and Paul. Paul and Gen. Pen. It's a Pen Plan!"

Jack answers with that silent raise of one eyebrow. Whether his implied judgment is in response to my unprecedented peppiness or how overly interested I am in someone else's love life, I don't know. But it succeeds in making me feel sheepish.

"And did I mention," I add in an effort to redeem myself, "if we don't steer Gen toward Paul, she intends to go after the captain? I'm just trying to spare them both the embarrassment of that misguided effort."

"Well, that *is* a good deed." Jack leans back against the jump seat and studies me through cool blue eyes. "But what makes you think I'll even be there? Maybe I'd rather be on my own in my room."

"It's a twenty-four-hour layover on a tropical island," I say simply.

"Good point," he says. "Count me in."

Chapter 10

The entrance to our resort in Belize is lined with palm trees, the lobby filled with colorful flowers and bathed in sunlight. Through the back, the turquoise pool glitters. I can smell the salty spray of the Caribbean Sea. The lady at the counter gives us plastic wristbands, and a man with a tray offers us little glasses of orangey-peach juice. It's both tart and sweet, and I want to fill a CamelBak with it and sip it through a straw all day.

It's not a huge resort, but it has enough buildings to warrant a colorful little map. To get to the one that houses our rooms, we have to walk past the pool. Beneath the sun, in my polyester dress, I'm hot but not unbearably so. In a bikini, it will be exactly the right temperature. Gen squeezes my arm, and I grin at her and nod. I know exactly what she's thinking because I'm thinking the same thing. It's 3:26 P.M. If we hurry, we can still catch a couple of hours of sun. I slip around Jack, and Gen pushes Pilot Paul to the side. We start to run.

The wheels of our roller bags bounce on the stone-paved path. Laughter burbles up through my throat, making me gasp. Sea air fills my lungs. I'm glad Captain Ballinger stayed behind to check out the workout facility. He'd be appalled at our lack of professionalism. I can feel Jack's eyes on me as my heels wobble beneath me, but I don't care. Dark strands of hair slip from my braid and stick to the beads of sweat that trickle down my neck, making my skin prickle once I enter the air-conditioned building. I stop in front of room 132, leaning against the door as I heave in deep breaths.

"Meet me right here in five minutes," I say, waving my key card at Gen.

"Make it four." She shoves her card upside down into the reader.

The room is airy and beautiful. It's accented in shades of teal with beach scenes on the walls. The curtains are pulled open to a balcony. I can't see the Caribbean, but the thick bushes with hot-pink flowers make for a beautiful view. I pull the luggage rack out of the closet and throw my bag on top before shimmying out of my dress. My navy bikini with the little red and white sailboats on it is at the top right corner of my suitcase, exactly where it's supposed to be. My flip-flops are beneath it. Before I head out, I take my watch off and slip it in the pocket of my dress so I'll remember to put it on in the morning.

Gen's door opens the moment I step out of my own. My head tilts as I take in her swimsuit. Black strips of material crisscross her torso, strategically covering the naughty bits. It looks like it's been drawn on, and I find it impossible to comprehend that she's navigated her way into it in such a short period of time. It would've taken me twenty minutes and a video tutorial from one of those *Fifty Shades* movies.

"Were you wearing that under your uniform?" I ask.

"I'll never reveal my secrets." She starts down the hall, and I fall in beside her. "Do you like it?"

"It's magnificent."

Gen beams. "Should we go to the pool or beach first?"

"I told Jack we'd meet them at the pool." It was my first concession to the Pen Plan, and voluntarily agreeing to see Jack felt weird enough that I considered scrapping the whole thing. "I'd like to get some food."

"Perfect." She slows in front of Paul's door and nods toward Jack's. "You can tell him we're headed there now, and I'll let Pilot Paul know."

I glance down at my exposed chest. I could've sworn this suit used to cover more of it. I should've worn a T-shirt, at least to walk around in.

"They'll find us," I say, speeding up instead of slowing with her. Having someone see me in a bikini at a pool feels a lot more incidental than showing up at that someone's hotel room door wearing what is basically a bra and panties.

Thankfully, Gen follows me without arguing.

Outside, the loungers are wooden but painted white. They have yellow cushions on top. We set up on a stretch of empty ones that face away from the sun but toward the sea. There are umbrellas, but the palm trees behind us provide most of the shade. I pick a chair with a little table next to it. It has a menu on top. I study it while Gen plays with the straps on her suit, shifting them so there's a little less breast exposed up top but an emergence of underboob. Somehow, it looks more X-rated than normal cleavage, which I'm sure is her intention.

"What's our discount here?" I ask. The prices are surprisingly low for a resort, but the seafood nachos sound best, and they're one of the most expensive things on the menu.

Gen reaches for the menu. "I don't know. Thirty percent? I think that's what they told us at the front desk."

I let her snatch the menu from me, and I lean back,

stretching my arms over my head. Something cheerful and beachy that I don't recognize plays through the speakers behind us.

"We'll save money on drinks, though," Gen says.

I tilt my head toward her, and she opens the massive beach bag between us. It's neon orange with black skulls outlined across it. There are at least thirty mini-bottles of liquor inside. I gasp at the sight of them and jerk upright. "Gen!"

"What?" Gen pulls a massive pair of sunglasses with squared-off edges out of the bag and slides them on her face. Hopefully—although probably not—to hide her shame.

"Please," I say, "tell me you didn't steal those from the plane."

"I didn't steal these from the plane."

My eyes narrow. "Where are they from?"

"The plane." Gen holds her hand up as I groan. "But I didn't steal them! I had a bachelor party in my section on the flight in. So, obviously, I was going to give them a couple of free rounds. But then I thought about it, and if we were at a bar, would I really be buying drinks for them? No. They'd be buying drinks for me. So, I took them."

I groan again. "You took them from the company who gives us a paycheck."

"No." Gen elongates the word like I'm the dumb uncle who can't understand basic logic. "I took them from the guys in the bachelor party."

"The ones who never got the drinks from you."

"But they *would* have. Just like they *would* have bought drinks for me if it were the other way around."

It's a mental yoga exercise I can't possible bend my mind into, so I just shake my head at her outstretched offer of a tiny rum. Gen shrugs and drops it into her lap before pulling out a can of pineapple juice, also from the plane. I watch in wonder as she shakes it, pops the top, takes a glug, and dumps the rum in. She tilts it back up to her mouth.

"Mmm," she says, licking her lips. "Piña colada!"

"It's a miracle you haven't been fired yet."

She laughs. "Do you have any idea how many good letters I have in my file? Passengers love me."

In the glare of the sun, she is a study in black and white. Platinum hair cascades down her back, wild and unruly. The stark strips of her suit cross her skin like something from a bondage porno. Only her lips have color, two slicks of crimson paint. If we were actually friends and I brought her to our house, Alexander would hide the valuables.

"You are very loveable," I say, meaning it.

Her smile widens, and her eyes slide past me. "Oh, fun! The boys are here."

I swing around and see Jack and Paul walking into the pool area. They stop at the table of towels, giving me time to study them. They're both tanner than they have any right to be. It's December, for heaven's sake. I glance down at my pathetic winter skin. It glows white like it's attempting to light passage out of the shade. There's a faint line across my waist from the tights I wore on the plane. I reach for it, rubbing at it like it can be erased. My eyes slide back to Jack.

Some people look smaller once the layers of their uniform are peeled away. Not Jack. He looks larger. He's not overly muscled, but the ones he has are clearly defined. He has six abs to Alexander's eight. But where Alexander's are tight and pinched, the result of a strict diet and forty-five minutes of cardio per day, Jack's look casually strong. I can picture him doing sit-ups while laughing with a group of guys at a gym.

Not that I would. Picture him, that is.

I deliberately tear my gaze away and focus on Pilot Paul instead. He's thick but less pudgy than I expected. He looks solid and manly. If he were standing next to anyone else, I'd feel confident in my ability to steer Gen toward him, especially now that the captain has disappeared. Jack might be a problem, though.

I slip my legs over the side of the chair, turning toward Gen so my back is to them.

"Paul looks good," I say in a low voice.

"He does." Gen lifts her sunglasses and studies him.

I shrink, mentally pleading with her to be less obvious. If they're looking at her, there's no way they don't know we're talking about them. Despite my embarrassment, I forge on.

"And Jack?" My question comes out in a whisper.

"Mmm." Gen nods. "I'd like to suck caramel sauce out of his belly button."

My stomach sinks. "So, you're interested in him?"

"Like, *interested* interested?" She waves a dismissive hand. "Too nice."

An unbidden snort surges through my nose. "*Nice?* Jack Stone? What do you need? Your men to come with a warning label? Crossbones and flashing danger lights?"

"It's not a requirement," Gen says. "But it does sound exciting, doesn't it?"

I laugh and lie back in my chair, peeking back toward the guys. They're unexpectedly close. Jack catches me looking, and I jerk my eyes away and pull my sunglasses down from the top of my head. I fidget with them anxiously. They used to be my favorite pair, but now I feel self-conscious of them. They're cat-eyed, and Alexander has proclaimed them silly.

"Well, hello, you sexy man-beasts." Gen wiggles her eyebrows.

Paul blushes adorably and hovers in front of us. I tilt my glasses up and widen my eyes at Jack before tilting my head toward Gen.

"Right," Jack says in the least covert way possible. He plucks the towel from Paul's hand and tosses it onto the lounger next to Gen. "You can sit there."

Paul turns to him in surprise, but the wide, charming smile that has appeared on Jack's face immediately brings an answering one to his own. "Thanks!"

"No problem, buddy." Jack moves to take the lounger next to me, and my heart rate speeds up.

"Um." My eyes snag on the sharp relief of his triceps as he lays the towel across his chair. "You'd probably rather sit by Paul. I'm planning to read, so I'll be boring company."

"I'd love to sit next to Paul," he says. "It's well established how nice he is. But now I've committed myself to playing right-hand man to Cupid. It's called *priorities*, Ava."

My eyes jerk toward Gen, but she's too busy rifling through her liquor collection to have caught Jack's reference to what's supposed to be a secret plan.

"And you did a good job," I say, lowering my voice in an example of what discretion looks like. "He's sitting next to her now. So, there's no reason you can't sit next to him."

"But there is. If I'm over there, they'll talk to me. But if I'm here, deep in conversation with my charming, exceedingly friendly coworker, they'll have no choice but to talk to each other."

"But . . ." I trail off, unable to formulate a single reasonable argument against what is actually a surprisingly solid strategy.

The real question is whether I value my unrequested matchmaking endeavors over my own personal desire to be done with this man for the day. Sadly, years of conditioning have left me with an almost pathological need to pursue other people's happiness before my own. I sneak a peek at Paul and Gen and spot her passing a tiny bottle of whiskey to him. He looks delighted.

I sigh with defeat.

"I guess you'll get that conversation you were so eager for after all." Jack's lips curl up in a way that can only be interpreted as smug. "So, tell me, Ava. If you could change one thing about your life, what would it be?"

"Is that the only question you know?" I roll my eyes. He must realize I didn't answer it for a reason. His insistence on asking it again is just proof that he's using our unexpected alliance to torture me. "You read it in some icebreakers listicle online, didn't you? Or was it from a *Cosmo* quiz you've recently taken?"

"Actually, the quiz was from *Vogue*. And the article on how to dress right to minimize a large chest was life-changing." Jack peers down at the tanned expanse of skin below his neck. "Of course, mine is broader than their average reader's. But it's always a good idea to tone it down so as not to embarrass the scrawnier guys around me, don't you think?"

If his goal is to force me to notice the sharp lines that trace their way down to a V that leads into his swim trunks, I can only take comfort in the fact that he's too late. I drag my eyes away and wave at a uniformed man who has just served drinks to a couple across the pool from us. I'm going to need sustenance to survive this.

"I think it's a miracle you can walk upright when your ego's the size of a 747."

"What can I say? It's a talent," he says cheerfully. "Now, what would you change about your life?"

"I don't know. I'd have a different crew on my overnight in Belize?" I shake my head. "Scratch that. Gen and Paul are great."

"I'd be offended," he says, "if you hadn't already confessed how much you *need* me."

I roll my eyes.

"Now," he prompts. "This is the part where you ask the question back to me."

"Fine. If you could change one thing about your life, what would it be?"

His face grows serious as he thinks. My stomach tightens. I don't want to have a heart-to-heart conversation with this man. It was bad enough seeing him with his dad and getting a glimpse of how he grew up. I prefer him as a caricature, neatly defined in bullet points: Womanizer. Destroyer of Hannah's heart. Friend of Rex.

"I've got it," he says. "I would've hit the gas harder in the parking lot yesterday morning."

"I knew it!" The words explode out of me, and the approaching server stumbles in fear. "I knew you really were trying to get my spot."

That insufferable crooked smile makes an appearance.

"Good afternoon, my friends." The server waves with wide, anxious eyes. "Would you like to order something?"

I sit up. "May I please have the seafood nachos?"

"Of course."

"Those sound good," Jack says. "Do you want to split them?"

I snort. *Share?* With him? It's the most appalling idea I've ever heard. "No."

"But it's too early for dinner," he says. "If we get two orders of nachos now, we won't be hungry again until it's too late to eat a real meal."

I can't believe he's really trying to make this happen. Is this the kind of "we" he thinks I've invited by asking him to help me with Gen and Paul? Or has the conversation I've been blackmailed into participating in led him to believe I'd actually allow his filthy fingers anywhere near my plate of food? If so, I will make sure never to answer one of his invasive questions again.—*Where do you live?—Pass.—Do you like cookies?—Pass.—How are you?—PASS.*

"We are not sharing," I say firmly.

"They're quite large," the server offers.

"Hear that, Ava?" Jack parrots the server. "They're quite large."

"I'm very hungry, though," I tell the server. "Famished, in fact."

"But you're so small. And our kitchen is very generous." The server smiles proudly. "You will be pleased to share such a mountain of food."

My stomach sinks as I realize this is a battle I will not win. I'm not capable of disappointing this stranger. Not when he looks so pleased with himself and his generous kitchen.

"Yes." I sigh. "You're right. We'll share."

I flip to my side so I don't have to see Jack's triumphant expression. "Hey, Gen. Can you mix up one of those piña coladas for me?"

My need for liquor has officially grown large enough to outweigh my principles.

Chapter 11

I lift the makeshift piña colada can to my mouth, but it's still empty. I've downed the entire thing before the nachos have even arrived. I'm a lightweight and can already feel a pleasant warmth expanding from my belly up into my chest. I lick the sweet, sticky juice from the top of the can.

"What are your favorite kinds of movies?" Jack keeps lobbing these stupid questions at me. It's like I've been roped into a game of verbal tennis.

"Ones where the unlikeable coworker gets shipped off to a different country." The rum has sucked the venom out of my tone. My answers are a half-hearted effort at this point. My eyes drift to half-mast. If I concentrate, I can almost hear the roar of the sea over the music.

"I didn't realize that was a genre," Jack says wryly.

"Oh, yes," I say. "The unlikeable coworker always gets sent to some isolated forest or something where they can't bother anyone else. It's usually cold, and there's not much food. They get sick. Like, deathly ill. And then an angry bear shows up."

"So, these movies are considered thrillers."

"Comedies. For the audience, at least. I don't think you're getting just how unlikeable the coworker really is."

"I see." Jack pauses for a blissful moment, and I use the reprieve to roll over toward Gen and Paul.

"Gen," I say, "do you like dogs?"

"Who doesn't?" she asks.

I smile. "Paul has a golden retriever! Paul, do you have any pictures to show her?"

Paul's head tilts with confusion. Belatedly, I realize he's never told me he has a dog. I just decided he seemed like the kind of man who did.

"You're supposed to be letting them talk." Jack whispers the words before resuming a normal volume. "And now you're supposed to ask me a question. Do I really need to remind you every time?"

"Apparently so." I roll over to face him. "All right, Jackson. What kinds of movies do you like?"

"Romantic comedies."

"Never heard of them."

"Sure you have," he says. "The main characters are often at odds. But there's this spark between them that has the audience rooting for them to get together. In the end, they overcome their differences and share the kind of kiss that makes the sky erupt with fireworks."

My stomach swoops, probably from the rum. "Sounds like fantasy to me. There are wizards, right? Pointy hats and sparkly wands? I guess I have seen a couple, but I prefer things more rooted in reality."

"Like bear attacks?"

An unwanted grin tugs at my mouth. "Exactly."

I turn back toward Gen and Paul, but they're talking animatedly about something that sounds suspiciously like sports. It doesn't seem like that could be romantic, but who's to say what revs other people's motors?

"What do you like to do in your free time?" Jack asks.

I groan. "Can't you guess?"

"Hmm." Jacks fingers tap his efforts at thought against the plastic table between us. "You plot the demise of unlikeable coworkers?"

"I don't believe in violence, Jackson. I'm satisfied with a little light sabotage."

"Like sneaking into their house and putting all of their clean clothes in with the dirty laundry?"

"And replacing their shampoo with hair-removal cream."

"You could swap their aspirin out with laxatives," he says.

"I intend to."

Jack laughs, and I suppress the urge to join him.

"What's your favorite food?" he asks.

"Any food I don't have to share."

"That sounds a little greedy, but okay." Jack lets a few seconds pass. "I'm sure you're about to ask what mine is, so I'll just tell you. It's pizza. But my *favorite* pizza is the Chicago-style deep dish at Firenzo's near the airport. They sell it by the slice, and I stop there after every trip. Whether I get in late or early, whether I'm hungry or not, I can always make room for a slice of deep dish."

"For me, it's those gas station cherry pies that are wrapped in the wax paper," I say.

"That's your favorite food?"

"No. They're disgusting. I'm pretty sure they're ninety percent high-fructose corn syrup and red food coloring." I hesitate, suddenly wishing I'd kept my mouth shut. Things feel like they're taking an uncomfortably earnest turn. Jack's cheek is resting on the lounger, though, his attention fully on me, and I don't know how to wrap this up. "But they're my pizza slice. I stop and get one after every trip."

"If you don't like them, why do you get them?"

"I don't know. I guess they remind me of road trips as a kid. At some point, we'd always stop and get gas station pies. It's probably the worst thing you can eat in the car—inevitably a blowout will lead to cherry goo all over your fingers—and every time I finished one, I swore to myself that I'd try something different the next time we stopped. But . . ."

"But you never did?"

"The thing is," I admit, "high-fructose corn syrup and red food dye might not be good for you, but they taste *really* great."

"Do you ever get them when you're not traveling?"

"Never." That would be like eating a deep-fried Oreo on a random Tuesday afternoon when everyone knows such gluttony is reserved specifically for the state fair.

"So, it's not really the pies. It's the tradition."

"No." I'm not sure what I'm arguing about, but I know instinctively I don't want to agree with him on this.

"I think it's cool. You've turned flying into a continuation of your childhood travels, and you celebrate each trip with a cherry pie, just like you did growing up."

"No, I didn't." My shoulders stiffen. "I don't."

"All right." He shrugs, and his cheek leaves the towel and turns back up toward the sky.

I stare at his profile, feeling compelled to convince him of something I can't quite put my finger on. Thankfully, I'm spared the embarrassment of a one-sided argument by the arrival of the nachos. The server was right. It's a heaping plate of food. I tug myself upright, but my body feels lazy from the piña colada.

"See?" The server sets the plate on the table between us, his smile proud. "Three people could share this."

"It looks fantastic," I say. The words *thank you* get caught in my throat as Jack hands him a credit card. "What are you doing?"

Jack stretches his legs around the sides of the table. "Eating."

"I'm paying for the nachos," I say. "I ordered them."

Jack glances up at the server, who looks nervous. "Take the card." He looks at me. "Happy birthday."

"It's the lady's birthday?" The server's nervousness is replaced by glee.

"The big four-oh," Jack says. "Doesn't she look great for her age?"

My eyes narrow. "I'm not—"

"Don't be embarrassed," Jack says, interrupting me. "The alternative to aging is dying. You're just leveling up, sunshine."

"Nachos!" Gen pops up next to me, and Paul peers over her shoulder. "Can I have some?"

I'm too busy turning back to scowl at Jack to think through my answer.

"No." Jack and I say the word in unison, and the server backs quickly away.

"Is that . . ." Gen leans close enough for me to feel her breath on my back. "*Shrimp* on your nachos? Gross. Never mind."

Jack is already pulling a homemade tortilla chip from the stack, taking a hunk of white cheese and one of the shrimp. I swing my legs over the side of my lounger, but there's nowhere for them to go. His legs are too long. They're taking up all the space.

"Do you mind?"

"Not at all." He winks and shovels the entire thing in his mouth.

I push his legs out of the way with mine. We're all tangled limbs and sticky skin. My body heats up as I glare at him, waiting for him to cede some territory. He doesn't. Instead he reaches for another chip. He's scooping up another of the precious shrimp. If I don't get in there, he'll eat them all. It's the parking space all over again. Jackson Stone clearly has no respect for basic laws of civility.

I grab a chip and sweep it under the shrimp on his, taking it for my own. Jack growls, and his eyes fly up and lock with mine. I smile and shove the entire thing into my mouth. It's delicious. The salsa is spicy, the cheese is creamy, and the shrimp is the perfect savory addition. I chew like a savage, smacking my lips with satisfaction when I'm done. Jack watches it all, his mouth slightly open in shock at my unapologetic theft.

It's not until I reach for the next chip that he snaps out of it. He snags the exact one I'm aiming for, and the battle is on. We ravage the plate, shoving towering chips into our mouths in a mad frenzy. Spices explode on my tongue, and the chips slice at the top of my mouth. My eyes water, and my belly extends with pleasure. It is a full-body experience and, without question, the most satisfying meal of my life.

When we're finished, the plate looks like the remains of a battleground. The broken bones of fallen chips splattered with the bloody chunks of pico de gallo.

"You guys are animals," Gen says, a hint of awe in her voice.

Hearing the two of us grouped together returns me to sanity. I jerk my legs away from Jack's, stretching them across my own chair. They're sweaty in the spots that have been pressed against his skin, and the wind brushes against the dampness. Chill bumps rise in its wake. *I have Jack on me.*

I have been contaminated.

I need to dip my body in bleach. My eyes dart toward the pool. Chlorine should work. It's strong enough to combat pool pee, isn't it? That's only slightly less disgusting than Jack sweat. Gen's legs are on one side of my chair, and Jack's are still on the other. Like a weirdo, I scoot toward the end of my chair and stand up. I leave my glasses on my towel and run for the pool. Without pausing at the edge, I dive in.

The water rushes over me, cool and cleansing. I open my eyes as I slice across the bottom, blinking through the sting. When I see legs in the distance, I come up for air. Someone cannonballs into the water near me, sending water flying everywhere. Gen pops up from beneath the surface, black streaks of mascara lining her cheeks. I laugh and rub my own, hoping my mascara is as waterproof as it claims. I tug the hair tie from my braid and slip it on my wrist as Gen doggy paddles toward me. Behind her, Jack and Paul run toward the pool.

"Duck!" I yell the word at Gen before sinking to the bottom. Their bodies hit the surface like bombs, and the water whooshes in my ears. My hair flies around my head, a cloud of dark, celebratory eels. I put my foot against the bottom and shoot myself back up.

"Marco!" Gen shouts the word, her eyes screwed shut against a puddle of mascara. I look around, but the guys haven't resurfaced yet.

"Polo!" I shout just as Jack's head pops out of the water.

He sweeps the water out of his eyes and grins before squeezing his lips together in a show of silence.

"A Jack Polo is on your left," I cry. But Gen is already headed my way.

"Marco," Gen calls again.

This time Jack shouts "Polo" with me like he's a good player, but I'm already screwed. Even Paul's belated "Polo" can't reroute Gen. She's churning toward me like the Terminator, and my splashing attempt at escape only seems to fuel her. One more cry of "Polo" brings her crashing into me. She gropes me like a conquering pirate, dragging me underwater.

It's so absurdly aggressive, I start to giggle, and the bubbles that escape my mouth return in the form of chemical-tasting water. I cough it out as firm hands wrap around my waist, pulling me into the warm air. I spit out water and more inappropriately timed laughter.

"This isn't rugby, Gen." Jack says sternly from behind me. The heat of his skin hovers just off my back, and his hands don't let go. "And you." He turns me around so I'm facing him. "You're supposed to wait twenty minutes after you eat before swimming."

My body sways against his, my shins slipping against his leg. I exhale some kind of cough-scoff, and for a moment, I'm terrified I won't be able to keep my legs from wrapping around his waist in an effort to stabilize myself. But then I inhale my first pure drag of oxygen and regain control of myself. My lips curl up, and my eyes drift closed as my hands slip up his arms.

"Marco," I whisper before slapping both palms against his firm chest. Using that broadness he's so proud of, I launch myself backward. "You're it!"

I relish the moment of stunned silence that comes before his shout of "Marco" hits the air.

"Polo," I call, backpedaling furiously.

I wipe the water out of my eyes and spot Jack going after Gen. She squeals and cheats by ducking beneath the water. He slaps at the water where she just was. A whistle pierces the air. I swim to the side and hoist myself up on the smooth, warm edge. The whistle sounds again, sending a group under one of the umbrellas scuttling toward the beach.

"There's something going on in the sand," I call behind me. "Everyone's going down there."

When no one responds, I turn back to find Jack holding Paul in place while Gen plows toward him like a steamship.

"What if it's a gigantic whale? Or one of those water-skiing Santas?" I hoist myself out and head toward the path that leads down to the beach. Water drips from my body, hitting the ground like the start of a rainstorm as I walk. I try to run my fingers through my hair, but it sticks to them, thick with chlorinated water. Past the palm trees, the Caribbean stretches out, a beautiful swirl of turquoise and navy. I ogle it, slowing as I approach, soaking it in. Gen catches up and grabs my arm, dragging me forward.

The sand is hot but not scalding. There are about twenty people crowded around the man with the whistle. As we get closer, the beat of salsa music emanates from an old-fashioned boom box on the sand behind him.

"Line up in rows," the man with the whistle says. "But leave enough room to shake your hips!"

"It's a dance lesson!" Gen starts to run, and I sprint with her.

She pushes through the group, inserting herself into the first row. I try to deviate and stick to the back, but I can't stand the disappointment on Gen's face when she turns and sees me. With a sigh, I duck my head and tunnel toward her. I'm surprised when I discover the guys right behind me. Once again, it ends up with Gen and me in the middle, Jack beside me and Paul beside Gen.

The lesson begins. It starts simply at first, but soon we're combining hip shaking with the step work. My breasts bounce with the effort. When I try to make them stop, the instructor eases in behind me and puts his hands on my waist.

"Let your body move with the music," he orders, yelling over the pulsing drumbeat and sultry trombones. "Feel the rhythm."

Heat floods my face, and I peek at Jack in my peripheral. His entire head is turned my way, his gaze locked on my breasts.

"Eyes straight ahead," I snap.

"I was just trying to see what it looks like to feel the rhythm," Jack says. He drags his eyes slowly up to my face. "This is a learning experience, you know."

"Learn by someone else's example, peeping Tom."

Jack shrugs and looks to his left, where a girl with long legs and a bright smile shimmies in response to his attention. She lifts her arms into the air and does a sensual turn so he can appreciate the smooth expanse of skin beneath her thong. I tug my eyes away from them, focusing on the moves. I'm just starting to feel like I have them down when the instructor orders us to partner up.

Paul turns toward Gen, but she turns toward the man behind her. I can't imagine why. He's middle-aged with a potbelly, Bugs Bunny swim trunks, and neon reflective sunglasses. Jack's head jerks toward me, and both of our eyes narrow. I feel a moment of satisfaction that, somewhere over the course of his reluctant participation in the Pen Plan, Jack seems to have actually become invested. He steps forward, but I beat him to it, flying toward the cartoon rabbit enthusiast and claiming him as my own partner and cutting Gen off in the process.

"Ava!" Gen's hands go to her hips.

"What?" I widen my eyes with innocence. "Paul's free."

She shrugs and turns toward him. His smile is like a kid's at Disney World. I steel myself and turn to face my own partner. He's short, probably about five foot five, but still taller than me. His skin is oily, and so is his expression. It says he's noticed our little catfight over him, and he's feeling confident he's worth it. I wrinkle my nose and look toward Jack, but he has ended up with Bright Eyes.

"Harry," the guy says, pointing at himself before taking my unoffered hand in his. "And you are?"

"Ava." I try to slip my hand from his grip, but he holds tight.

"Sweet Ava." He licks his lips. "Sensuous Ava."

My stomach sours. I consider an escape, but the instructor has already started calling out orders. Harry wiggles his hips to the beat of the music. He looks like a seal trying to shake itself dry.

"Get close to your partner," the instructor says. "Share your rhythm with them."

Harry tugs me toward him. His body is slick with sweat. I swallow back a gag. He spins me in the sand. I try to spin away, but he keeps a firm grip. He dips me, and his hand wanders. He pulls me back up and thrusts his hips. Something hard presses against my belly. I gasp and try to rip myself free, but he's stronger than he looks.

A shadow falls across us.

"That's enough dancing for you," a deep voice says.

I look up, and for the first time ever, I'm relieved to see my coworker. Harry's pudgy hand squeezes low enough on my back that he's venturing dangerously near butt territory.

"Get your own partner." Rather than look up at Jack, he stares at my breast.

"I just did," Jack says calmly.

I look over at Bright Eyes, but she's already been snatched up by someone else.

"Bye, Harry," I say.

Harry tears his eyes away from my chest. They slide past my face to Jack, who smiles at him in a way that offers no room for argument.

"Bye, Harry," he says.

Harry's shoulders slump.

"It's your loss, sugar tits," he says as he backs away. "He might have the looks, but *I've* got the moves." He punctuates the claim by jerking both of his fists toward his waist and thrusting out his pelvis. With one turn of his heel, he waddles away.

I laugh, but it's tinged with discomfort. Does Jack's rescue necessitate a verbal show of gratitude? It feels like it does, but I hate the idea of being the damsel in distress. We all know he's no knight in shining armor. Or, if he is, he's shined it up so as to attract the gazes of all the girls in the village.

"So," Jack says, his expression serious. "It's unfortunate that you'll have to settle for my looks. I'd steal his moves, but they're too slimy to get a firm grip on."

"Funny." My voice drops to a mumble. "Thanks for coming over, though. I thought he was going to steal third base before the end of the song."

"Yeah, well. I would've done it sooner, but . . ."

"But you were enjoying watching me get groped by a man-sized bovine?"

"No," he says. "I wasn't sure which one of us you'd prefer less."

His confession hits me in the chest, and my eyes drop to the sand. I don't know why it makes me feel so bad. I haven't made any effort to hide my feelings toward Jack, so it should hardly be surprising to hear the message has been received.

"You're not dancing." The instructor singsongs the words,

reaching for Jack's hands. He presses one to my waist and puts the other on my shoulder. Jack's expression tightens like my skin has scalded him, but it's not that bad. Our height difference is so extreme, my face lines up with his chest. It's like staring at a blank, although well-defined, wall. Jack could be any man with tan skin and pleasantly bulging abs. We both just need to use our imagination.

"Come on," I say. "We'll dance a little. How bad could it be?"

"If you're capable of letting me lead," he says, "we might even have some fun."

I sneak a look up at his face, and the corner of his mouth tilts up.

"Are you trying to tell me you're the one with the moves, Jackson?"

He answers by falling into the dance the rest of the group is doing. His steps have extra flair, though. I struggle to keep up at first, but his grip is firm, guiding me with the beat. Once I'm able to keep up with him, he adds some flourishes. A spin. A dip. I throw my head back, exhilarated.

The breeze off the sea sends my hair flying around my head. The beat of the song fills my ears. Jack swings me back up and away, then twirls me in until I'm pressed against his chest, skin on skin. Our eyes meet, and my stomach fills with butterflies. He spins me away from him again, but catches me by my waist before I can go too far. Our feet return to mirroring each other, and I laugh, feeling wild and alive.

Sweat is dripping down the back of my neck by the time the lesson ends. Jack must be hot, too, because he doesn't wait to hear what the instructor says. He just grabs my hand and starts running for the sea. I run with him, two steps to his one just to keep up. We hit the water and plow into it, struggling to stay upright against the waves. I give in and pull my hand away, diving headfirst into one. It crashes over me and fills my ears with the sound of a rushing train. I push through, rising and diving again, until the waves become rolling hills.

Before long, Gen and Paul join us. We splash each other and play until eventually the sea wears us out. Then we float, letting the rise and fall of the waves lift us to the sky and bring us back to earth, again and again. I stare up at the perfect blue sky, wondering how it's possible there could be more to life than this. And by the time we turn to go back inside, I've come to the terrifying realization that it's not possible. Up and down like the waves, to the sky and back to earth again, that's what life is for me. I might not have chosen it, but it has unquestionably chosen me.

Chapter 12

I trail behind as we walk through the sand toward the pool, my mind racing with the enormity of what I have to do. I can't call Alexander because the data charges are astronomical. I never added international coverage to my plan because who wants to be reachable if you've managed to escape to a place far enough away to be *un*-reachable? That's half the magic of exploring other countries. Not being uncontactable, but being in a different world, untethered and free.

Plus, who needs to make a call these days? It's better to video-chat him on the VC app. If I can't wait to have this conversation with him in person, at least it can be face-to-face.

Jack slows and falls into step beside me. "Are you okay?"

"Yeah." I try to summon up something to be annoyed with him about, but I'm too distracted to give it my all. "I'm fine."

"You sure?"

"Yes." I glance up at him, and the concern on his face causes the last of my defenses to crumble. "It'll be finc. Thanks, though."

I pray I'm right. Grabbing my stuff from the pool, I tell my coworkers I'm going to shower.

"Dinner at seven?" Gen asks.

"I might be late," I say. "Order without me. I'm still pretty full from those nachos."

"You're coming, though, right?" Jack reaches for my wrist, his fingers circling it loosely but managing to stop me in my tracks.

I meet his eyes, wondering absentmindedly if it was the forced intimacy of the dancing that has made it seem natural for him to touch me like this.

"Probably not," I admit.

"But what about your plans?" He emphasizes the last word. "Tropical islands? Sheepdogs? Pens?"

"You wanted to put sheepdogs in pens?" Gen pulls her chin in so it looks like she has two more. "That's weird. You should wait for a Texas layover to get into something like that."

"The plan is still on." I turn to Jack but avoid his eyes. "You'll just have to take the reins for a while."

It's not a lie. There's a chance my conversation with Alexander will go well, and an hour from now, I'll be sipping a piña colada while encouraging Gen and Paul to play Seven Minutes in Heaven. There just happens to be a much greater chance I won't. I duck my head and hurry away.

The room is darker than I left it. The sun isn't down yet, but it's no longer strong enough to stretch its rays through the window. I shower and put on pajama pants and a T-shirt, hoping to present a picture that will indicate to Alexander this is about the job, not some desire to have fun in strange cities without him. I climb onto the bed and build a wall of pillows behind me to lean on. With a deep breath, I open the app and press the only contact in it. It's my favorite picture of Alexander. He's not smiling, but he's wearing a collared shirt with the top two buttons undone, and his hair is uncharacteristically mussed.

I took it when he was in the middle of a big case. He'd been working round the clock and had barely had time to eat. I got takeout from his favorite restaurant, Salzone's, and showed up at his office in a trench coat I bought just for the occasion. Underneath, I was wearing nothing but a bra and panties. I'd never done anything like that, and I'd been terrified he'd think it was trashy, but I was determined to wipe away some of the stress that had been straining his brow.

Alexander laughed when he untied the trench coat belt and spread it open.

"You crazy girl," he said. "Who wears a blue bra with pink panties under a trench coat?"

My stomach sank as I realized this moment was exactly the kind of situation he'd given me those matching lace sets for. I couldn't imagine why it hadn't occurred to me when I was going through the door. But my bra wasn't blue; it was teal, my favorite color. And I'd thought the pink panties complemented it well.

"I should've worn the black lace ones you gave me," I said.

"Are you kidding?" Alexander gripped the lapels of my coat, pulling me toward him. "Look around this office. There's nothing but black and white and gray in here. I need all the color I can get."

I felt so special that day. In a world of black and whites, I was Alexander's color. My hand strokes the soft cotton of my teal T-shirt. Hopefully I still can be.

He answers on the fourth ring, and my heart leaps into my throat, causing my "hello" to come out strangled.

"I didn't expect to hear from you tonight," he says. "Did you make it to Belize?"

"I did." I hesitate. *Do I say it's beautiful here? Do I tell him how much fun I'm having?* Either admission is likely to color the message I have to deliver. "I ate seafood nachos."

Alexander shakes his head. "Leave it to a vacation resort to find a way to make seafood unhealthy."

"Yeah." I fake a laugh. *Say it, Ava. Just say the words.*

"Are you already in for the night?" he asks. "I thought your crew members would want to do something special to send you off."

This is it. A neon sign blinks overhead, flashing, *This is your chance.* I have to tell him. Squeezing my eyes shut, I summon my courage.

"I was tired," I hear myself say. *I'm a coward.* "The sea wore me out."

Alexander smiles. Unlike Jack's, his is straight and even. It is the thing that first drew me to him. It shines with self-assuredness. It's the smile of someone who is used to things working out in his favor. It promises, by his side, the world will be equally fortuitous for you.

"That sounds fun," he says. "Maybe we can go to the beach for our honeymoon."

If it weren't for his use of the word *maybe*, I might believe him. It's his lawyer loophole, though. *Maybe we can skip the gala this weekend and go to Ro's birthday party instead. Maybe I'll leave work early Friday and we can catch that exhibit you've been wanting to see. Maybe you can choose a new paint color for the new bathroom.* I've experienced enough of Alexander's maybes to know they're nothing more than the metaphorical carrot on the stick, designed to keep me looking forward to the future.

Alexander knows I love the beach, just like I know he finds it hot, dirty, and boring. It doesn't matter, though; he doesn't actually want to go anywhere. We've planned five weekend getaways since we've been together, and he's canceled every one of them. Usually he cites a work emergency, but the truth is Alexander doesn't like the unknown. He doesn't want to stay in a hotel where someone else has slept. He doesn't want to eat in a restaurant where he doesn't know what dish is best. He likes routine and creature comforts. I used to find it endearing. Lately, though, it has begun to feel a bit stifling.

Not for the first time, I find myself wondering what, exactly, it was that made Alexander choose me in the first place. Sure, maybe I claimed to want to quit my job and live a different kind of life. But nobody as smart as he is picks a partner who only has the *potential* to become what they want. He was drawn to me because, while he's in an office eighty hours a week, I'm out experiencing the world. In the same way I long to absorb some of his stability, Alexander wants to vicariously visit the beach without ending up covered in sand. Our differences are what make us work, but if I leave my job and spend the rest of my life in his condo, waiting for him to come home to me, I won't be the person he fell in love with anymore.

"I don't want to quit my job." My words explode out of my mouth. I freeze in the wake of them, shocked they're out there between us. I'm amazed I've had the courage to say them aloud.

For a moment, Alexander looks equally shocked. His eyes flick from side to side like he's reading the information from a legal brief. Slowly, they focus on me.

"That's understandable," he says. "You've been doing this job for nine years. Change is always scary. You just have to focus on what comes next, Ava. You're going to be a wife. Maybe, soon, even a mother. This chapter is closing, but the next one will be better. It will be about us."

"But I'm not sure I can be my half of *us* if I'm not me. Flying—travel—I think it's part of who I am. Without it, I'm worried I'll disappear."

"You won't disappear," he says confidently. "You'll grow. You'll improve."

"Can't I do those things while having a job?"

"Ava." Alexander exhales his disappointment with the word. He says it like he expected better of me, like he hates to say it but we both know I'm being a little childish.

"I want to marry you," I say. "I just don't understand why it has to be either-or."

"I don't understand why you're turning this around on me. You came into this relationship talking about how you wanted to settle down. You couldn't wait to stop flying. Do you honestly think I would've pursued a future with someone who intended to stay gone all the time?"

"But I'm not gone all the time. I fly three days a week. I'm only away two nights a week." I bite my tongue to keep from saying the rest, but I can tell by the look on his face he hears it anyway. *You work thirteen-hour days, five days a week. You go into the office on weekends. Between the two of us, there's no contest who works more. You win by a landslide.*

"I don't understand this focus on semantics. What's changed? The job you're suddenly defending is the same job you've always blamed for the problems with your friendships. It's the thing you've always claimed has kept you from putting down roots. You moved into my condo with a couple of suitcases and a box, Ava. How many twenty-eight-year-old women do you know who can fit their entire life into the trunk of a car?"

"Maybe I'm a minimalist. Is that so bad?"

"It's not bad at all. I'm sure your parents would make the same claim, and they seem very happy with the life choices they've made. But I do listen when you speak. I know how hard it was for you to grow up in the care of people who flitted around the world in search of adventure. Can you blame me for not wanting to raise a child the same way?"

The comparison stings. "We don't have a child."

"But we will. Unless that's another thing you've changed your mind about without consulting me?" He manages to keep any venom out of the jab he's delivered. It's just a question that deserves to be answered. A lawyer's tactic. He wants to know how undependable I've become. How many of my promises were uttered through lying lips. The witness on the stand has been proven unreliable.

"I still want to be a mother." My voice has grown wobbly. "Maybe if I had a child, I'd realize I want to quit flying after all." I'm not lying; it's entirely possible I would. But my mind is already being invaded with reminders of all the mothers I've flown with over the years. So many of them get rid of most of their trips each month but keep one or two, claiming those couple of nights in a hotel bed are the key to maintaining their sanity.

Alexander's eyes narrow as if he's reading my thoughts. To his credit, he chooses not to argue the point. Instead he makes it about himself.

"Am I supposed to build my life around a maybe?" His voice grows clipped, like he's a teacher assigning a task. "Explain to me what changed. Tell me exactly why you've decided you need to keep flying. Maybe, if you can make me understand, I'll be able to better determine if I can trust you to make the right decision in the future."

The request—*demand?*—sparks little embers of anger in my belly. I tell myself it's just Alexander's lawyer training revealing itself, but there's so much in his words that bothers me. I don't like the insinuation there's only one right decision, or that it just happens to be his. I don't like the expectation that I have to defend my career choice, especially when I'm expected not just to accept his but also to attend his work functions in support of it. Most of all, I don't appreciate his condescending tone, or the fact that it's not the first time I've heard it directed my way.

But I am not a person who fights, not with anyone, really, except for one particular coworker who I've hated long enough that there's no risk to it. I am smaller than that, weaker. My fear of rendering myself disposable is too great. So I force myself to answer, because he's told me to. Because, somehow, I can't help needing to make him understand something I'm almost certain he should simply respect.

"I didn't realize how much flying meant to me," I say. "When I needed a job, it was my only option. I felt forced into it, so I assumed I'd be grateful to leave. But now that the time has come, and I've been able to let go of my resentment, I've realized that somewhere along the way I fell in love with it. I enjoy being in the air, and exploring cities I've never been to, and ordering room service on my overnights. I love working with different crews and chatting with passengers. I like airport eggs."

"Eggs?"

Alexander cuts my answer short with his question, and there is something so patronizing in his tone, it sends the little sparks in my belly flying higher. *Eggs.* Such a silly thing. But we both know I'm not actually claiming to want to keep a job for the eggs. It's about appreciating a satisfying start to a three-day trip. It's about routine, which is something he, of all people, should understand. But he's not looking for understanding. He's looking for a crack to take advantage of. He's looking for a way to win this conversation and get his way.

My chin juts out.

"Love me, Alexander." For maybe the first time ever, I am the one giving the orders. "Love me for me. Love me as the flight attendant with the nomadic childhood and the free-spirited parents. Choose to marry the girl in the mismatched bra and panties. Choose me for who I am, not who you wish I would be."

I meet his eyes and feel the wetness that has seeped into mine over the course of my plea. Never has a conversation left me more vulnerable. If Alexander can't do this, he's not the difference I've been searching for. He's just another person in my life who gets to pick and choose when he wants to have me.

"I love *you*." My voice cracks. "Will you marry me?"

He tilts his head, and for a moment, I actually believe I'm going to get the happy-ever-after.

"Are you going to quit your job?" he asks.

The question hits like a punch in the gut. A tear breaks free and slips down my cheek. "No."

He frowns. "Then I'm sorry, Ava."

I close my eyes. "So am I." The flood gates open, and I begin to cry in earnest, but it doesn't matter.

He's gone.

I CONTINUE TO stare at the phone long after he's hung up. It's a black hole, a visual representation of a future that used to be filled with sepia-toned scenes of domesticity. Silently I beg it to brighten with the light of an incoming call. *Change your mind.* Tears trickle down my cheeks. *Please, just want me. Don't disappear on me.*

I crawl beneath the covers, pulling them over my head. I am the child in the backseat, forgotten. I've been left behind again.

I pray for sleep, but rather than dreams, my head is flooded with memories. Alexander, the night we met, at one of his work functions. I'd gone with a friend as a favor. He needed a plus-one. I borrowed a dress from Ro, a silken thing, the pale lavender color of lilac petals in the light of dawn. I felt like a princess.

I spotted Alexander the moment I walked in. His suit was tailored so sharply it looked like armor. Our eyes met across the room, and he smiled. The entire room brightened, and my heart began to race. People crowded around him, drawn like moths to a flame. I forced myself to turn away, not wanting to be one of the many clamoring for this beautiful man's attention.

I sipped my champagne and nodded, pretending to understand the small talk of overly educated professionals. My dress was strapless and cut low in back, and I imagined it was the gaze of the man with the dark eyes that made my bare skin tingle. Still, when he appeared at my side, my breath hitched with surprise.

He slipped the empty glass from my hand, replacing it with a fresh one. It was the thoughtfulness of the act that undid me. The fact that he'd noticed, and rather than offer a drink, he'd taken action. It made me feel seen. Cared for.

Later, after we'd talked the night away and absconded to a balcony that overlooked the Chicago skyline, we each confessed to our loneliness.

"I spend too much time in the office," Alexander admitted. "When I'm not there, I'm at these kind of things, talking to the same people I spend every day of my life with."

"You must meet women, though," I said. He was so handsome. I imagined they spotted him in the street and followed him into coffee shops, finding ways to chat with him in line.

"I don't want women." He smiled wryly. "I'm boring. It's my fatal flaw. I hate variety. I just want the one. I want a life of sames. The same person by my side. In the same home forever. Living the same days again and again, until they're so well-worn they're like an old cotton T-shirt against my skin."

My stomach soared. It was like he'd found the blueprint I'd sketched as a child and stretched it out in front of me, a map to my perfect life. I knew it with every fiber of my being. I'd found the man I was going to marry.

I never imagined we'd end up here.

Chapter 13

I wake up the next morning to the growl of my stomach. My heart pounds as I grab my phone. It's 8:12. There's one missed message. My stomach leaps, and I click on it with bated breath. **News? Sounds interesting!** It's from Ro, a belated response to my eager text. My stomach falls, then growls again.

I was too sick with heartache last night to eat, but the dancing and swimming of yesterday has caught up with me. I turn on the lamp next to my bed and reluctantly swing my legs to the floor. I refuse to open the curtains to the balcony, though. I don't want to see the sun. I don't want any proof this day has begun. If I can just block it all out, maybe it will still be yesterday. Yesterday, I was still engaged. Yesterday, someone wanted to spend the rest of his life with me.

I rifle through the nutrition bars in the top pocket of my food bag. They all look tiny and insubstantial. I want real food. I do not, however, want to go outside searching for breakfast in a world where today is today. I open up the food bag's cold compartment. The frozen burrito bowl on top has defrosted, contaminating everything with the smell of garlic and onions. It looks disgusting. It's perfect.

Thankfully, the plugs are the same as back home, so I don't have to find an adapter for my HotLogic. I dump my burrito atop the portable hot plate and tap twenty minutes into the timer on my phone. The screen shows there have been no new calls in the last two minutes. I double-check the volume. It's still on. I pace the room. Alexander and I have broken up. *Haven't we?*

The exact words—*it's over*—were never said. Shouldn't details have been discussed? There are so many questions that need to be answered. Where am I supposed to go tonight when I land? To his house, where we sleep in the same bed? What about tomorrow, when his parents expect to come out to dinner with us to celebrate our engagement?

I click on the VC app, and my finger hovers over his picture. *He's the one who hung up on me. Why should I have to call him?*

It's a childish point. But I don't want to call him. The truth is, I'm not ready for the answers to any of my questions. I doubt I'll like them.

Beyond the immediacy of tonight, there's a slew of other questions straining against their leashes. Would I really start over again in Chicago? Maybe this is exactly the excuse I needed to try something new. I could move to Denver and spend my weekends hiking. It's not a violation of my childhood aspirations if it's not my choice to leave, is it? I was willing to stay in Chicago. I was willing to live with Alexander forever. He's the one who decided I could only stay if it was on his terms.

The timer on my phone goes off, and for a moment, I'm certain it's a call. My fingers shake so badly I can barely press the button to stop the noise. I feel too sick to my stomach to eat my burrito bowl. I draw lines in it with my plastic orange travel spork before finally giving up.

Today isn't yesterday.

As much as I wish it wasn't, today is today. It's the first day of my broken engagement.

But it's no longer the last day of my career.

IT'S MIDMORNING, THREE hours before I have to go inside to shower for work, and the sun is already baking my skin like raw cookie dough. I'm lying on a lounger by the pool, attempting to read. Paul showed up a while ago, but I convinced him to deliver breakfast to Gen's room. I suggested he find something sugary and decadent. "No girl can resist a man who knocks on her door with sweet offerings," I told him, imagining a regretful Alexander appearing at mine with apology doughnuts. If I can't have such happiness for myself, at least I can manufacture the moment for someone else.

I pick my phone up for the hundredth time. Still nothing. I should respond to Ro, but I don't have news anymore. No *good* news at least. Technically, friends are supposed to be the people you turn to in times like this, but I'm not sure Ro is really a friend anymore. At least I don't have to tell Meredith. She'd probably be secretly pleased, thinking someone as undependable as I am never deserved a man as stable and wonderful as Alexander in the first place. There's no question she'd take Alexander's side about my job.

"Nice glasses." Jack appears from nowhere and tosses a towel onto the lounger next to me.

"Thanks." I mutter the word, fingering the curve of the cat-eyed lens. "They're silly."

"No, they're not," he says. "You look like one of those

quirky girls who plays a ukulele and writes lyrics that sound like poetry."

"Whatever." I can wear them all the time now, if I want to. Alexander never has to look at them again.

"Did you get some sleep last night?" Jack stretches the towel out, his abs flexing as he bends. If any women were with us, they probably wouldn't be able to stop themselves from tucking singles into the waistband of his navy swim trunks.

I wish he'd go away. We crossed a line yesterday, with our stupid Pen Plan and our dancing. Now he assumes I'm some new recruit to his fan club, eager for his false compliments and banal conversation. But I'm not interested in either, and I certainly don't want to answer any of his stupid questions. If I open my mouth, there's a good chance I'm going to end up crying. He's the worst. I hate him.

I hate him. It feels good to remember. Any thought that isn't about Alexander is an improvement. I lean into it, letting my mind do a deep dive. It sails past Hannah and her heartbreak and all the women Jack slept with to make sure she'd forever regret falling in love with someone like him. For the first time, I don't stop it short of the memory of Jack and Rex laughing in the airport. I zoom in, expanding it until it fills my head. Jack Stone and Rex Blackwell. Two of a kind. They make me sick.

"Can't you find another chair?" I motion at the expanse of empty seats. "I'm tired of having to pretend to find you tolerable."

"Ouch." Jack's tone is light, but his face tightens. "I know we have our whole love/hate thing going on here, but you're taking it a bit far, don't you think?"

"I don't think I'm taking it far enough." I lift my book over my face and peer into its pages. "If I were, you'd be gone."

I feel a twinge of guilt as he silently grabs his towel and turns away, but I use the image of him and Rex to push it down. At the time, I hadn't realized why Jack was talking to me that night. I thought he was just a friendly fellow crew member. A nice guy. *Silly, stupid me.*

Rex and I had been together for almost eight months by then. I'd met him on a trip. In my defense, I knew immediately he was someone to be avoided. He was a pilot, co-captain of the tribe of wanderers I'd never aspired to join. Plus, his name was Rex Blackwell. It's still the dumbest name I've ever heard, and that includes Stake. I mean, Rex, really? Does he expect people to believe it's short for something? Tyrannosaurus?

I'll give him one thing, though: Rex was charming. And funny. I laughed all the time with him. I giggled my way through our first date. I tittered nervously when I realized our lifestyle—the spontaneous weekend trips to San Diego and endless nights on the road—wasn't so different from my parents'. I threw my head back and guffawed with relief when I realized it was possible to be okay with that. So many years running from my destiny when all along I could have simply embraced it.

I even laughed the day I was rerouted, my duty day extended by four long hours; they were sending me to Seattle, the same hotel Rex was in. I could surprise him. Rex loved surprises.

Checking in, I searched the pilot sign-in sheet for his name. Room 317. I stopped there first, thinking there was no point in dragging my bags to my own room. He wasn't there, though, so I dropped my bags off, changed out of my uniform, and went to the restaurant. The bar was packed, but I didn't see Rex anywhere.

"Well, hello," I heard behind me.

And that was the first time I laid eyes on Jack Stone.

I wish I could say I was unaffected by his shockingly blue eyes and that dark mess of hair, but I wasn't. Jack smiled a devil-may-care smile, and not for a moment did I consider trying to dampen the grin that sprang up on my face in response. *Silly, stupid me.*

"You look thirsty," he said. "Can I get you a drink?"

"I'm actually looking for my boyfriend." The words took more effort to get out than they should have.

"What a coincidence. I'm looking for my girlfriend. I think you might be her."

Our eyes locked, and we both began to laugh.

"Sorry," he said. "It was too good an opportunity. I couldn't resist."

"You should probably try harder next time." I heard the unplanned lilt of flirtation in my tone and pulled my hand from the lock of hair I'd begun to twirl. "Um, I'd better go."

"Wait." Jack reached for my arm, and his touch sent a tingling sensation across my skin. "Stay for one drink. My airline gets a discount here. I'd hate to miss an opportunity to take advantage of their generosity."

He grinned in a way that should've alerted me to who I was dealing with. Only a true charmer could make getting a drink feel like a mischievous opportunity to play Bonnie and Clyde. But instead of spotting Jack for who he was, I found myself focusing on the discovery that I might spot him again in the future.

"If you work at Northeast Air," I said, "I already have the same discount."

"So, we're coworkers, are we? That's fortuitous. Let's pretend that, instead of offering you cheap vodka, I approached you because I recognized you as a fellow Northeasterner."

I laughed in spite of myself. "Maybe we should pretend you approached me because you wanted to help me find my boyfriend. Any chance you know Rex Blackwell? He's a pilot."

Jack's friendly expression grew suddenly shuttered. "He's the pilot on my trip, actually. He was here earlier, but he just walked out a few minutes ago. I think he might have gotten a call."

"I should go find him," I said.

"His jacket is still on that stool. I'm sure he'll be right back."

I hesitated, unexpectedly torn. It had been a long day, and a cold drink and some light banter was more than a little tempting.

"You know what they say about being lost," Jack added. "The best way to be found is to stay in one place."

It was the realization that Jack was still holding my arm that settled it for me. If a cold drink and some light banter was what I wanted, I certainly didn't have any excuse in finding it with a man I'd just met. Nobody was up for a good time more than Rex.

I shook my head and pulled free. "Enjoy your night."

I could feel his eyes on me as I walked away. My awareness of him was proof I'd made the right decision. I hurried toward the elevator.

This time, the door to Rex's room wasn't fully closed. I rapped my knuckles against it, and it shifted beneath them. A moan slipped through the gap, and my stomach clenched with intuition before my brain had any inkling of what was going on. I hesitated in the hallway, my hand still lifted to the door. Slowly I eased it open, my heart in my throat.

The curtains were open, lighting the room with a purplish glow. Rain patterned against the windows. Discarded clothes led a path across the floor. The starched white shirt of a pilot's uniform. A crumpled flight attendant's dress. On the bed, Rex writhed atop a long-legged woman. Her satisfied moans filled the room, the new soundtrack to the shattering of my heart.

The memory squeezes at my chest, making it ache with old pain. I glare across the pool, where Jack has relocated and is talking to a group of girls. He thinks I don't know what he was doing with me in the bar that night, but I do. He was stalling me, covering for his buddy. I suspected it later that night, but I didn't know for sure until I spotted him and Rex walking side by side at the airport the next morning. The long-legged woman was with them, and I watched her say something that made them both laugh. *Two of a kind.*

Like Jack's ex, Hannah, I'd get to learn how many of my coworkers Rex had slept with. The information was meted out to me in bits and pieces over the next year. A whisper here. A confession there. There are still flight attendants whose eyes shift away when they see me. I can see the guilt on their face, but it's the pity I hate the most.

No, scratch that.

It's guys like Jack and Rex I hate the most.

Chapter 14

We've been sitting on the runway, waiting to get out of Belize for almost half an hour. The plane is disgustingly hot. I'm on the jump seat in the back, trying to convince a passenger to overcome his need to use the lavatory and return to his seat.

"We're on an active taxiway, sir," I say. "If you go in there, I have to call the captain, and per FAA regulations, he has to turn off the engine. We'll lose our spot for departure."

"But I have to pee." His whine is much more in line with a toddler than the grown man he's masquerading as.

"I understand that," I say. "What I'm trying to explain—"

Jack's voice breaks through the speaker, and the man's head jerks up like he's being spoken to by a higher power.

"We do need all passengers seated at this time," Jack says in a smooth yet commanding voice that reminds me of the pilot he used to be. "And by 'all passengers,' I am referring specifically to you in the back. Everyone, please turn around and direct the lost man forward so he can find his way to his seat."

Over a hundred people swivel around and begin waving their hands. The man turns red and glares at me before hurrying back down the aisle. Laughter follows in his wake.

Perfect. Twenty bucks says I'm the one who ends up with a complaint letter in my file. I fight the urge to call Jack on the interphone and inform him I was taking care of it. But we haven't spoken since my comment at the pool this morning. Working back here together during flight promises to be a delight. Thank goodness it's the last day of this trip.

I'm headed back to real life. Soon I'll have to talk to Alexander. I need to know if I'll be renting a hotel room tonight, or if I still have a place to live. I have plenty of time to stew in my worry because another ten minutes pass on the runway without movement. If Jack hadn't embarrassed him so thoroughly, the man with the tiny bladder would probably be back by now.

In the cabin, the natives have grown restless. The whispers of complaint crescendo to a loud whine. People begin turning around and calling questions back to me. I offer worthless responses. *I'm sure we'll be taking off shortly.* I can feel the fake smile on my face deteriorating into a grimace. *Any minute now.* It would be nice if I knew something, but until we hear from the pilots, we're as much in the dark as everyone else.

Once again, Jack's voice comes across the speakers.

"Ladies and gentlemen," he says, "we're getting quite a few questions up here. I haven't heard from the captain yet, but I have done the math. We've gone about two hundred fifty feet in the last thirty minutes. By my calculation, we'll arrive in Houston sometime around October of next year."

There's a moment of shocked silence before the cabin erupts into laughter. I fight back my own smile. As everyone settles into their seats, the interphone dings, and it's Captain Ballinger's voice I hear when I answer.

"Unfortunately," he says, "we've run into a problem with the plane. Please tell the passengers we're heading back to the gate."

....

I BLINK, HOPING against hope I misheard the Ops agent's words. But she's already repeating them, and they haven't changed.

"All passengers will be rebooked on tomorrow's flight," she says in a bored voice.

We've been sitting at the airport for over an hour, just as uncomfortable and uninformed as the passengers, but they respond as if we've made the announcement ourselves. I wince beneath the shower of complaints hurled our way. It's as if everyone has convinced themselves we've snuck into the airport overnight, popped the hood of the plane's engine, and started ripping wires out while gleefully cursing their plans. We're only the airport servants; it's inconceivable to them that we might've had plans of our own.

Captain Ballinger ends his call with Scheduling and turns to us. "They're grounding the plane for maintenance. It will be back in service for tomorrow's flight, and we will be its crew."

"But I've got a pole dancing class in the morning!" Gen reaches for the captain's phone.

He rears back like it's his nether region she's aiming for rather than his international calling plan. "What are you doing?"

"I need your phone. If I don't cancel, I'll have to pay for the class."

"Use your own," he says brusquely.

My mind spins, drowning the two of them out as they begin to argue. This is terrible. If I had any hope of bringing Alexander around to my side, it's officially gone. He'll use this to prove his point: as a flight attendant, I'm absent, undependable. His righteousness will be justified. And our engagement dinner. Is it on? Is it off? It doesn't matter because I won't get home in time to attend.

He'll probably go anyway. I can see the whole night play out, as clearly as if it's lit on a screen. The servers whisking away the place setting in front of my empty seat at the table. The gaping hole an inverse shrine to my absence. His mother's feigned concern. *You dodged a bullet, darling. Would you really want to marry someone who can't be bothered to show up to the wedding events?*

A tiny, deviant part of me sighs with relief. *An extra night on a tropical adventure*, it says, *sounds like a lot more fun than a stuffy restaurant with Alexander's parents.* I shush it and focus on Alexander's disappointment instead. It feels less selfish.

And it distracts me from having to acknowledge he might not care about my absence at all.

I DON'T BELIEVE things can get much worse until I walk into my hotel room and my new roommate steps on my heel. In nine years of flying, I've never once had to share a room with someone. I've never even heard of other flight attendants having to do so. It's an offence. A travesty. It is, apparently, what happens when your plane breaks down and the hotel only has four available rooms.

"If they were gentlemen," Gen grumbles, "the pilots would've offered to share and let us have our own rooms."

"But think of poor Paul. Would you want to share a room with Captain Uptight?" I hold up my hand when her eyes brighten. "Wait. Don't answer that."

"He's so sexy, though. I bet he'd take my clothes off just so he could properly fold them."

"Why do you have this thing for Captain Ballinger? Can't you just like Paul?" I'm not sure if it's our sudden status as roommates that's caused me to give up all effort at subtlety, or just my desire to see someone—anyone—find the happiness I've recently lost. "He's so great."

"I suppose. He's a little weird, though, isn't he? He brought, like, five kinds of muffins to my door this morning. And when I invited him in to come in, he was all, 'No, I don't want to intrude. I just wanted you to have a nice breakfast.'"

"That doesn't sound weird. It sounds sweet. Like he respects you."

"Which is weird," she says. "Which side of the bed do you want?"

I look around. The room is identical to the one I had last night, only this time there's a view of the Caribbean through the balcony. I'd be happier with two double beds. I wrinkle my nose at the king-sized in the center of the room. Gen strikes me as a cuddler.

"Maybe I'll just sleep on the floor," I mutter.

"Don't be ridiculous." Gen does a backward dive onto the bed, bouncing on her butt. Her shoes are still on. They probably have seagull poo on them. "I haven't had a sleepover since I was a kid. We're going to have so much fun!"

I can only imagine what mischief a young Gen was capable of getting into during a sleepover. The grape juice must've been spiked with her mother's vodka. Everyone probably borrowed her black clothes to TP the neighborhood houses.

"If you're expecting to play Truth or Dare," I say firmly, "you'll be doing it alone."

"Ooh! Truth or Dare. That sounds fun."

I consider asking if she minds if I use the luggage rack, but her roller has already toppled backward, spilling the contents of her tote onto the floor. I'm pretty sure she's not going to bother to pick her stuff up, much less heave it onto a rack. Gen kicks her shoes off but leaves them on the bed. I take the rack for myself.

"Grab those leftover minis out of my tote," she says. "Let's get this party started."

"I need to use the bathroom." At her whine, I roll my eyes and grab a bottle of Baileys off the floor. "Give me a few minutes," I say, chucking it at her.

I close the door tightly behind me and set my hands on the counter, staring into the mirror. The strain of the last twenty-four hours is getting to me. My eyes are bloodshot, the red contrasting with the now bluish version of hazel in a way that makes them frighteningly colorful. My cheeks and forehead are lightly burned from all the sun I got this morning. The humidity has thickened my hair, and unruly tendrils have escaped from the braid. My eyes widen as realization dawns. I don't look devastated. I look wild.

It's the last possible image I want to present to Alexander. I tug the braid out and run my fingers through my hair, pulling it straight and patting it down until it's soothed into something more presentable. My fingers shake as I pull the phone out and open the VC app. I give myself one last look in the mirror. *You can do this.* I take a deep breath and click on his picture.

For the first six rings, I stare at the phone. On the seventh, I distract myself by surveying the bathroom. It has a wooden counter and a wooden floor. The sink and towels are white. The tiny bottles of shampoo and conditioner have an orange flower on them. I sniff it and guess it to be a combination of hibiscus and lemon, but it turns out to be vanilla tangerine.

On the twelfth ring I reach for the plastic shower curtain. I slide it open and study the white tile inside. I'm closing it—the sixteenth ring—when I finally admit to myself Alexander is not going to answer.

I end the call and sink down to sit on the closed toilet lid. I stare at the wooden slats of the floor. What now? Texting is an option. I'm not sure how one types something like this in a text, though. *My flight got canceled. I don't know if I still live with you, but if so, I wanted you to know I'm not coming home tonight. And I don't know if we were still having our engagement dinner tomorrow night, but if so, I'm not going to make it.*

I might as well just type *None of this is important to me* because that's certainly how it will be interpreted.

Ignoring the frugality instilled in me by a lifetime of struggling to make ends meet, I take my phone off airplane mode. For some reason, my mom is still number one on my speed dial. Scheduling for Northeast Air is second, ranking it two slots higher than the man I'm supposed to marry. It feels like a sign. Of what, I don't know. That I'm not supposed to quit my job? Or that my priorities have been wrong all along?

I press number four and wait for Alexander to answer. My stomach sinks on the third ring. My grip has grown tight by the fifth. On the seventh, it will go to voicemail.

"This is Alexander," he says, his words clipped and curt.

My heart squeezes in my chest.

Alexander has never once answered a phone without looking at the number. He is playing professional. Really, he's angry. I can tell by the coldness in his tone. I'll never understand that about him. I get warm when I'm angry. Flushed with frustration. Hot with shame. Sweaty with defensiveness. Alexander goes arctic.

"It's Ava," I say quietly.

"I'm aware. How can I help you, Ava?"

"Really?" I sound embarrassingly small. "This is how you want to play it?"

He sighs. "No, of course not. None of this is playing out how I want it to. I'm probably going about it the wrong way. I'm just not sure how to talk to you now. Haven't we said everything there is to say?"

"We still have lots to discuss, Alexander."

"Such as?" There's a shift in his voice I don't like. It carries a hint of knowing. It is presumptively triumphant. "Has something changed on your end?"

"Actually, it has." I squeeze my eyes shut. "My flight has been canceled. I'm stuck in Belize. I don't fly out until tomorrow afternoon."

"Interesting." It's clearly not what he wanted to hear. The triumph in his voice has iced over. Reindeer could frolic comfortably in the frost it produces. "I wish I could say I was surprised."

"I'm staying because my flight got canceled, not because it was my choice."

"But your trip was supposed to end today. Are you really claiming there are no other flights out of Belize?"

"I'm telling you I have to work the flight out of Belize tomorrow," I say. "It's called an unscheduled overnight, and it's certainly not my first. This is a part of what I do for a living, Alexander. Delays, reroutes, unscheduled overnights. They're all part of it."

"Exactly. Yet you see no reason that a profession like that isn't conducive to a stable home life?"

Frustration roars through me. I'm not sure how the people

who really are on the stand manage to restrain themselves from grabbing the judge's gavel and chucking it at him. "Four days out of the week, I'm nothing but the stable one! I'm there, sitting patiently in your condo, just waiting for you to get home."

"But the rest of the days you're gone. Half the time, you're completely unreachable. Look at where you are. In another country, when you were supposed to be going to bed with me tonight. And what about our engagement dinner? You would've just missed it? My parents were coming. Would they have been expected to act like it's normal to celebrate a wedding when the bride can't even be bothered to show up?"

"I wouldn't—" I inhale deeply.

"What? You wouldn't have missed it? Or you can't help that you're stranded in another country? Which scenario am I supposed to seek more solace in?"

He pauses as if to wait for my answer, even though he knows he's left me with no good options.

"Forget it," I say. "This is pointless."

"Enjoy your beach vacation."

It's too much. His righteousness. His coldness. His insistence on treating me as an opponent across the courtroom rather than the partner he's chosen for life.

"I will." This time, it's my voice that's like ice. "But I'll be certain to make it back on Saturday to clear my stuff out of the condo. It would be nice if you could find somewhere else to be until late afternoon."

"Consider it done. And my ring?"

A hot laugh rips from my throat. Of course he thinks of it as *his* ring. It was never really meant for me, was it? Alexander knows I wouldn't have chosen anything like it. He wasn't considering me when he bought it. He was more concerned with what his partners would think. Those four carats did more to symbolize his success and wealth than they ever could've done to represent our love for each other.

"It's all yours. I left it in the guest bathroom."

"You're not even wearing it?" His voice rings with incredulity.

He probably expects me to feel guilty, but I don't. I'm glad I've managed to surprise him. For once in this relationship, it feels good not to meet his expectations.

"Nope," I say. "I guess it just wasn't a good fit."

The screen goes silent as he disconnects the call. Or maybe I do it first.

Maybe we've done it in unison, finally synced up after all this time, united in the moment that will keep us apart rather than the many that could have kept us together. With shaking fingers, I put the phone back into airplane mode. This time, it's not nerves that are causing them to tremble. It's adrenaline.

I don't feel anything I should feel. Not devastation. Not rage. Not even relief.

I feel feral.

All my life, I've made myself smaller around the people I love. Somehow I even managed to stop growing at a mere five feet. Tiny enough to be portable. Quiet enough to blend into the furniture. Agreeable. Easy. Whatever it takes to keep them from leaving me behind. Anything to keep them from wondering why I'm still there.

Finally, there's no one left to be small for.

I swing the bathroom door open, and it bounces off the wall. The boom of it fills the room. Gen jerks upright on the bed, her eyes widening as I scoop a mini-bottle of tequila off the floor.

"Are you okay?" She sounds more excited than concerned.

I nod, focusing on the tiny screw top of the bottle. With a satisfying pop, it rips free. I tilt it up to my mouth and choke down every last drop. It burns my throat like fire. A hot, cleansing flame.

"Ava?" A hint of worry creeps through her enthusiasm. "Do you want to talk about something?"

"No." I cough the word out. "You were right before. We're in freaking Belize. We should have some fun tonight."

Chapter 15

Gen and I leave the room because we have nothing to mix the liquor with. It doesn't matter. The tequila I chugged has already circulated around my head, leaving everything in its wake pleasantly woozy. Because there's no longer any reason to save it, I've put on my wedding dress. It sways in the sea breeze, soft material sweeping against my legs like it's dancing. The fact that it looks appropriate rather than too fancy for the beach tells me no reasonable wedding planner ever would've signed off on it anyway.

The sun is deep into its final descent, streaking the sky with its reds and oranges and pinks. Music fills the air near the tiki hut by the pool. The stools at the bar are full, but Gen pushes her way between two guys wearing worn-out baseball caps and colorful swim trunks. The air is immediately hotter among all the bodies. They look at her like she's a mermaid who has wandered onto the shore.

In her tiny shorts and black sequined tank top, she glitters dangerously. Gen is not a mermaid; she's a shark. I bet she enjoyed letting Stake break her heart. I bet it hurt like hell and was terrifying in its intensity, but she let it consume her just like she does every joy in her life. Gen is a person who is not scared of emotions. She embraces them. The good and the bad. The delight and the rage. It's impossible to imagine her making herself small or worrying about being left behind. She's so big, she's impossible to escape.

"Take my seat," the guy at her arm says. His voice is deep and carries a Southern drawl.

"And here I was, thinking chivalry was dead." Gen's crimson lips stretch into a predatory smile.

"Not in Texas." He tips his hat playfully. "They teach us right."

Spotting me as he stands, he nudges his friend to get up with him. I nod my thanks and climb up onto the rickety stool, facing the bar. Gen slides onto the seat next to me, facing behind us where the guys are hovering. Clutching my dress to my thighs, I twist slowly toward them.

"I'm Damon," says the guy who gave up his seat for Gen.

"And I'm Robby." The guy in front of me smiles.

My eyes flick back and forth between them. They could be twins. Damon has dark hair and Robby is blond, but other than that, they're interchangeable. They both have the same beefy build with shoulders that stoop forward. On their left biceps are the same tattoos, block lettering with what I'm guessing is some kind of mascot behind it. They look like ex-college football players, probably recently graduated.

"Let's get some beers for the ladies," Robby says, waving over my head at the bartender.

I spin back around and lean my elbows on the smooth wooden bar. The bartender nods and pours the daquiri he's just blended into a plastic cup. He tops it with a straw and slides it to a woman a few seats down from me before returning.

"Four beers?" The bartender grabs some plastic cups from the stack, and I notice, like me, he's perfected the art of palming the correct amount without counting. We're soul mates in service, united by the love of our craft.

"Actually," I say, "can I get a tequila sunrise? Or wait. Is there any kind of local cocktail?"

"You're thinking of a Belize Breeze." He smiles, a flash of white against dark skin. He probably had dimples as a child. Now he has deep grooves that indicate a lifetime of laughter. "How does coconut rum, fresh pineapple juice, and cherry liqueur sound?"

"Perfect," I say, smiling back at him.

"The same for me, love muffin," Gen says, swinging me around. "But can we get a couple of tequila shots first? To set the mood."

"What mood are we aiming for?" the bartender asks, already reaching for the bottle. "Are we celebrating something?"

Aside from my broken engagement? Well, there's also my impending homelessness. And the devastation of realizing the man who was supposed to love me for the rest of my life tapped out about sixty years shy of the end goal. But at least I know where I stand, which, for clarification's sake, won't *be at an altar.*

"Hell yeah, we are," Gen says. "We're celebrating broken planes and free vacations in Belize!"

"Make that four shots," Damon says. "On our tab."

"Avian sabotage and a free vacation? I'll make it five." The bartender winks. "On the house."

He lines them up and we lift them in the air.

"To broken planes," the bartender says.

"To broken planes!" I shout it out with the rest of them, and we all laugh before tipping the cups up. The liquor hits my throat, and I let the fire burn its trail to my belly before squeezing the lime between my teeth.

The hum of conversation around the bar grows louder. Our mood is contagious. The lady next to me introduces herself. Despite the fading light, she's wearing sunglasses that reflect my image back to me.

The bartender mixes up our Belize Breezes and places them in front of us. They're beautiful, yellow at the top but pink at the bottom. They taste like candied fruit, and I drink mine far more quickly than I should. It works some kind of wonderful magic that turns everything funny, even Robby's childish frat stories.

When I look down, my cup is magically full again. This, too, makes me laugh. Time gets wobbly, stumbling forward to the rhythmic beat of bongo drums. Our group grows.

My stomach growls audibly, informing me it's time for dinner. But my stomach is stupid. And boring. It's not time for food. It's time for group cheers and drinks that taste like paradise. I ignore my stomach and order another Belize Breeze instead. The bartender serves it with another round of shots. It's perfect timing because my throat feels normal again, coated by sweet nectar. I prefer it when it burns like the fire I've set to my engagement. I tilt my head forward and touch the tip of my tongue to the straw.

"What are we cheers-ing to?" The voice comes from behind me, and I jerk upright, recognizing it immediately.

"Jack!" I swing around on my stool and lean toward him. I tilt too far, though, and find myself falling forward.

Jack catches me against the hard expanse of his chest, his arms wrapping around me. He's wearing a worn T-shirt that's soft against my cheek and smells like soap and summer. I snuggle into it for a moment before putting a hand against his shoulder and pushing myself back upright.

"You're here!" I grab my shot and thrust it into his hand. "Cheers, everyone! To Jack!"

"To Jack!" They lift their cups, calling it out like a rally cry.

Jack lifts an eyebrow, and I shrug. Someone could probably shout, *To forest fires!* right now and it would be parroted cheerfully. We're here to celebrate. Any excuse will do.

"You usually look annoyed when I show up," Jack says suspiciously, still holding his little cup of tequila. "Why do you seem happy to see me?"

"I like fighting with you," I say.

"Can't you fight with anyone else?"

The question makes me laugh. Haven't I just tried that? For better or for worse, I've just allowed myself to fight with Alexander, and now we'll never speak again. Fighting can only be considered fun with someone like Jack, when you can be confident your life will be better once they disappear from it entirely.

"Nope." I lean forward and boop him on the nose, but my finger slips to his lips. They are full and firm, and I can't drag my eyes away from the way my finger perches between them. "It has to be you."

Jack's eyes darken. He slips his hand around my wrist and holds it in place. His lip curls up, and with the speed of a panther, he touches the tip of his tongue to my finger and bites it. It's just a small nip, but I feel it deep down inside my belly. It's shocking, and I gasp at the audacity of his assault and the unwanted pulse of desire it produces.

"You shouldn't be so sure you're going to win," he says.

I rip my hand free, and Jack lifts the shot to his mouth and tilts it up. I order myself to turn away, but my gaze is riveted to the slip of his tongue between his lips.

"I think we should get some food," he says, breaking the spell.

"I would, but I'm currently busy drinking." I turn to find my two-toned drink and notice Paul hovering beside Gen and Damon. "Pilot Paul! Do you think you could break our plane again tomorrow? I love it here."

"I'll see what I can do." His face is adorably sunburned.

"Thank you. You're the best." I drop a hand on Damon's beefy shoulder. He's leaning into Gen, likely bragging about another great thing he did on the football field. "Pilot Paul is the best," I inform him. "He thinks Gen is a beautiful, exciting firework. If you don't, you're not good enough for her."

Gen's mouth falls open.

"All right," Jack says, taking my arm and guiding it away from Damon. "Food. Let's order the same thing and race. You like to try to eat faster than me."

I do like that.

As tempting as Jack's suggestion is, I think I might be too hot to eat. The crowd around the tiki hut is three rows deep, and people are blocking any airflow. I grab my Belize Breeze and slip off the stool, pushing through the crowd, out to where I can feel the wind from the water.

Above me, the sky has turned black. The moon is a tiny sliver, but the stars are brighter and denser than I've ever seen them in Chicago. Maybe, if Alexander could see them like this, he'd realize my job isn't just delays and reroutes. He'd understand it's also moments of unexpected beauty. Or maybe he wouldn't. Maybe that kind of understanding is something he's never had any desire to achieve.

I start toward the palm trees, heading to the flickering flames of the tiki torches that line the sand. A couple is blocking the path, debating over whether they should stay for another drink or leave to see the bioluminescence. The guy's dreadlocks hang in his face, shadowing his features, and he has one of those travel-sized guitars slung over one arm. The girl has a tattoo that stretches from her shoulder to her waist and skinny, tanned arms that gesticulate wildly as she argues. He's in swim trunks, and she's in a string bikini that is losing the war against her butt cheeks.

"You said an hour," she says. "It's been almost two."

"You're talking about the bioluminescence?" I ask. I've read about the tiny fish-things that glow in the dark, but I've never seen them in person. It's something I've always wanted to do. "Are you going to see it now?"

"We were going to see it twenty minutes ago," the girl says, pulling a pack of cigarettes from the woven bag on her shoulder. "But someone always has to get his way."

"We're here, aren't we?" The guy steals a cigarette from her and lights it before passing the lighter and pack back to her. "I wanted a fishbowl from Tandy's, but you wanted to see your bartender boyfriend."

"Because he always gives us free shots, which is a lot cheaper than a fishbowl from Tandy's. Anyway, those fishbowl drinks are for tourists."

He scoffs. "We've been here for all of a month, Celeste. You think they don't still consider us tourists?"

I raise my hand like an eager schoolchild. "Can I come? To see the bioluminescence, I mean. Not to get a fishbowl. Although we can do that first if you want to. It sounds yummy."

They both turn to me, offering me a clear look at their faces. Celeste's is surprisingly pretty, in a natural, un-made-up kind of way. His is mostly covered by an unkempt beard.

I trust them. At least, I'm willing to pretend I do. I'd really like to see the glowing fish-things.

"Um, no offense, but who are you?" Celeste exhales a stream of smoke as she eyes me.

I wonder what she sees. A happy, carefree tourist? Or a girl who's endeavoring to drink her heartbreak away? "I'm Ava. I'm a flight attendant who disappoints people and changes my mind about very important things."

"She's weird," the guy says. "That could be entertaining."

"She's drunk," a low voice says. "Ignore her."

I spin around and find Jack behind me once again.

"Ignore *him*," I say, pointing at Jack. "He's a cheating cheater who cheats."

"He cheated on you?" Celeste's free hand goes to her hip.

"Yes," I say.

"No," Jack says at the same time. He looks at me, his eyebrows shooting up in surprise.

"Well," I amend, "he tried to cover for the guy who was cheating on me. Isn't that the same thing?"

"Yes," the guy says, just as Celeste says, "No."

They turn to each other.

"Seriously, Celeste? You're siding with Abercrombie on this one? If I helped some guy cheat on one of your friends, you'd set me on fire."

"It's Jack, actually," Jack says. "And I did no such thing."

"He did," I say. "He tried to stall me in a hotel bar so I wouldn't go to my boyfriend's room and catch him with another flight attendant."

"I did not!" This might be the first time in our brief acquaintance that I've seen Jack look completely stunned.

Dreadlocks lets out a low whistle. "All right, let's go."

"What?" I'm pretty sure all three of us ask the question in unison.

"I'm Eddie," he says, lifting his cigarette to his brow and flicking it out like a salute, "and I'll be your tour guide for the evening. It sounds like we'll have a lot to discuss."

"Bye, Jack." I wave at him.

"Oh, Abercrombie's coming, too," Celeste says, starting down the path.

"Damn right." Jack stalks past me. "Abercrombie wouldn't miss this for the world."

I glare after him and take a long chug of my drink before giving in and stumbling after them.

Chapter 16

Cold wind roars in my ears, and my hair whips around my face. The only thing that makes it tolerable is the fact that my hair is whipping against Jack's face as well. He's next to me on the middle plank of the rickety wooden speedboat. Celeste is on the plank in front of us, and Eddie is in back, manning the engine.

One of my hands is consumed with the effort of keeping myself from flying into the water, and the other is trying to hold my dress to my legs. In my drunken state, I'm doing neither well. My skin is covered in goose bumps. We hit the thousandth bump, and I grip the board beneath me. The bottom of my dress flies so high it hits my face.

I can feel Jack's laugh in the shake of his shoulder against mine. Mercifully, the boat slows. I cover myself back up and make a point of not looking at him. We haven't spoken since we got on board; it's been too loud. I can tell he's mad at me, though. He hasn't looked at me once, not even when my panties were on display.

"Quiet, everyone," Eddie says, as if there's a single person on the boat who's speaking. "The passage to the lagoon is narrow, and I need to make sure nobody is on their way out."

Celeste turns on the flashlight and points it toward the dark hole in front of us. I hold my breath.

"We're clear," she says.

Eddie moves the boat slowly forward into a canal lined with spindly tree trunks. In a matter of moments, we're surrounded by blackness. The temperature rises by at least ten degrees. The only light is a concentrated circle from the flashlight on the water in front of us. Apart from the rumble of the motor, it is eerily quiet.

"All right, Jack." Eddie's voice echoes across the water. "The time has come. There have been some allegations lodged against you. I think the exact accusation was that you're a cheating cheater . . . who cheats."

Celeste laughs, and I cringe. I've never even heard rumors of Jack being unfaithful. Calling him that probably says more about my inability to separate him from Rex than it does about Jack. Still, isn't helping a cheater cheat basically the same as cheating?

"I've never cheated on anyone in my life," Jack says firmly. "I have no idea why I'm on trial here."

"But you did try to help Rex cheat on me."

"What are you talking about?" Jack throws his hands in the air. I can't see it, but I feel the whisper of air that comes off the movement. "Rex Blackwell? I don't even like that guy. He's always telling stories about how great he is. It's like watching a show made up entirely of commercials for itself."

For a moment, I'm distracted by the truth in his observation. Rex always did love the spotlight. I'm not sure why he ever thought he could be satisfied playing to a one-woman audience. I spent months after we broke up trying to figure out why I hadn't been enough, but maybe it was never about what

I was lacking. Maybe it was simply a numbers issue. After all, what true performer wouldn't rather play to a full house?

Not that I'm making excuses for him. The guy stomped on my heart and kicked it into the gutter; there's no excuse for that. My eyes narrow, and my attention returns to Jack.

"Then," I say, "what's your explanation for that night in the bar?"

"I don't know what I'm supposed to explain. I saw a beautiful girl, and I tried to talk to her. Sue me."

My mouth drops open, and I squint, trying to spot some sign of mockery on his face, but there's nothing but darkness. He is a foot from my face, and I can barely see his outline.

"Sounds reasonable to me," Eddie says. "Weird little Ava, do you disagree?"

"I do," I say, barely resisting the urge to add *your honor*. "What Jack is failing to mention is that he *started* talking to me because I was alone, and heaven forbid a former pilot pass up the opportunity to flirt with a woman. But he *kept* talking to me because he discovered who my boyfriend was and didn't want me to go upstairs and catch his little pilot buddy sleeping with one of my coworkers. Men like them have to look out for each other, you know."

Jack groans. "Can you please not refer to that man-whore as my buddy? Tequila burns when it's coming back up. And I really don't appreciate being lumped in the same category as him either."

"I saw you two at the airport the next morning," I say. "You *high-fived* right in front of me. It was a total bro fest. I was scared to get any closer for fear I'd have to hear you comparing conquests and get caught in the middle of all the chest-bumping."

"Sure. Because why wouldn't you think that? There's no chance we would've been talking about weather or flight loads or any of the hundred more normal options two crew members might choose to discuss. First flight of the day, in uniform, walking through a crowded airport. That's exactly when I like to get into locker-room talk with a relative stranger."

"I'm sorry, my tiny, odd friend," Eddie says, "but I think I'm swinging to Abercrombie's side on this one. You hear that, Celeste? Once again, I've been forced to admit to your superiority in judgment."

"I know you can't see my face," Celeste says smugly, "but I'm currently wearing my 'of course you are' expression."

"And just so we're all clear on the events of that morning," Jack adds, "the high five happened because our crew had been rerouted into an eleven-hour day, which Scheduling had just informed us was getting pared down to half that."

As foolish as Jack's initial speech made me feel, the added details were a mistake. He's just overplayed his hand.

"So," I say, "you expect me to believe you remember everything about that particular moment, despite the fact that it was just a normal trip for you. Forgive me if I find that a little hard to believe."

"Normal?" Jack scoffs. "Who said it was a normal trip for me? For the sake of professionalism, I had to be friendly with a guy I couldn't stand. And I felt like a jerk high-fiving him when I was secretly wishing I could see his girlfriend's gorgeous smile again. Obviously I didn't realize then that you're only capable of smiling at me in bars, when you're looking for other guys or drunkenly cheers-ing me."

"Well . . ." I stall out. I'm not sure I believe him, but I do know better than to fall for his flattery. "That's a relief."

"What?"

"That you understand it was just the booze that made me toast your arrival."

Silence stretches for a moment, and then Jack lets out a little snort of laughter.

"Have you ever had a thought you didn't say aloud?" he asks.

His certainty in my answer is comical. I've spent most of the last year holding back thoughts. *I don't want to wash the sun off my skin before I get into your bed. I prefer to shower in the morning, like I'm starting each day anew.*

It's not as much fun to watch TV when you break down every scene, declaring the plotlines unrealistic. Can't you just allow us to be swept away by the story?

The Starlight is gaudy. And pretentious. And I don't want the people you work with to be at our wedding because they're painfully, unbearably boring.

"Yes." Maybe it's the booze that makes the confession slip out. Or maybe it's just the realization that I believe him—that I don't have to respect the way Jack conducted his own relationship to admit I've been wrong about his involvement in mine. "Normally I'm the queen of holding things in."

"Well, that sounds way less entertaining for everyone." Jack must have heard something in my tone because his has softened. "But this is not a normal night, Ava. We're not supposed to be here. In Belize. On this boat. It's a tear in reality. A stolen moment. So, what do you say? Can we toss our weapons overboard and just allow ourselves to enjoy it?"

I nod, knowing he can't see it. Still, I could swear he does, and I can feel his answering smile in the darkness.

"If you threw your weapons overboard," Eddie says, "they'd turn blue."

"What?" I shift to turn toward him, but my eyes are drawn up to the sky as we enter the lagoon. The stars are even brighter now after the darkness of the canal. They twinkle brilliantly, lighting the still water with their shine.

"Beneath us," Eddie says.

I look over the side of the boat and am shocked to see a glowing trail of blue under us.

"They get brighter when agitated," Celeste says. She bends over the wooden edge and swirls her hand in the water. It blooms to life, glittering with blue.

I hold the edge of the boat with one hand and lean over, but the alcohol has rendered me less than stable, and my arm is shorter than hers. Jack's arm slips around my waist, hovering lightly against my side. My stomach dips at the unexpected contact. I tense for a moment and feel the answering uncertainty in his hand.

"Thank you," I whisper before bending over the edge.

The water is shockingly warm. It swooshes through my fingers, transforming into something glowing and alive. I squeal with delight, swirling my hand deeper into the water. Jack laughs, his grip on me tightening.

"Check this out," Celeste says.

I pull myself upright just as she cannonballs over the front of the boat. The water explodes with color. I gasp and begin to applaud. Jack slaps his hands together, piercing the air with a stadium whistle that echoes over the water. From behind us, Eddie jumps in, much closer to us than Celeste. Warm water hits my skin, trickling down my back.

"I want to go," I say.

"Let's do it." Jack tugs off his shirt and tosses it onto the board Celeste was sitting on. The starlight dances across his abs. I feel a strange urge to trace the pattern with my fingers.

"I'd have to go in my dress," I say. If it were any other dress, I'd be fine with that. But I love this dress. Even if it *was* supposed to be the thing I wore to start my new life, it also fits perfectly in this one.

"You can't. If your clothes are wet on the way back, you'll freeze. Just go in your bra and panties. They have to provide more coverage than that tiny thing you were wearing yesterday."

I roll my eyes, but I can feel the flush spreading across my cheeks. "My bikini is not tiny. It's perfectly average-sized."

"Hey," Jack says with a wink, "no complaints here."

"This is why I'm not nice to you," I say primly.

"Niceness is overrated. At this point, I'm considering anything less than active aggression a win. Avert your eyes." He reaches for the button of his shorts.

My eyes widen, and I jerk my head away just before the sound of a zipper hits my ears.

"I'm not wearing a bra under my dress," I admit, staring at the slick of water in the bottom of the boat.

I hear a hitch in Jack's breathing.

"It's fine." His voice is strained. "We won't look. Right, guys? Nobody is looking at Ava when she jumps in."

"I might look," Celeste says, her head bobbing above the water.

"Keep it in your pants, woman." Eddie sighs and leans his head back so he's floating. "Why's it always got to be me explaining to you that women aren't objects to be ogled?"

I peek up at Jack. His shorts have come off, and he's down to material so flimsy, I can see the lines of the landscape beneath it. As much as I wish I didn't have to admit it, what's underneath looks impressive.

"I can take my boxers off if it will make you feel better," he says with a sly smile.

"It won't."

"I was just thinking it might be more comfortable. You know, if we both went skinny-dipping."

"Yes!" Celeste says. "Let's all skinny-dip!"

Before I can argue, the water around her begins to glow with the movement of her body. Seconds later, her bikini top comes flying in the air and splatters at my feet. The bottoms follow closely behind. I can't decide if I'm horrified to see her suit in front of me or impressed by her aim.

"Because I don't really know you guys," I say, "I feel the need to formally state that there is zero chance of this turning into an orgy."

"You're preaching to the choir, my strange miniature friend," Eddie says. "I'm not saying weirdness is sexually transmitted, but until it's been scientifically proven not to be, my dick is guaranteed to be skittish around the likes of you."

Eddie follows up his offensive assurance by shimmying out of his swim trunks and sending them arcing through the air. They hit the back of the boat and slip down the side into the water. It welcomes them with a yawn of blue.

I arch an eyebrow. Surely he doesn't need help from someone as weird as me. But Jack slides around me, and the boat sways from side to side as he moves to the back and leans over the edge to grab the trunks. He tosses them to the floor and turns to face me.

"We're doing this?" he asks.

I hesitate. "Seems like it."

He smiles, his teeth gleaming against the night. I blink at the sight of him, nearly naked already, a mere foot away from me. His body is so perfect, it almost hurts to look at it. Almost, but not quite. My gaze traces the lines of his smooth skin, down to the triangle that points south.

"Here we go," he says.

I pull my eyes away and will them forward until I hear the splash of water. It glows around him, a beacon summoning me. I turn away from them, and without giving myself a moment to hesitate, I slip the dress over my head. The air hits the skin that's been covered, and it feels like freedom. I fold the dress and place it on the board I've been sitting on, then slip my panties off and drop them on top. With a shriek, I jump overboard.

The water consumes me, blooming into neon. It is strange and wonderful. I wave my arms and watch blue shoot from them like I'm emitting secret powers. My laugh skips across the water like a flung stone, the salty water slipping into my mouth. Jack does a flip, and I spot the muscled cheeks of his butt as they skim above the water.

I splash at them, and Celeste retaliates for Jack by splashing at me. Some overspray hits Eddie, and he sinks from his floating position and pops back up with a handful of water. We shriek and duck to avoid his spray. Jack is waiting when I come back to the surface. A wall of water hits me in the face, and I gasp and laugh as I slap it back at him. Water flies between the four of us, and our shrieks fill the air.

"I surrender!" Jack shouts the words when the three of us turn on him.

I laugh and sink beneath the surface, feeling the water caress every part of my body.

It's not the first time I've skinny-dipped. When I was eleven, we lived in a trailer in Kentucky for a while. It belonged to one of my parents' friends, and he kept it in a field behind his house. There was a pond nearby, and I spent most of my days out there alone. My parents kept saying they were going to buy me a suit but couldn't seem to remember to actually purchase one.

The first few days I was at the pond, I just dangled my feet in the water, wishing I could go in. Eventually, temptation got the better of me. I held my nose and jumped in, still wearing my jean shorts and tank top. It wasn't bad, but the wet shorts rubbed on the walk back to the house, leaving red bumps scattered across my inner thighs.

"Let's go shopping tomorrow," Mom said when I asked her again. "We can get some doughnuts, too."

The next morning, I awoke to an empty trailer. I checked the table for a note, but they'd forgotten to write one. I wasn't worried—I knew they'd be back—but there was a fire licking up my spine as I walked to the pond. The sun burned at my scalp as I crossed the grass, but it was that little flame inside me that sent sweat trickling down my neck. I reached the pond and ripped my clothes off, right there in the open, not even checking to see if this time, magically, someone else had come to swim.

My parents had returned by the time I got back to the trailer that day, but I never asked them for a swimsuit again. For almost two months, I played naked in that pond. I pretended I was a wildling raised by wolves. I was a slithering creature of the sea. I was shipwrecked with the Swiss family Robinson. I taunted the world with my recklessness, daring someone to catch me. If they did, I might have been embarrassed, but at least for a minute, I wouldn't have to be alone anymore.

I spin in a slow circle, taking in these people I've somehow ended up with. It feels just as good as my eleven-year-old self imagined it would.

Chapter 17

Eddie is the first person to climb back into the boat. I avert my eyes as he towels off his naked body. Jack and I are treading water as Celeste regales us with tales of their travels. She and Eddie have been on the road for about two years. After six months of picking blueberries for free lodging in Australia, they found themselves low on funds. The incredible snorkeling, unique food, and friendly locals have made them fall in love with Belize, she says, but it's the low cost of living that initially drew them here.

"We were going to take a ferry when we arrived." Celeste's face bobs above the water, lit by stars. The water around her glows with the flow of her hands. "We flew into Belize City and were going to ferry straight to this island called Caye Caulker, and all over the world, that's what you do, right? You take the slow boat, packed like sardines, instead of the fast one, because it's always cheapest. But we were headed to the dock, and our taxi driver is chatting with us, and he laughs at us when we tell him our plan. 'For only a few dollars more,' he tells us, 'you can get there by plane.' And I swear, we didn't really believe him, but he was so enthusiastic about it that we just agreed. So, we end up at this tiny airport, and sure enough, for fifty dollars we get on a plane."

"Fifty dollars each?" I can't help needing specifics. So many of my nights growing up were spent hovering at the edges of a circle of travelers. In the living rooms of strangers or on folding chairs around a bonfire beneath the light of the moon, the stories would fly, verbal road maps to the next adventure. And nobody could just listen. They needed to know all the details, followable bullet points already worked out by someone else. Because the kind of people my parents were drawn to were not the planners of the world. They were the wanderers.

"Nope," Celeste says. "Fifty total. And there were no lines or jetway. Just a six-seater on asphalt, like a taxi with a propeller. They toss our bags underneath and usher us in, and there are two other people already seated. And then we just take off. And we're flying over the sea and these thick trees that look like rolling carpet, and it's the most incredible view I've ever seen. And, too soon, we land on this grass runway, a little field surrounded by palm trees. And there's a bamboo hut on stilts on one side of it, but no airport or anything. And the pilot turns around and waves us out. We get our bags from under the plane, and he takes off, leaving us in this field all alone. There's not another person on the ground. No signs. Nothing to say that we're even on Caye Caulker."

"Were you freaking out?" Jack drifts closer to me.

When his blue glow threatens to collide with mine, I wave my arms in the water, propelling myself backward.

"Not really," Celeste says.

"She was totally freaking out," Eddie says from the boat. He pulls his little guitar from its waterproof bag and strums it in response to our laughter. "She thought we'd been stranded on a deserted island and were going to have to craft spears from bamboo to fish with. Be honest, Celeste. Didn't you have some weird thing about monkeys? You were convinced you were going to have to fight them for their bananas."

Celeste splashes at him, and Eddie bends over the guitar, covering it with his body.

"Careful," he says. "I made seven dollars playing this thing on the beach the other night. If you ruin it, you'll have to come up with a new retirement plan for us."

Before she can respond, he begins to play a song. It's a slow, sweet choice. The melody slips across the still water, filling the air.

"So, what happened?" I lay my head back against the water and stare up at the sky. "Did you find civilization?"

"We did," Celeste says. "We walked for a while and eventually heard music. It led us to the shore, where we found all the hotels and restaurants. We spent a couple of nights there until this big wooden sailboat pulled up to the shore, offering a three-day trip to Placencia for cheaper than what we were spending on our room."

"And that, my friends, ended up being some of the best snorkeling we've ever done," Eddie says. "Right up there with the Great Barrier Reef. At one point, Celeste had a stingray below her and a shark above her. I could almost see the water around her turn yellow."

"Gross! If anyone peed themselves, it was you." Celeste swims toward the boat and hoists herself over the edge, giving me an eyeful of her butt. "Where's that whiskey?"

I slip underwater, holding my breath, stalling. I'm not ready to go. I want to stay here all night and snorkel in the lagoon at dawn. I want to hitchhike on a plane and land in a field surrounded by palm trees. I want to fight monkeys and steal their bananas. I'm not supposed to want any of these things, but I do.

A rare pang of homesickness hits me. It's not for any of the temporary housing I've lived in over the course of my life; it's for my parents. They'd love every moment of this night, and I'd love sharing it with them. Two fellow adventurers who know me instead of a guy I can't stop fighting with and a couple of backpackers who probably won't remember my name tomorrow.

It's a silly, pointless longing, though. Even if my parents were here, they'd inevitably drift away. They'd follow the neon trail of a fish or something, and I'd end up waiting in the boat for them, terrified we wouldn't get back in time for my flight. It should be different as an adult, but it's actually worse. I can't allow myself to be sucked into their magic anymore. The stakes are much higher now.

I pop my head out of the water and gulp in the fresh air. Laughter burbles from my throat. I'm a twenty-eight-year-old woman still wishing for my parents; clearly, I need to make some friends. Real friends. Friends who can accept me for who I am, the person who won't always be around. The person who can't always be small for them.

"What's so funny?" Jack waves an underwater hand at me, sending a slush of water slipping softly against my bare breasts. "Did you get tickled by a fish?"

I fight my instinct to propel myself away again. Instead I stay still, allowing the glow of our blues to dance. If my plan really is to embrace being a flight attendant—which, considering my willingness to tank my relationship over the decision, seems to have been rather adamantly decided—maybe it's time to stop relegating my flight attendant friendships to only the workplace. Pretending I'm not one of the flight tribe hasn't made it true. It's just kept me from developing real relationships with the only people in the world who completely understand my lifestyle.

"*You're* funny," I say, admitting it to myself as much as to Jack. "Sometimes, at least."

"Am I?" Jack's voice drops like he's picked up on the change in the air.

I study his face, lit by starlight. His often-tilted mouth, ever eager to break into a smile. His eyes that look dark now but I know to be the color of the sky. If I were to admit to myself that there are things about him I like, it wouldn't have to mean I'm susceptible to his womanizing charms. I am the person who has just had the strength to walk away from Alexander and his promises of stability and a lifetime of sames. I am strong; I look out for my own best interests.

"Yes," I say. "You are."

His smile flashes against the dark sky. "I wondered if you'd ever notice anything you like about me."

For some reason, his words cause my heart to speed up.

"I was just thinking we could be friends," I say. Rather than the offer I've intended, it comes out sounding more like a limitation. "I mean . . . look. What I'm trying to say is that it's possible I've misinterpreted what happened that night at the bar. If that's the case, I apologize."

"You apologize? Or you want to be friends?"

"Either," I say. "Maybe both?"

I owe him more than this paltry, reluctant offering. If Jack were Alexander, I'd be reciting all the ways in which I'd do better. If he were Meredith, I'd probably etch out my words of apology in calligraphy.

I can't do those things for Jack, though. Maybe it's just that our patterns have already been set. Or maybe it's that deep down, I know I'll never be able to fully separate him from the Rexes of the world and the carnage they leave in their pursuit of women. I can be friendlier toward Jack, but I could never truly be friends with him.

"I accept," he says. "Both the apology and the offer."

"Good."

"Should we hug on it?"

My eyes widen at the thought of his slick, naked skin pressed against mine. A small, nervous laugh escapes me.

"See?" His voice is quiet and serious. "You were right. I *am* funny."

Our eyes lock, and the night swells around us.

Maybe it's the Belize Breezes, or maybe it's just that Jack was right and we really have ended up in a tear in reality, but I lift my arm to the surface of the water. "Would a handshake work?"

Without a word, he edges closer and slips his fingers around mine. Blue flames spark between us. For a moment, I forget to paddle my legs. I drift dangerously close to full contact with him. Just as our blues swirl together, Jack lets go of my hand and sweeps himself backward. It's like the snap of fingers, the shaking of a shoulder designed to wake someone from a dream. It leaves me blinking and flustered.

"It's settled then," he says, the splashing of his hands too loud. "Friends."

I nod, too caught between worlds to be able to formulate a response.

Jack leans back so his head rests against the water, his face lifting toward the sky. I copy him, letting the stars fill my gaze until the entire world seems to twinkle.

"We probably shouldn't keep them waiting," he says.

"I don't want to go." I whisper the words like a confession.

"I don't either," he says, still facing the sky. "I want to stay here and catch a ride on a sailboat and snorkel with sharks and stingrays. I want to fight monkeys for their bananas."

I stare at his profile, grateful he doesn't turn toward me; it already feels like he has a direct line of vision into my soul.

"Me, too," I admit finally. "But monkeys are really smart," I add, uncomfortable with my confession. "I doubt that's a battle you'd win."

He doesn't look my way. "You know, I almost said no when you offered to be my friend."

"Because I say things like that to you?"

"No. Because I was worried if I said yes, you'd stop saying things like that."

Flipping over, he ducks underwater. I watch as long, muscular strokes propel him back toward the boat, a trail of neon blue in his wake. Slowly, I paddle after him, soaking in the last of the night, absorbing some of the neon magic for my own.

Jack climbs into the boat, and Celeste and Eddie don't bother pretending not to watch him towel off. Since their front-facing view is much more scandalous than mine, I feel little shame about indulging in my own little peep show. My eyes trace the length of his legs and the muscles that pop up on his back as he shifts to towel off a new part of his body.

He catches me looking, and my cheeks heat up, but I don't look away. If this night is a stolen moment, surely I'm allowed a few stolen peeks. Jack wraps the towel around his waist and takes a bottle of whiskey from Eddie, lifting it to his mouth. I reach the edge of the boat.

"Eyes captain-side, everyone," Jack says, lowering the bottle and swiping the back of his hand across his mouth.

"You mean port?" Eddie asks.

"I mean away from the naked woman who's about to come aboard." Jack turns pointedly away from me. Thankfully, Celeste and Eddie follow his lead.

Eddie begins to play another song. I climb into the boat and grab a towel. Without the speed of the boat and the chill off the sea, the air is warm. I swipe the water away quickly, but nobody turns around. Maybe it's Jack's guard-like stance. Or maybe Celeste and Eddie have seen enough of a show already. My dress sticks to my skin as I pull it over my head. I slip my panties on under it.

"Done." I settle onto the same wooden plank as earlier and reach for the bottle of whiskey.

"Your skin's still got a little bit of a blue glow to it," Eddie says.

"Really?" I study my arms.

Eddie laughs. "No."

I roll my eyes and tilt the bottle to my mouth. The whiskey hits the back of my throat, making me cough. It settles into a warm pool in the bottom of my stomach. Jack sits next to me, close enough to feel the heat radiating from his body.

"It's time," Celeste says.

For a moment, I'm certain she's going to take us on another adventure. My hands clasp together at the prospect. I sneak a peek at Jack and am surprised yet pleased to see the same flash of excitement on his face.

Eddie hands her the guitar and starts the engine.

"Time for what?" I ask.

"What do you think, my peculiar little angelfish?" Eddie swings the boat around. "It's time to go back."

WE'RE SILENT AS the boat eases through the dark entry back to the sea. It's not until we clear it that I realize how much the temperature has dropped. The wind breaks off the waves, growing icier the faster we go. I wrap the damp towel around me, but it only seems to make me shiver more. Tentatively, I shimmy my shoulders free of it.

That's cold, too.

It might be better, though. I pull it all the way off and tuck it between my thighs before wrapping my arms back around myself. They say skin-to-skin contact is the warmest, right? Does that include your own skin?

My hair might be the real problem. I've knotted it into a bun at the nape of my neck, but it's still wet. I begin to shiver, one of those deep shakes that tightens your back and curves your spine. Jack's arm goes around me, shocking me into stillness. He tugs me toward him, and I stiffen, resisting his pull.

He leans into me, his mouth hot against my ear. "Friends don't let friends freeze to death."

I fake a smile but ease up enough for him to slide me in front of his chest. I can feel Eddie's knowing gaze from behind us. Jack's arms wrap around me, one pressed against my stomach, the other over my chest. His forearms stretch over mine, skin to skin, his fingers wrapped around the backs of my arms. He rests his chin against the top of my head.

I'm surrounded by him.

It's both terrible and wonderful. Jack radiates warmth, and where his arms cover me, the wind can't reach. The shield he provides makes me want to slide into his lap and wrap his legs around me, too. In spite of myself, I push back further into him. Like I knew they would, his arms tighten around me. I resist the urge to twist my head and bury my face into the warmth of his neck. His fingers slip up and down the back of my arm, stroking it softly. I feel it through my entire body.

I tell myself to make him stop, but the communication lines between my brain and my body are frozen. In complete contrast to my orders, my fingers reach up to his arm. They stroke the outer edge of his forearm, tracing the groove of a muscle. When they reach his wrist, they start back up the path they've discovered.

I feel the tension in his chest at my back, but he doesn't pull away. Instead his other hand slides up my shoulder. Slowly, surely, it dips across my collarbone, feathering a line from one end to the place where it meets my neck. His finger slips up the delicate skin that leads to my jaw, and mine slides further up a hot trail of skin. I can't tell if it's his heart pounding against my back or if mine is just beating so loudly I don't recognize the sound anymore.

Up ahead, the lights from the hotel grow brighter. I slide my hand down the length of his arm, and he strokes the curve of my cheek. His hand trails back down my neck and dips low. My breath catches as it slides across my chest, just above the top of my dress. I want to push his hand lower. I want its heat on every part of me. Thankfully, the boat slows, approaching the shore before I can lose all illusion of control.

I lift myself upright, pulling myself from Jack's arms. His

hand slides across my back and down the length of my arm before letting go. With our physical connection severed, my brain begins to function properly again. To say it is displeased with the rest of my body's decisions would be an understatement.

It hurls truth bombs at me with poorly timed vigor: *Jack Stone is not the kind of guy you want to mess with. And* you—*you're just as fickle as him. You were an engaged woman yesterday. And today you're, what? Exploring a coworker's body like you're planning to re-create it from clay? Pull it together, Greene!*

My foot stomps at the watery boat floor in response, because it doesn't seem to be quite synced back up with my brain yet. In its opinion, my brain is overreacting and would benefit from realizing that being engaged yesterday doesn't make me engaged today. And considering Jack's already slept with a solid portion of my coworkers, I could've done a lot worse than—*gasp!*—touch his arm.

"We're going to drop you here," Eddie says, stopping shy of the beach. "Celeste, see if the Sharpie is in the guitar bag."

"Thank you so much for taking us with you tonight," I say. "It was magical."

"No problem, my odd miniature friend," Eddie says. "I'm sure we'll run into you down the road, and you'll end up taking us for a ride."

"It's possible, actually," Jack says. "In our line of work, we cover a lot of ground."

"Until next time then." Celeste reaches for my hand and uses a Sharpie to write a number across my palm. "We share that phone, so you'll always be able to get in touch with at least one of us."

"Thanks for everything." I wrap my arms around her bony

shoulders and squeeze her to me. It's strange to think I'll probably never see her again. But that's how it is in this world I've spent so much of my life determined to escape. You make friends faster than you ever dreamed possible, but they disappear just as quickly.

Jack presses a square leather wallet into my hand and jumps into the thigh-deep water. A second later, he holds out his hands toward me.

I shake my head at him. "What are you doing?"

"Carrying you to shore."

"Um, no, you're not." The minute I get off this boat, the adventure is over. The stolen moment must be returned to its rightful owner. There is absolutely zero way I'm departing from the tear in reality in Jack's arms; I want every memory of his skin against mine left on the other side before the fissure is sewn back up.

Jack's eyes narrow as if he's reading my thoughts. Just when I'm certain he's going to accuse me of being ludicrously stubborn, he grins.

"There's no reason for us both to get salt water all over our clothes," he says lightly. "If you were planning on carrying me, it would've been polite to let me know before I jumped in."

"I'm not carrying you," I scoff.

"Well, not now. It's too late for that. I'm already wet."

I turn to Celeste, but she just laughs.

"This round is going to Abercrombie," she says. "How are you supposed to argue with logic like that?"

With a sigh, I give in and lean forward, placing my hands on Jack's shoulders. They're broad and strong. If I had any upper-arm strength of my own, I could mount them like one of those things gymnasts twirl around on. Instead I let him swing me into his arms. My body presses against his chest. My face is too close to his. Now that we're back to real life, among civilization—now that I can see him—it feels uncomfortably real.

"Hurry," I say as he wades toward the sand.

Jack nods and slows down.

I fight the urge to bite his big, broad, stupidly muscled shoulder.

Chapter 18

"Well, that was fun," I say when he finally sets me down on dry land. I dig my toes in the sand and avoid his eyes. "I guess I'll see you tomorrow."

The corner of his mouth tilts up. "Are you hoping I'll pretend my room isn't across the hall from yours? Go ahead. I'll follow far enough behind so that, if anyone spots me, they'll assume you have a stalker. I'm sure you'll love seeing me get pepper-sprayed."

"Sounds like my new favorite show." I start toward the hotel.

"I'm really glad we're friends now," he calls out. "You're excellent at it."

I lift my hand, waving goodbye without turning back.

The little grope-fest in the boat has sobered me up enough to realize I need to go to bed. How am I supposed to properly agonize over the mess I've made of my life without a good night's sleep? Normal people don't respond to their canceled engagement by running off to swim with glow fish. They wallow. I wonder if Ben & Jerry's exports to Belize. I'm going to need a little rain tomorrow because all this sunshine and warmth is impeding my ability to properly mourn.

I glance back as I enter the hallway that leads to our rooms. As promised, Jack is about twenty feet behind me. His eyes are trained on the ground. I feel a pang of regret for ending the night so awkwardly. But apparently that's what I do now. I end things abruptly. Carelessly. It's a fact my ex-fiancé can attest to.

I reach the door and my stomach sinks at the realization I don't have a key. Because of this dress, I couldn't tuck one in my bra. I figured I'd be coming back at the same time as Gen. Wincing, I raise my hand to knock. I have no idea what time it is, but it feels like we've been gone for days. I rap my knuckles against the door.

"Problem?" Jack calls the word down the hallway.

"Shhh." I glare at him. "People are sleeping."

"I'm aware. You're the one who seems intent on waking them up."

I turn back toward the door, mentally pleading for it to open. Magically, it does. Gen leans into the crack. Her hair is tousled, and if I had to guess, I'd say she's using the door to hide her nakedness. *Perfect.* A cuddler and a nude sleeper. I'm so opting for the floor.

"I need an hour," she hisses. "I have company."

I crinkle my nose. "Damon?"

"Nope." She smiles through smeared crimson lipstick. "Pilot Paul."

"Really?" I can't help it; I'm too thrilled to be annoyed. "You're not going to break his heart, are you?"

"Right now, I'm just planning to break the bed." She looks so pleased at the prospect, I can't help but laugh.

"Go to Paul's room," I say. "He doesn't have a roommate."

"We would've, but we had to start here because someone had to be around to let you in."

"Well, here I am. Let me in."

"Sorry. You took too long. Now, we're kind of in the middle of something. Here . . ." Gen lets the door close, and I blink stupidly at the white wood until she pulls it back open and presses a key card into my hand. "Room 106. Watch a movie or something. Come back in two hours."

I look down at the key. "But you said one hour."

"My mom taught me to underestimate myself, but my therapist says that's something I should work on overcoming." Gen smiles and shuts the door in my face. This time, I hear the click of the lock.

A throat clears behind me. I turn slowly and find Jack leaning against his open door. He's smirking.

My hands go to my hips. "You think this is funny?"

"Do I think it's funny that you've been sexiled? No. Do I think it's funny that you've decided you like the person who has locked you out of your own room but somehow manage to have a problem with me, the one person whose door is wide open to you? Yes. Actually, I find that very amusing."

"I don't need your open door." I wave Paul's key at him. "I have a space all to myself."

"Don't let me keep you from it, then. Good night, *friend*." Jack flicks his fingers in salute and turns around, letting the second door of the night close in my face.

I huff and stomp past it. Naturally Pilot Paul's room has to be right next to Jack's. If it were up to me, I wouldn't share so much as a wall with Jack. He's probably already found a way to have women in there. I bet that's why he showed up at the bar so late. The smell of their perfume will have seeped through the vents into his neighbor's room, which is now my holding pen.

I slide the key into the slot, and a red light flashes at me. I twist the handle and pull anyway, but the door doesn't budge. It merely beeps its irritation at me. I slide the key again and pull. More beeps. I groan aloud and cross back to my door. When I try the key, green lights appear. I jerk it back out.

Gen has given me the key to our room.

I knock loudly, unwilling to enter and find myself witness to Gen's efforts to break the bed. Unsurprisingly, she doesn't answer. I turn and slump against the door. My eyes go to Jack's. I'd be willing to bet he's heard all the beeping and knocking. Any moment, it will open and his annoyingly knowing face will appear.

It doesn't.

Slowly, reluctantly, I approach his door. It's only an hour or two. As adamant as I was about the Pen Plan, it would be silly to throw a wrench in it now that it's found success. I lift my fist and knock.

Jack fills the door frame once more, newly changed from his wet shorts into a pair of sweats. His head tilts as he takes me in. For a moment, I'm certain he's going to make me ask for his help. But then a smile curls at his mouth and he steps back, holding the door open. I slip past him, careful not to make contact.

His room is identical to ours, which is strange, given I feel like I've entered a lion's den. His uniform is tossed over the chair, but other than that, the space is neat. I hover at the foot of the bed, not quite willing to sit on it. I'm not sure if the arm stroking on the boat was the result of residual glow fish pheromones or something worse, but I am fully aware it can't happen again.

"Sit." Jack waves at the bed as he passes me on his way to the minibar. "Do you want something to drink?"

Yes!

"No," I say, "thanks."

He smirks like he knows I'm too scared to mix booze and this kind of close proximity to him. When, exactly, did his womanizing ways begin to work on me?

"Food, then." Jack studies the offerings, then scoops them all up and dumps them on the bed. "Enough junk food must eventually add up to a full meal, right?"

My eyes go to the bag of chips, and my stomach growls audibly. I sink onto the duvet and grab for it. Ripping it open, I hum with pleasure as the salt hits my mouth. Except for the maraschino cherries I swiped at the bar, I haven't eaten anything since my burrito bowl this morning.

"I did try to feed you hours ago," Jack says, reading my mind, "but you were pretty intent on drinking dinner."

"I was trying to forget about my day." I shove three more chips in at once.

"Were the passengers giving you a hard time in the back?" Jack reaches for the Snickers, and my eyes narrow territorially.

"Not that bad." I watch as he breaks off half and folds the wrapper over the other half.

"Then why did you want to forget about your day?" He sets the other half on the bed in front of me, and I grab it with delight. "Was it the delay?"

I take a too-large bite of the Snickers, and a strand of caramel sticks to my chin. If it didn't taste so good, I might be embarrassed. Instead I close my eyes and chomp through the nougat and peanuts. This is the reason you're not supposed to drink on an empty stomach. I'm not a shark like Gen. I'm a bear. I use my paw to shove the rest of the bar into my mouth.

Jack laughs. "Ava?"

"What?" The word comes out in a mumble.

"Why was your day so bad?"

I open my eyes and find him staring down at me. It's weird. And uncomfortably intimate. "It doesn't matter," I say, waving him to the other side of the food. "It's over now."

"The day?" He doesn't move. "Or whatever was upsetting you?"

I scoot backward on the bed and fold my legs under me to create some space between us. Leaning forward, I swipe the pile of snacks toward me. I grab the Twix and rip it open. Jack holds out his hand, and I reluctantly pass him one of the halves.

"You're not answering my question," he says.

"I'm not." I don't want to. And not because he and Gen think I've been single this whole time. I don't want to answer Jack's question because, after the experience I've had tonight, Alexander and our failed relationship feel like they exist on a different planet. But if I speak them into existence, they'll crash into this one like a meteor.

"I have an idea," Jack says.

I open the bag of mixed nuts as he goes to the closet.

"Is this stuff expensive?" As I ask the question, I realize it's coming a little too late to be polite or helpful.

"Significantly cheaper than it would be in the States." Jack returns with a pack of cards and sits on the other side of the snacks, across from me. "I'll consider it a failure if we don't at least take a bite of each of them."

"Challenge accepted." We smile at each other. I wonder if, like me, he's considering a race. I'd propose it if I weren't already starting to feel full.

"All right." He pulls out the cards and begins to shuffle.

"We're going to play a game. Whoever draws the high card gets to ask a question, and the other person has to answer it honestly."

I scoff. Every time I indicate a lack of interest in getting to know Jack better, he takes it as a challenge. He's lucky he was born with such an appealing face because he's clearly not that bright.

"I'm not playing that," I say. "I don't even have any questions I want to ask you."

"You can ask me if I really tried to keep you from catching Rex that night. And I'll have to tell you the truth."

Our eyes lock. I'm already mostly convinced he didn't, but I've defined Jack by this one act for so long that the idea of knowing for certain is irresistible. It probably shouldn't be. I'm not sure why I care so much. But I can't help it; I do.

"Fine." I nod at the deck, and he sets it between us. I slip a card from the middle and turn it over. The ten of spades.

"Not bad." He flips the top card over and smiles.

It's a queen.

I groan.

"Why did you have a bad day?" he asks.

I peer into the bag of nuts and poke around for a pistachio. I should've broken down the door to Paul's room. At least there, I would've gotten a whole Snickers bar to myself.

"Ava?"

I exhale loudly. "Because I woke up this morning hoping there was still a chance with someone, but we ended up fighting, and I realized we weren't going to work it out."

Jack's expression turns guarded. "He didn't want to work it out?"

"You only won the answer to one question," I say.

Jack grabs a card and flips it over. I grin when I see that it's a five. I flip one over, and he grins. It's a two.

"He didn't want to work it out?" There's something about the way he repeats the question verbatim that makes me want to throw the nuts at him.

"I guess not," I say.

"Come on. You lost fair and square. Give me a real answer."

I consider quitting the game entirely. If it were anyone else, I would. But Jack's chin is tilted in challenge, and I can't stand the idea of backing down.

"If he did," I say, "he wanted his way more. If it were up to him, I'd be waiting at home for him, cooking his food and doing his laundry. I would definitely not be in Belize right now."

"He sounds like a loser."

"Unfortunately he's not. At all."

Jack flips over a card. It's a king.

"Seriously?" I am unsurprised when I flip over a four. "Did you rig this thing?"

"Shh. It's not your turn to ask a question."

"Fine. You can ask me if I hate you. That's an answer I'm willing to expand on."

"Sorry," he says. "I'd rather find out if you love him."

"Is that your question?"

"Does it not sound like a question?"

"Actually," I say, "no. It sounded like a statement."

"Are you stalling?"

I roll my eyes, but I am stalling, and I don't know why. Obviously I love Alexander. I was willing to commit the rest of my life to him. You don't do that unless you love someone. It's just hard to admit it because I'm mad. *Right?* I'm angry with him for not loving me enough, so my brain is tricking me by choosing to remember only the stuff I don't love about him. The way he sometimes speaks over me when I talk, finishing my sentences like I couldn't possibly have a thought original enough that he hasn't already thought of it first. How he always manages to get his way. His tendency to put a little too much gel in his hair.

"What if I don't? What if I just love what he represents? Would that make me a terrible person?" I brace myself for Jack's judgment—or, worse, some flippant remark that it's not my turn to ask a question.

"Not at all," he says quietly. "I doubt there's a person on earth who hasn't fallen for someone because they feel like they should."

"Really?"

"I certainly have," he says.

A wave of relief washes over me, and I reach for a card so Jack won't see how much his words mean to me. It's an ace of clubs. Finally it's my turn. I know what I'm going to say, but for some reason, there's another question trying to push its way to the front of the line. *Who did you fall for because you felt like you should?*

I shouldn't even care. I don't. Jack is always doing this, distracting me from my intentions, lulling me into a place of intimacy I never meant to enter. I push the question away.

"Were you trying to keep me from going to Rex's room that night?"

"No." Jack meets my eyes, and his are once again the color of the sky, so clear and blue it seems impossible he could be hiding anything in them. "I would never help anyone cheat on another person. I think cheating is the greatest hurt you could ever inflict on someone. Because you're not just doing something bad to them. You're sabotaging their whole life. You're letting them build a world around lies. And when they finally find out, they're not just going to be heartbroken; they're going to have to face the terrible fact that they've invested all of their time and energy into something that never really existed in the first place."

True. The tiny judge inside my brain lowers the gavel, finalizing judgment. I believe him.

I also agree with everything he's said.

My chin juts out defiantly as I grab my ace of clubs. Slowly and deliberately, I place it on top of the pile before flipping it over again.

"If you really mean that," I say. "If you know that falling in love and being with someone leads them to build their whole world around you, how could you take a bulldozer to Hannah's?"

Chapter 19

I'm putting my nose where it doesn't belong, and I know it. This is not my fight. But maybe it is. Aren't he and the other Rexes of the world responsible for the way us Hannahs feel when we're forced to share a jump seat—thigh to thigh—with someone who knows you used to be in love with the man they're sleeping with? Isn't it their fault we shrivel inside as we break down some girl's every feature, every word, trying to determine what she has that we were missing?

"What?" Jack's eyes flick back and forth like he's trying to read my words in the air to make more sense of them.

"You didn't want to be tied down. That's your choice. But did you have to be so incredibly insensitive?"

"Again, I say, *what*?"

"High card." I point at the ace of clubs. "You made the rules. So, here's the question: How many of your ex's coworkers have you slept with?"

"You do realize," he says dryly, "that I didn't make any rules that might indicate you could pick an unbeatable card and just keep playing it, right?"

I grab another one and hold my breath as I flip it over.

Nine of diamonds. Jack turns over the Jack of hearts. I groan at the irony. He meets my eyes and tosses it to the side before flipping over another card. It's a five.

"You're up," he says. "You're sure you want to open the door to questions about our sex lives?"

My stomach flutters at the idea.

"Yes," I say, trying unsuccessfully to make my voice firm. "How many women has Hannah had to work side by side with, knowing they're sleeping with the man she thought loved her?"

"Zero." Jack says the word with infuriating confidence.

"You can't know that!" I think of all the whispers I've encountered since Rex and I broke up. The women who have confessed, and the coworkers who have taken it upon themselves to confess on their behalf. Entire three-day trips of mine have been ruined by ambushes in the lounge or security lines beforehand. "How many Northeast flight attendants have you slept with?"

"I'm going to ignore the fact that you didn't earn another question," he says calmly. "I'm also going to choose to overlook the fact that this seems to be veering into interrogation territory. I'm not sure why you care so much about who I've slept with at our company, but the answer is one. You clearly know who she is, so I'm assuming I don't need to clarify?"

"You're lying." I exhale the words in a whisper. "Game's over. I win."

"What am I missing here?"

"Say it. Tell me I'm the winner." I'm so disappointed in Jack. But I'm even more angry. He tricked me into sharing things when he never intended to play fairly. It's like being mentally mugged. And I gave up the goods so easily.

"Ava?"

"Forget it." I grab the cards and flip them to the same side so I can shuffle them.

"I don't want to." Jack puts his hand over mine, pushing gently until the cards are pressed against the bed between us.

I stare down, distracted by the unexpected contact. His hand is so much larger than mine. And warm. Why is his body always so warm? And why have I now touched it enough to be able to attach the word *always* to that observation?

Resistance causes me to stiffen. Physical touch is to Jack what lawyer tactics are to Alexander. I'm so easily led, I'm basically Lassie. No collar required. What I wouldn't give to be Cujo instead.

"Hannah told everyone," I say, yanking my hand out from under his. "She must've, because I've never even met her, and I heard all about it."

"All about what?" A tightness pulls at Jack's face. It's an expression I haven't seen since that night in the deli.

"All about how you broke up with her because you couldn't be committed to one person. How you're working your way through all the flight attendants at Northeast."

"Is that what I'm doing?" His gaze drifts toward the ceiling. "We have what? About twelve thousand flight attendants? So, at least eight thousand of those are females. Huh."

"Huh?"

"Well, that's a very high number." He glances down at me. "At least you know I'm not lacking in ambition."

"Gross."

"It's not true, Ava." He sighs. "None of it. I met Hannah right before I left the Air Force. When she talked me into applying at Northeast, I decided not to pursue anything with her because I didn't want to be involved with someone I worked with. Obviously, my mind eventually changed and we got together. But seeing how that ended, do you really think I'd put myself in that position with another coworker? Much less eight thousand of them?"

"Maybe?" I don't know. Men aren't notorious for thinking with their brains. "If what you're saying is true, why is Hannah telling everyone something else?"

"Because she's angry that things didn't work out the way she wanted them to?" He shrugs. "Because if she can convince herself that I couldn't commit, it will make her feel better about her inability to commit to me? Because it wasn't enough to break my heart, she has to punish me for being unable to forgive her?"

"She broke your heart?" It's not the question I mean to ask, but it pops out anyway. I can't imagine Jack with a broken heart. He seems unbreakable. "How?"

Jack's expression turns wary. "It's just an expression."

"So, she didn't break your heart?"

"You know what?" He crosses his arms over his chest like he's building a layer of wall between us. "You seemed pretty comfortable with your version of the story. Let's just leave it as it was."

"I just . . ." I trail off because I don't have an excuse for my prying. *I just want to know the truth*? But why? So that I can forgive this man for something that has nothing to do with me? So I can convince myself Jack Stone is someone other than who I thought he was—someone different from Rex?

I reach for a card and flip it over. Six.

"It's a low card," I say. "You'll probably win."

His arms stay crossed. "It's not my story to tell, Ava."

"Isn't it? I'm asking about your relationship. I'm asking how *your* heart got broken."

"But—"

I cut him off. "Flip the card over, Jack."

He shakes his head, but his hand reaches out and flips a card over. It's a three. He has to answer my question.

"What really happened between you and Hannah?"

"You won't repeat it?" His eyes search mine. "She's dealing with enough. I don't want to cause problems for her at work."

I nod, even though I find it baffling that he's so concerned about privacy when Hannah's been running her mouth like an auctioneer. "Nothing leaves this room."

"Fine." He sighs, and I can see his discomfort in the stiffness of his shoulders. "We were together for over a year, and I thought we were really happy. Actually, that's not fair. We were really happy. I know we were. But Hannah loved to drink. She was a nightmare to go out with because we'd always get to that point in the night where I had to follow her around. If I didn't, she'd end up behind the wheel of a car, or stuck between the toilet and the wall of a bathroom stall. Or, as I would eventually discover, in someone else's bed." Jack's eyes flick toward the ceiling again. "More than once, it was a pilot I ended up having to work with. Only I was serving passengers in the back of the plane while he was up front flying it. I was still a pilot when Hannah and I met, so you can imagine how that felt, holding myself up and comparing who I was to who I'd become. Feeling less than eight other men. Eight 'mistakes.' But at some point, we can't still pretend it's a mistake, can we?"

"No." It doesn't even occur to me to wonder if Jack is telling the truth. I recognize the unwarranted shame—the feeling of being found lacking—that comes with being cheated on; I've felt it myself.

"I mean, a number that high elevates it to hobby status. The woman cheated on me recreationally."

"By karate standards," I admit, "she probably would've earned a red belt at least."

He lets out a short, mirthless chuckle.

"That was rude, wasn't it?" I grimace. "I should've just said I'm sorry."

"Are you?"

"Am I sorry that happened to you?" It's not a question I even have to consider. "Yes. Very, actually. I know how it feels, and I wouldn't wish it on anyone."

"Hannah knew she needed to get sober. She said she needed me by her side. When I told her I couldn't be, she was more angry than heartbroken. I guess she decided to rewrite history. Make me the bad guy. It's classic Hannah. In one swoop, she was able to discredit me in case I decided to tell the truth and also skew the odds against me being able to move on with someone new."

I let out a low whistle. "That's evil."

"That's what I loved about her."

"You loved that she was evil?"

He laughs at the incredulity in my voice. "Not exactly. I loved that she followed every impulse she ever felt. She was electric."

"It sounds scary."

"It could be, at times. But at least it was real. There was no veneer to chisel through, no politeness. When she was mad, I knew it. When she loved me, I felt it. I think that's what made it so easy to walk away in the end. The cheating hurt, but that wasn't what killed us. It was the fact that she hid it."

"I don't know," I say. "Cheating and hiding it. It sounds like two sides of the same coin to me."

"Maybe. And I'm not saying I could've gotten over the cheating. Not eight times, at least. But I would've at least understood it. I'd been with her enough times when she was drunk to know how out of control she got. I'd sat with her the next morning as she'd try to sew together the pieces of the night she'd blacked out. The secrets, though. I never even imagined someone as real as her was capable of that. It was like falling in love with someone because they're tall and pulling off their pants one day to discover they've been tottering around on stilts the entire time you've known them."

"It always comes down to pulling the pants off, doesn't it?"

Jack tilts his head. "You're uncomfortable."

"What?" My head nods, even as I say, "No."

I am, in fact, growing profoundly uncomfortable in the wake of all this sharing. I'm growing even more uncomfortable at the ever-shrinking, suddenly blank list of reasons to hate Jack Stone.

"You are," he says. "You get quippy when you're uncomfortable, and your eyes turn a grayish-blue color, which is very different from the grayish-green they turn when you're feeling competitive. So, what is it? Are you keeping secrets? Or are you just feeling bad that you've been picking fights with me for no reason?"

Both.

"Neither," I say.

"That's it, isn't it?" He looks delighted with his intuitive reasoning. "That's why you've been so mean to me. You thought I was a man-whore who tried to help your ex cheat on you."

"Okay." I roll my eyes. They're beginning to tire from

being on spin cycle for so long. "It's not like I've actually been *mean* to you."

"No? There have been points over the last couple of days when I seriously considered investing in a bulletproof vest."

"If they go on sale, I'd still grab one. There's something very irritating about your face, you know. Not everyone has the same amount of restraint I have."

"My face?" His hands pat curiously at his cheekbones. "It's irritating?"

"Violently." I'd feel a lot better about being in this room with him if there really was something wrong with his face. In actuality, it might be one of the most perfect faces I've ever seen. Which is, actually, very irritating, so my point stands.

"I think you like my face."

My eyebrows jerk up, and I huff out a little laugh. "You probably also think Eddie and Celeste were calling you Abercrombie because you look like a model. But really they just meant you smell like a teenage boy and your shirts are too tight."

"I think you like how my shirts fit." Jack's mouth widens into his full, crooked smile. "And I think you like me."

My heart begins to race. "Well, we both know you're not that bright."

"Aren't I?" His expression turns serious, and he leans forward, his eyes trapping mine.

They're intent, darkened to a stormy blue, and I can't seem to pull my gaze away. My stomach swirls when he takes my hand in his. Slowly he slips his fingers between mine. The pad of his thumb traces a line up the center of my palm, and goose bumps rise across my arm.

"You're probably right," he whispers. "I must've been imagining things."

He lets go and pulls away, leaving me with a pulsing sense of loss. My fingers press against each other, trying to re-create the sensation of his hand over mine. It doesn't work, though. They just feel empty. My face heats with frustration and embarrassment. If I didn't think Jack would find a way to read something else into it, I'd tell him exactly how much I hate him right now.

"Let's play Speed," he says.

"What?" I shake my head, trying to knock the unwanted haze of lust away.

"The card game. Speed. You know the rules?" He must take my blank stare as a no because he begins to explain how to play.

If it weren't so annoying, it would be comical. I grew up playing Speed. What I actually need explained is how Jack just went from holding my hand back to shuffling cards in less than two seconds. It's fine, though. Great, even. I'm happy to compete with him. In fact, I'll be even more satisfied when I'm beating him.

While he's shuffling, I slip my legs beneath me so that I'm kneeling instead of slumped over. Jack glances up from the cards and catches me. His lip curls with amusement. I pat at the hem of my dress, ignoring him. I might not be comfortable, but I'm in a better position to slap the cards. It's my fighting stance, alert and predatory.

"You ready?" He slides half the pile in front of me.

I nod and grab them.

"Go!"

We both start flipping cards, fast and furious. I have never wanted to win more. Two kings top each other, and we slap. My hand lands just under his. The rush of adrenaline causes me to shriek with triumph. My eyes widen at the noise, and we both start to laugh.

"If someone comes knocking," Jack says, "I'm telling them you're the one who woke them up."

"It's your room, sucker." I collect my cards smugly.

"Go!" He shouts the word before I'm fully ready, and I hiss.

We start flipping again, but we're both too frantic, so the cards aren't landing in their piles. They're scattering all over. Still, I spot the two nines and my hand dives toward the pile. So does his. It lands first, but I weasel mine in under.

"Nope." He tries to push my hand out of the way.

"What?" I feign innocence, but I can't stop the laughter that comes burbling out.

"Remove your hand, cheater. You're not taking this one."

"That's funny. From the way I'm touching the cards, it feels like that's exactly what I'm doing."

He grabs my wrist and tugs, and my hand slips off the pile. My body shifts toward him, and my other hand reaches for his chest to stop myself from falling. We both freeze. Our eyes meet, and the room goes silent. The temperature rises by ten degrees. Like the oxygen has left the room, our breathing turns ragged in unison.

Jack's grip on my wrist tightens, and my eyes drop to his mouth. I drag them back up, only to discover his gaze is locked on mine. My tongue, still vacationing separately from my brain, slips across my lips like an invitation.

Jack's brow furrows. "I can't kiss you," he says hoarsely, "if you don't like me."

"I like hating you." My voice comes out weakly. "Is that enough?"

He uses his grip on my wrist to wrap my arm around his neck.

"For now," he says, sliding his hand around my waist.

His eyes meet mine before his mouth does. Sharp sapphire and terrifying in their intensity. He looks like he intends to win this one, and I wish I didn't want him to. I tilt my chin, and his lips touch mine. They're soft but firm with a hint of demand. For once, I'm not the one instigating the challenge. Jack spells it out with hot swipes of his tongue. *Like me. Want me like I want you.*

If my mind is still resisting, the rest of my body seems to have given up the fight. My breasts strain against the thin material between us. My hands curl into his hair, tugging him closer. My knees push forward, settling on each side of his legs so I'm straddling him. He groans and pulls me harder against him before leaning forward. We fall like a tree, me on my back and him on top of me. Our mouths never stop touching. They're dancing. Or fighting. Whatever it is, it's my new favorite activity. I want to train for it. I want to win gold at the Olympics for it.

I pull my mouth free, but rather than behave, it takes the opportunity to explore. It slips down his throat, and my teeth nip at his skin. It's still salty from the sea, but somehow the scent of his cologne lingers. Leather. Cedar. It's like the woods and the sea have collided, creating the greatest place on earth. I could set up a tent on his Adam's apple and live the rest of my life in this very spot. I lick the divot where his collarbones meet and feel the vibration of his moan. He yanks me back up and crushes my mouth with his. My fingernails dig into his back. He presses against me and my leg wraps around him, urging him closer.

"Okay," he says into my mouth. He pulls back for a moment, but then returns for an even deeper kiss. He pulls away again. "Okay," he repeats.

"Okay, what?" My hand slips to the back of his neck, and I tug him toward me. To my surprise and tremendous irritation, he resists. "Kiss me, you fool."

He laughs and drops his face to my neck.

"I can't." His breathy words tickle my throat.

"You're right," I say. "I didn't want to say anything, but you're really not great at it. We should practice."

He groans and rolls off me, leaving my body mourning the loss of his heat. His arm falls over his face as he settles on his back beside me. The first prickles of reality hit, spiky and hot like embarrassment. He didn't feel what I just felt. Now that he's won, he's no longer interested.

"I wish we could," he says, "but we have a problem."

"What's that?"

"Pay attention, sunshine. I've already said it more than once. You don't like me."

My eyes drop to the duvet. Is that true? Jack has already said he doesn't believe it, and I no longer have any reasons to claim it. Still. Things have been easy under that premise. Safe.

"Mm-hmm," I murmur noncommittally.

"If we're going to change that, you're going to have to get to know me better."

I picture my new camping spot just west of his Adam's apple. "Isn't that what I was doing?"

Jack grins and pulls me toward him. Reluctantly I allow him to roll me into his side. I rest my head on his chest, and his fingers slip through my hair. His heartbeat thrums against my cheek.

"I live in Boulder, Colorado," he says. "I was in Chicago until a couple of weeks ago. A few weeks before that, Hannah showed up at my apartment, drunk out of her mind. I didn't let her in. The next morning, I found her passed out against my door. Snoring, so I knew she was alive, but she slept right through me leaving. I started driving. I wanted to get away for a while, to clear my head, but the farther away I got, the more I knew I didn't want to go back. I needed a clean break. A week later, I found myself talking to a guy in Boulder who had a new rental opening up in his building. I agreed without even seeing the apartment. I mean, those mountains. That sky. Who cares where you sleep when you're surrounded by beauty like that?"

It's a sentiment I've heard my whole life. Hearing it again both terrifies and thrills me. Rather than lean into it, I pivot away, focusing instead on practicalities. "So, why are you still based in Chicago? Shouldn't you be Denver-based?"

"The transfer just completed. This is the last trip I'll work out of that base." Jack smiles. "See? Your parking lot will be safe now. I've already got my car packed. When we get back tomorrow, I'll drive to Boulder and leave Chicago in my rear-view mirror."

I blink at his stupid, cheerful face, trying to understand the point of all this. We could be kissing right now. A meaningless, primal meeting of needs. Why is Jack acting like I need to get to know him? Why is he trying to make me like him if he's only going to leave anyway? It's a cruel game, one I've played too many times to count, and I think I might hate him for it.

"And that's it?" I ask. "I'll never have to see you again?"

"We fly for free, Ava. If you'd just pretend there might be something between us, there's no limit to how much you'd have to see me. But I don't want to play this game anymore. I want to be allowed to like you. And I want you to like me."

I sink deeper into him, pressing my face into his side. The world goes dark, but Jack doesn't disappear. I can still feel him with me, strong and firm. He's not, though. He's the guy who gets in his car and drives away. He disappears. And he's right. I like him in spite of that.

I don't know when it happened, but I'm worried I always have. I think I saw it in him that first night at the bar. I took one look at his crooked smile and that dark hair—windswept like he'd been driving with the windows down—and I recognized him as one of *us*. The wanderers. The people I've tried so hard not to be like, even though I can feel the fibers of them woven into my skin. My restless feet, leading me out of my room on overnights, out into the world.

Maybe it's not the worst thing in the world to admit to liking Jack Stone. I'm always searching for forever, but maybe, just for a moment, I can detour into the temporary. He said it himself. Chicago is in his rearview mirror. After this trip, he can be in mine.

"Fine," I say into the soft cotton of his shirt. "What do you want me to say?"

I brace myself for his demand. *I like you.* I can already tell saying it is going to feel like admitting defeat.

"I want you to tell me where you live."

I look up in surprise, and he laughs.

"How can we like each other if we don't know the basics?" he asks. "So, tell them to me, Ava. Let me know you."

He says it like it's the simplest thing on earth, when really, it's the most unanswerable thing he could ask. Before this trip, I lived with Alexander. Now, I have no idea.

"I guess," I say slowly, "I live in Belize."

I'm not trying to hide anything or avoid a complicated conversation. I just want to meet Jack's goal. He says he wants to know me, but nothing about my past relationship speaks to the real me. If anything, living with Alexander was my attempt to become someone else.

"Come on, Ava."

"Really." I meet his eyes. "Growing up, my mom always said the only way to be happy in life is to make your home where you are."

"Did you travel a lot when you were younger?" His voice has softened, and his hand begins to stroke my arm.

"I did. We traveled so much, my house became the place I felt the least comfortable. If I'm being honest, it still is."

"Which is why you currently live in Belize?"

It's such a simple question, so perfect in its understanding, that I find myself beaming in response.

"Exactly." I kiss him, not to stop the conversation but because of it. Because he cares enough to ask the questions. Because he understands my answers. Because I don't have to be who I want to become. Because he seems to appreciate me for who I am.

Jack must understand the difference because this time he doesn't stop me.

Chapter 20

I jerk out of my dream to the sound of someone calling my name. Gentle fingers stroke my arm. My eyes fly open, and my hand reaches to wipe away the drool dripping from the corner of my mouth. Jack is lying on his side, facing me.

"Sorry," he says, "but we have to get up."

I blink with confusion. "It's afternoon already?"

"Actually, it's 6:30."

"In the morning?" At his nod, I groan and roll over, burrowing my face into the pillow. We stayed up talking forever last night. There's no way we've had more than a couple of hours of sleep.

Jack tugs at my arm. "Come on. We're going to miss departure."

He's so bossy. I have no more interest in getting up right now than I had last night in stopping kissing so I could "learn to like him." But stop we did—I was lucky he didn't build a pillow wall between us—so now it's my turn to be difficult.

"Our flight doesn't leave until 3:15," I grumble. "We don't lobby until 2:00. Do you even know how time works? Are you still drunk?"

"I was never drunk. You'd drunk all the liquor in the bar by the time I arrived. Now come on. I want to take you somewhere."

I press my face into the pillow in a show of resistance before rolling over. Jack stares down at me with a determined expression. He's so cute with his eyes all sleepy and his hair crazier than ever. I can't look at him anymore without thinking about everything I learned last night. He's no longer Jack Stone, breaker of hearts and stealer of parking spots. Now, he's the older of two brothers who used to skip school and sneak into the baseball stadium during home games. He's the boy who lost his mother to cancer a few years ago. He's the man who thrilled his father by going into the Air Force, only to disappoint him by choosing to fly C-130 cargo planes instead of becoming a fighter pilot.

"I was able to fly medical equipment in when it was desperately needed," Jack told me, his eyes bright at the memory. "Water when people were dying of thirst. Dad thought he was mad that I wasn't trying to blow people up, but when he found out I was separating from the military? Well, if he didn't hate lawyers even more than he hated me, I'd be legally disowned right now."

It wasn't, like I meanly assumed, bad behavior that ended Jack's flying career. Three and a half years ago, his plane was attacked by small-arms fire during a delivery. It blew out the swing window on his side of the cockpit, compromising the vision in his left eye. He could still fly, but he'd never do so professionally again.

"Then Hannah told me about her job. It was hard to imagine giving up the sense of purpose that came with being enlisted, but they'd stuck me behind a desk, and it was even harder to face a lifetime of being trapped in a cubicle. I knew Dad would never accept it, but he's never had an easy time accepting anything about me. He can't understand why I'd rather talk than fight. Why would he understand that I'd rather fly than sit?"

I sigh at the memory, and Jack grins like he knows he's about to get his way. He gets out of bed and crosses to my side, pulling me up.

"You need to change into your bikini," he says. "Do you want to sneak into your room to get it, or do you want me to?"

"Are you out of your mind?" I allow him to sweep my legs over the side of the bed. "We can't go in there. What if they're still at it?"

"You or me, Ava. Those are your options."

I open my mouth to argue, but I can see by the set of Jack's jaw it's pointless. This battle is going to swing his way. Adding up all the personal facts he cajoled out of me last night, he's way ahead on points. I'm going to have to find something to push me ahead, or it's possible he'll end up winning the entire war.

"I'll go." There's no way I'm giving Jack a chance to see Gen naked, even though she'd probably enjoy the opportunity to show off.

"And who knows," I add with a smile. "Maybe I'll even come back."

I savor the surprise that falls across his face as I sail past him. He's saying something as I scoop up the key and leave, but I let the door close on his words. It's a small but enjoyable victory, made sweeter by the fact that Jack himself made it clear last night he has no interest in any kind of truce. He teased me mercilessly when I told him about the time I used permanent marker to give myself a beauty mark on my left cheek. And after I made myself vulnerable enough to explain the reason I hated my name, he had the audacity to whisper "Good night, Aviana" as I was falling asleep in his arms.

I smile, too distracted by the memory to hesitate before sticking the key in my door. It swings open quietly. Inside the balcony doors are open, letting in the sea air and the light of the rising sun. Clothes are scattered across the floor. On the bed, Gen's bare leg is draped across Pilot Paul's thighs, just below his naked butt. I freeze and drop my eyes to the ground, but there's no sound of stirring or gasps of surprise at my presence.

Laughter burbles up inside me, but I hold it in and scurry toward my bag, praying I won't wake them up or accidentally get another eyeful of something I don't want to see. With my suit and flip-flops in hand, I turn back toward the door. In spite of myself, my eyes swing across the room. Gen lifts a hand in a wave but makes no effort to pull a sheet across herself. Her lips stretch into a smile, the crimson all kissed off.

"I think I'm in love," she says, not bothering to whisper.

Laughter leaks out of me like the release of a tire valve. "It was that good, huh?"

She stretches like a cat, baring her breasts. "Better."

I lift my hand to my eyes in case she intends to bare any other body parts. "I'll just leave you to it then," I say, hurrying toward the door. "And don't worry. I'll knock before I come back in."

"Good idea." Her words slip through the door as it closes behind me.

Across the hall, Jack is leaning out of the door to his room.

"Come on," he whispers. "You need to put your suit on. We're going to miss it."

"Miss what?" I race around him and hurry into the bathroom, unsurprised when he doesn't answer me.

I feel giddy with anticipation as I whip the dress over my head and kick my panties under the sink. It doesn't matter what we're doing. I'm just pleased there's one last adventure to be had before we leave Belize. I bet Jack wants to swim while the sun rises. Maybe the waves are the highest in the morning. I turn toward the mirror as I tie the top around my neck, and I see that my eyes are sparkling and my cheeks are flushed.

Once again, I look wild. There must be something in the air here. Without the threat of Alexander seeing it, I can admit it suits me. The salt water has left my hair in beachy waves. My eyes are almost fully green, a miracle that only occurs when I'm especially delighted about something. The corners of my mouth are tilted up like I'm just waiting for a reason to laugh. I look *happy*. I can't remember the last time I saw myself like this.

Jack bangs on the door, and my reflection jumps. Bright white teeth flash through her smile. When I open the door, Jack grabs my hand and pulls me out. He's wearing a faded Ramones T-shirt with his swim trunks and has flip-flops on his feet.

"I need to borrow a shirt to wear as a cover-up," I say, resisting his pull.

"No time." His grip on my hand tightens, and he tugs me out of the bathroom and through the door. When we hit the hall, he begins to run.

I give in and run with him, focusing on keeping up. The sound of our footsteps fills the hall. My breasts bounce in my flimsy suit, and I have to double my stride to meet the length of his legs. The sunlight is blinding when we burst through the door at the end of the hallway, and I drop my eyes to the ground, letting Jack guide our path. We go past the pool and through the palm trees and run through the sand. My side is beginning to cramp by the time Jack slows. I suck air into my lungs and look up to see a boat full of people.

"Stay here for a minute," Jack says.

Before I can ask any questions, he lets go of my hand and strides toward a man in an orange shirt with *Snorkel Belize* written across it. On the boat, another guy in an identical shirt is handing out cups with pink juice in them. A woman wearing a neon tank top and a fanny pack holds one behind her back and uses her free hand to snatch another. The sun is gaining strength, filling the sky and reflecting off the waves. Jack shakes the man's hand, and I spot a flash of color as money slips from Jack's palm to the man's. The man smiles and waves me toward the boat.

"Let's go," Jack calls out to me.

I shake my head, but he's already walking toward the water. It takes him a moment before he realizes I'm still standing where he left me. He jogs back, his long, muscular legs slicing across the sand.

"It's snorkeling." Jack slows to a stop in front of me, looking pleased with himself. "You said you wished you could go."

"I did." I hate the way the air seems to leak out of him. "I mean, I do. But not today, Jack. Not when we have to lobby at 2:00. What if we don't get back in time?"

"Weren't you the one who was just calling me drunk for not realizing how much time we had?" His confidence returns. "We'll be fine. And remember those girls I was talking to yesterday?"

I shake my head, but we both know I remember. Jack was

across the pool from me, still sulking from how rude I'd been, and the girls had crowded around him in their skimpy suits and unfairly tanned skin. Their flirty laughter was so loud, I couldn't even pretend to read over it.

"Well," he says, "they'd just come from this tour. It's a morning thing, seven to eleven. That leaves us with a full three-hour buffer."

"Still." I hesitate, wanting to go along with him but knowing I shouldn't. On travel days, you can't put your schedule in someone else's hands. It's a rule. What if the boat driver decides he fancies a trip to Cuba? I'm not sure I'm capable of tying him up and taking over the boat so I can get us back here. "I don't think it's a good idea."

"It is." Jack takes my hand and laces his fingers through mine. Slowly, he walks backward, hypnotizing me with the stroke of his thumb as he pulls me with him. "Trust me."

Like a drooling drunk, I allow him to guide me. He's the Pied Piper, and his thumb is playing the music that speaks to my soul. *This guy.* He's a problem, and I know it. One look at his eyes tells me. What man has eyelashes that thick anyway? You can't trust someone who could be in a Maybelline commercial without even using mascara. Yet somehow my feet push forward, sand flicking up from my flip-flops and hitting my calves.

If I'm being honest with myself, I want to go snorkeling every bit as much as Jack does. I want to see fish the color of rainbows. I want to ride in this big boat and feel the sea breeze whip through my hair. I want to continue last night's adventure for as long as possible.

Jack climbs aboard first and holds out his hand, his grip firm as he guides me up. Continuing to hold my hand, he skirts around the other passengers, leading me to an opening along the side at the front of the boat. The guy with the drinks offers us one as we pass, and I'm relieved to see Jack shake his head. Technically, it's nine hours before we fly, and the rule is no drinking within eight hours of working. Still, I'm glad to discover Jack isn't the type to press it until the last minute. Some people are, and those are the kind of people you've got to watch out for.

The sun is burning off the chill in the air, but it still lingers over the water. Goose bumps scatter up my arms. Jack spots them and tugs his shirt off, insisting I put it on. Once I have, I lean against the edge of the boat and face the water, propping my arms up on the railing. Jack settles in behind me, his stomach pressed against my back, arms draped over my shoulders, resting on mine. As always, he radiates heat. I sigh and melt into his warmth.

Even after everything that was said last night, it's easier to accept the shift between us when I'm not looking at him. There's no reminder of how attractive he is. How untameable he looks. How much power he has to break my heart. I don't have to acknowledge that he's not the kind of person you settle down with. I can just enjoy the way his skin feels against mine, the undeniable chemistry that crackles between us.

"Have you snorkeled before?" Jack's words drift over my head.

"Several times," I say to the sea. "You?"

"Once, in the Bahamas."

"My mom jumped overboard in the Bahamas."

"What?"

"She thought she saw a dolphin, and she got so excited, she jumped in." My words catch in my throat as I start to laugh.

"We weren't even stopped at the time. The captain was so furious he turned around and took us back before we could snorkel. Mom kept apologizing to my dad and me, but we couldn't stop laughing long enough to forgive her. My dad started calling her the flopping seal, and she really did look like that when she went over. There was no diving, nothing graceful at all. She just kind of hurled herself overboard."

"She sounds like a riot."

"She'd make a great friend," I admit.

"What about a mother? Did she make a great one of those?"

"Sure." I hesitate, and the boat starts to move. "But . . . I don't know. I guess I always thought parents were supposed to make you feel safe."

"And yours didn't?"

"Mine made me feel nervous."

"Why?"

I stare out at the water. It's getting darker as we head out deeper. The turquoise has turned to navy. The waves are less choppy, though. They swell in small soothing hills. A seagull keeps pace with us, darting ahead, then swooping back around. The wind gets stronger as we pick up speed, but Jack's body is blocking me from most of it.

"Ava?" He dips his head and speaks into my hair. "We don't have to talk about it if you'd rather not."

"No, it's fine." So I had an unconventional childhood. Who didn't? "What was the question?"

He hesitates. We both know I remember the question. "Why did they make you feel nervous?"

I shrug in his arms. "They were just spontaneous, I guess. Always running off. I never knew if they'd remember to take me with them. They always did, of course. But sometimes I wasn't even sure if I wanted them to."

"What do you mean?"

"I don't know. It just messed stuff up when I went with them. I missed things. Things with friends. Classes. Important tests. My parents were the reason I had to take this job, but they were also the reason I almost lost it."

"How so?"

"I no-showed for a flight." Just saying the words makes me cringe.

"You didn't even call Scheduling?" Jack looks surprised. "You must've been terrified they'd fire you."

"I was. But there was no cell service. My parents had talked me into going to a friend's house with them. It was one of those days where our crew got to the hotel before noon, and I had all day to do nothing. When my parents called and just happened to be nearby, it felt like fate. I didn't think to be worried when they wanted to pick me up. I was just happy to get to see them. But they didn't tell me their friend lived out in the desert, nor did they tell me they were driving his car. The four of us were sitting in his backyard when he disappeared to get beer. He didn't show back up until the next day. They thought it was hysterical. I *was* hysterical. And that pretty much sums up our general life dynamic."

Jack's grip on me tightens. "That's awful."

"Sometimes, yeah. But I've had some great times with them, too. I guess I'm just trying to figure out how to find the balance in my own life."

"Meaning?"

I pause, trying to formulate an answer. It feels like an obvious question, but it's one that's never been asked of me. I've never actually spoken to anyone else about this. I've never really even let myself consider there might be a balance. I've just been hell-bent on building a life that's the opposite of my parents'. Until yesterday, I couldn't allow myself to face the fact that life on the road might be permanent. That I might want—maybe even need—it to be.

"I just," I say slowly, "would like to find a way to feel both free and settled at the same time. If that's possible."

"It's possible." Jack says the words with so much confidence that I can't help laughing.

"You think?"

"I *know*. When do you work again?"

"Um." I shake my head in response to the whiplash subject change. "I've got a trip on Tuesday."

"So, you're off this weekend?"

"Yep." *I was supposed to be off forever.* The reminder hits me like a slap in the face. Marriage. Alexander. How would he feel if he could see me moving on so quickly? With someone so unsuitable to the life goals I had claimed to share with him? It's hard to even consider it because Alexander belongs in a different world. This is a different planet from the one where I was engaged to him. I can't imagine him here any more than I can imagine the sea parting and a herd of giraffes strolling between the resulting walls of water.

"Then, let's do something," Jack says. "Do you like to hike?"

"I love to hike."

"Perfect. We're going hiking this weekend."

"Where? In case you've forgotten, I live in Chicago. Or were you thinking I'd spend my days off flying to wherever you happen to be?"

"Well, we do have great hiking in Colorado. But if you don't want to go there, I'll come to Chicago. Or we can meet in Seattle and drive to the mountains. Whatever you want, we can do it. Just say the word."

Jack puts his arms around my waist, turning me around to face him. My back presses against the railing. My hair tickles at my cheek. Sky blue eyes meet mine.

"I'm serious, Ava. There's something here. You want to be free? Go exploring with me. You want to be settled? Let's sit down and have a cup of coffee. I know we're just getting to know each other, but let's find out where that could lead. Just give me a weekend. That's a small enough thing, right?"

Our eyes lock. It's another contest. Who will blink first? Who will concede in the battle of the weekend? Is this a battle I even want to win?

I don't know how the stakes have escalated from this trip to a weekend so quickly. Belize is easier. It has a built-in timer. Different world, different planet, and all that nonsense. But *this*. I've taken this chance before—this glittering promise of something different, something even better than what I believed I wanted—with Rex. And look how that turned out. I ended up a walking bruise on two stunted legs. Not that it's Rex's fault I'm short. But really. The man certainly didn't make me walk any taller.

Still, I know enough to trust that Jack is no Rex. He may run off to the next great adventure without me, but I doubt he'll do it with another woman in tow. It's just a matter of if I can handle the uncertainty. Or, more importantly, if I want to.

"A weekend?" I try to say it coolly. Confidently. Like I'm playing hard to get rather than reeling with terror. Instead it comes out a bit mousy.

"A weekend. It's just a date, Ava. An extended date. Nobody's talking marriage here. We just met."

His eyes sparkle like he's teasing, but he can't possibly know how hard his words hit me. I was willing to commit the rest of my life to someone who didn't make me feel half of what this man makes me feel. The anger. The frustration. The amusement. The excitement. The lust. They might not all be good, but they're the ingredients that make up passion, and that's something I haven't allowed myself to lean into in . . . well, ever.

"What about your car?" I ask. "Weren't you supposed to drive all your stuff back?"

He waves my words away like a meal he's decided he's no longer hungry for. "I'll do it when we get back."

"I'd like to see the Grand Canyon," I say, averting my eyes.

The truth is, I planned a trip there last year. A surprise for Alexander. With my airline discount, I booked a car rental at the Vegas airport for twenty-eight dollars a day. Meredith lent me her tent—this was right before she decided I wasn't the kind of dependable friend she needed—and I splurged on a backpack big enough to carry provisions for day hikes.

It was just supposed to be a small getaway, but I was so excited. Our entire relationship, Alexander had paid for everything. Meals. Gifts. He even offered to take over my rent, a gesture I couldn't accept for a multitude of reasons. It meant everything to me to be able to do this one thing for him. But the day before we were supposed to leave, Alexander casually dropped the news that he had to work after all.

It was the first time he ever saw me cry. Not the first time I'd cried since we'd been together, obviously. I'd had bad days, like everyone does. But I'd learned enough to know better than to show people that kind of ugly emotion; it makes them uncomfortable. It makes them want to run away. Not Alexander, I discovered. To him, my tears were silly. They made him laugh.

"Sweetheart," he said, stroking my cheek. "We'll have a

million opportunities to go to Vegas. I can book a room at the Venetian. Maybe we'll buy front-row tickets at Cirque du Soleil. You could go on a shopping trip so extravagant we'll have to pay someone to carry your bags."

I don't think he ever realized Vegas was just meant to be the entry point of our trip to the Grand Canyon.

I'm certain he never realized I'd much rather stay in a borrowed tent than at the Venetian.

"The Grand Canyon?" Jack brushes a flyaway strand of hair from my cheek and drops a kiss in its place. "Sounds like we have a plan."

Chapter 21

The boat is a flurry of activity. We've arrived at our first stop, a tiny island filled with palm trees. There's no snack stand or souvenir hut, just green fronds shading brown sand, a swirl of turquoise water lapping at its banks. The raw beauty is breathtaking.

Without speaking, Jack and I continue leaning against the boat's edge, soaking in the view while the rest of the crowd fights over a pile of flippers and snorkeling masks. This is the nautical version of the deplaning process we've witnessed a thousand times. Only instead of a plane full of people trying to jam their bodies and bags into a three-foot-wide aisle, the floor is rocking and the luggage is up for grabs.

In other words, it's chaos. There's clearly more than enough equipment for everyone, and the race is a show of its own. The grabbing hands have managed to separate the paired flippers, and everyone is shouting size numbers.

"My baby needs another small one!" The woman with the fanny pack bellows the words into the crowd. She waves the lone kids' flipper in her hand, hitting an elderly man in the back. She doesn't seem to even consider apologizing. She's furious no one understands the gravity of her situation. She's raising a prince with not one but two feet, and he has the right to be dual-flippered *now*!

The tiny baby prince—who looks to be at least six years old—picks up a large flipper and shoves his arm into it. He swings it wide and slams it into her knee.

"Get in there!" Fanny Pack yells the words at another small child, a girl a couple of years older than the prince, and points the flipper toward the pile.

The scraggly haired girl shrieks out a war cry and dives in. Literally. She hurls her body on the pile of plastic, bony arms and legs spread wide, attempting to cover it from the rest of the scavengers.

Laughter bursts from my throat, and I slap my hand over my mouth, but it's too late. Fanny Pack hears and turns to me with a glare. I look to Jack for protection, but he's turned toward the sea in an attempt to hide his own laughter.

I avert my eyes, playing possum, but Fanny Pack and I both know I've been caught. For the next ten minutes, I try to mind my own business, but I'm riveted by their family. Now Fanny Pack is trying to take pictures.

"Look at the camera," she orders the two kids and their miserable-looking dad.

The kids slap their finned feet loudly against the boat floor.

"We're having fun," Fanny Pack shouts. "Look like you're having fun!"

The prince tugs one fin off his foot and slings it overboard as the girl flips the camera off with both middle fingers. I try my best, but the laughter explodes out of me. Jack reaches for my shoulder and spins me toward the water, but not before I see Fanny Pack jerk toward me, laser beams of rage shooting from her eyes.

"Memories," Jack says, slinging an arm around me. "My

mom always wanted to document everything when we were growing up. It was a competition between my brother and me, an ongoing game of who could most effectively ruin her pictures. Of course, then she died, and we would've given anything to go back and let her have whatever she wanted."

My laughter sputters out. I look up at Jack, but his face is smooth and easy, like he'd just informed me his mom usually packed peanut-butter-and-jelly sandwiches in his lunch box.

"But you were just kids," I say carefully. "It's not like you intended to take anything away from her."

"True. But that's what you do when you feel powerless in the face of something like death. We focused on the things we had control over, the things we could've done differently. My brother even set up an Instagram account a couple of years ago, just because he knew how much she would've loved seeing the pictures of his life. I couldn't do it, though. I tried, but it was too hard. Too little, too late, I suppose."

"Oh, Jack." The words slip out of me, whispered and worthless.

"Don't worry." He offers a small, reassuring smile. "Talking about her doesn't make me sad. It's just the way it is."

"And you want to be able to remember her without having to filter the truth." It's a guess, but I say it like a fact so he doesn't have to elaborate if he doesn't want to.

"Exactly."

The expression on his face makes me feel like I've won something precious, and I find myself beaming inappropriately in response to such a serious conversation.

"My parents had a policy about pictures," I say, attempting to cover for my smile. "They were adamant about authenticity. It didn't matter if we were in front of the most perfect scenery in the world; if we'd argued on the way there or one of us was sad about something, they wouldn't let us take a picture of everyone smiling. They said it would just create a false memory."

"I like that."

"Me, too," I admit. "Of course, the flip side to it was we didn't end up with many pictures."

"Because someone was always unhappy?"

"No. Because the best memories, the ones we'd most want to remember, were always the times we were having too much fun to think of picking up a camera."

Like my parents, I don't own a scrapbook. I don't even have a small stack of pictures held together by a rubber band. I've only held onto one single photo. One perfectly preserved memory I keep on the nightstand by our bed. Alexander changed out the frame while I was out of town—something black and sleek to match his decor—but it still feels like mine.

It's from a road trip my parents took me on when I was thirteen. We were driving through New Mexico, and I spotted a hot-air balloon through the backseat window. It was a million crazy colors, a floating rainbow. I shrieked with excitement, even before I spotted the other one. Then there was another. We kept driving toward them, and soon they were everywhere. We found out later it's a festival they have, an annual thing, but in the moment, it felt like it was just for us, some secret glimpse of magic. We pulled over at a lookout to get a better view, our faces turned up to the sky, the sun warm on our skin like a hug from the universe.

On our way back to the car, a woman stopped us. She said she'd taken a few pictures and asked if she could email them to us. We'd forgotten about her before we even left the parking lot, but a few days later, my mom opened her in-box to find the best surprise we'd ever gotten. The woman had captured us in the perfect moment. Our faces lit with elation. Our hair lifted in the wind. A bright blue sky as our background, balls of color hovering like promises.

"I wish we could take a picture right now," Jack says. "I'd like to remember this moment."

I wish we'd had a videographer following us around since last night. I want to remember every adventure we've shared. The bioluminescence. The game of Speed. Kissing. This boat.

"You don't have your phone?" I ask.

He shakes his head. "I left it in the room. No international plan."

"Same." I left mine on the bathroom counter. Hopefully Gen and Pilot Paul haven't decided to use it to record any X-rated memories of their own. "I have a feeling we won't have a hard time remembering these memories, though."

"True." He smiles and tilts his chin toward the snorkeling gear. "Are you ready to make some new ones?"

I nod and follow him to the picked-over pile. Without a crowd around, it only takes us a few minutes to grab our equipment and suit up. The man who was handing out life vests has gotten in the sea to lead everyone else to the coral, so we slip down the ladder without them. The water is cold enough to make my breath catch in my throat. I give into it, sinking under so my body will acclimate. Salt water barrels down the tube attached to my mask, filling my mouth. I wave my flippers and shoot to the surface, coughing it out.

"You all right?" Jack treads water near me. At my nod, he starts backward, toward the opposite side of the island as the crowd. "I don't want to get kicked in the face by a tourist. There's got to be fish over here, too."

I hesitate, looking back at the group. Jack is right; they're on top of each other, colorful air tubes bunched together like candles on a birthday cake. I lower my face into the water and blink through my goggles before starting after Jack's bright orange flippers.

The sun shines through the water like a spotlight, illuminating the school of neon fish in front of us. I feel the vibrations of Jack's voice, and when I look up, he's pointing down toward the seabed. I follow his finger and spot the massive stingray hovering above the sand, its edges flapping like Dumbo's ear, pretending to be harmless. Squealing, I swim toward it, but veer left so I don't actually get closer. Jack swims over it, and I squeeze my eyes shut.

When I open them again, he's left the stingray in his wake. His head is above water, and his legs dangle beneath him. I swing wide around the ray and swim to his side. Jack's mouthpiece dangles past his jaw and I spit mine out, too. The sun hits my face, making the little crystals of salt tingle against my skin.

"Look," Jack says, pointing toward the island's shore. "Monkeys."

"Really?" I paddle closer and am delighted to see two beneath a palm tree. One picks something up and puts it back down.

"If there are monkeys," he says, "there must be bananas."

I catch his meaning immediately. Jack wants to fight the monkeys for their bananas. At the very least, he wants to pull a banana off a tree and eat it in the wild like a castaway. Celeste's story was too good. It's made us want to do more, to lean into the adventure.

"We can't," I say reluctantly. "We should get back to the group."

"Or . . ." Jack's eyes are so bright, they shine through his fogged-up mask.

I laugh. "Or nothing."

"Or . . . we could just go to shore for a minute. Glance around. Meet the monkeys. See if they're willing to share."

I shake my head, but he's already stuffing the mouthpiece back in and tilting his face toward the water. Before I can say a word, he's under and propelling himself toward the bank. I glance back at the group, but the trees are too thick to see through, blocking my view of both. I consider going back without Jack but instead sigh and start after him.

He's kneeling on the hot sand in front of the monkeys when I catch up. They're facing him down, skittering forward and back again, not willing to come too close but too curious to run away. Their tiny monkey eyes barely glance my way as I approach.

"Hi, little guys," Jack says in a soft voice. "Where do you keep your bananas?"

One of them chatters loudly like he's trying to answer.

"Can you do a backflip?" I squat next to Jack and wait for the monkeys to answer. When they don't, I ask, "Maybe a cartwheel?"

"They live on an island," Jack says, "not in a circus tent. You want to ask if one of them has cymbals next?"

"Actually, I was going to see if they wanted to borrow yours."

"Funny. If I were in the circus, I think we both know I'd be the lion tamer."

"And I'd be?"

"The lion." He grins so adorably, I only half want to press my hand to his side to see if he topples over. "Obviously."

I roll my eyes and stand up, stepping toward the trees. The ground beneath them is peppered with shade and sunlight.

"These are tall," I say, scanning the tops of the palm trees. "Wouldn't the bananas be too high to reach anyway?"

"I don't know. I've only ever seen bananas at the grocery store."

I press farther into the mass of them, and the world quiets and gets louder simultaneously. The trees block the wind and the hum of the sea, but new noises take their place. The rustle of leaves. The buzz of insects. The crack of a stick beneath my heel. I spot a coconut on the ground and bend down to grab it. It's weirdly furry.

"Jack!" I lift it above my head like a trophy. "Do you think we could break this open?"

I lower the coconut and study it. It's so weighty, so substantial. So different from the grated white snow that's sprinkled over cake frosting. It looks like the kind of thing dinosaurs would have in their nests.

"I'm sure we could figure it out." Jack's voice comes from closer behind me than expected.

My skin prickles to attention as he reaches around me and plucks the coconut from my hand. I turn to grab it back, but he's not running away. He stays firm in front of me, still and solid. Our eyes meet for a moment, but mine are already tugging downward, drawn toward the wall of tanned skin. Without tearing them away from the sight, I reach around him and wrap my fingers around the coconut. To my surprise, he doesn't jerk it back.

"Aren't you going to try to keep it from me?" Disappointment colors my question. I thought the coconut was an excuse. We'd wrestle and shriek and pretend to want some stupid furry dinosaur egg, all so we could end up with our arms around each other, our mouths too close to resist touching.

"No." Jack lets go of the coconut completely, and I clasp it without any sense of victory.

I move to step back, but Jack's hand slides around my waist, holding me in place. His other hand moves up my arm, leaving a trail of fire in its wake. It slips behind my neck and into my hair. His eyes drop to my lips, narrowing with concentration as he gives a small tug on my hair. My chin lifts, and the coconut drops to the ground as his mouth lowers to cover mine.

I want to inhale him. It's like the sun has infused his skin, and now he's all heat and brightness. He devours my mouth as I press closer to him, wanting to feel him everywhere. The hard expanse of his chest. The jut of his muscles. Skin on skin, still slippery from sunscreen, our limbs entwined.

I gasp when his hand pushes under the triangle of my bikini, cupping my breast. With a grunt, he lets go and yanks the flimsy fabric to the side so I'm exposed, the sea air brushing against my sensitive skin. With another flick of the wrist, the other breast is bared.

"Beautiful." He breathes out the word before dipping his head to cover one nipple with his mouth. His tongue swirls in a way that makes my knees weak.

He must feel how close I am to falling because he looks up.

"Your eyes are fully gray right now," he says. "Dark gray."

I try to respond, but I've devolved to my basest form, nothing left but sensation and desire. Words are lost to me.

"They're the same color when you're mad at me." Jack's head drops back to my breast, teeth nipping in a way that makes my body tremble.

He holds me in place and drops to his knees, his lips moving slowly down my stomach. There's a sound in the distance, but I'm too focused on his mouth's path to comprehend it. Jack pulls back and tilts his head, but my fingers tighten against his neck, tugging him forward.

"Wait," he says. "Is that . . ."

The panic on his face cuts through the haze of lust. I force myself to focus. I know that sound.

"The engine!" Jack jerks upright, his eyes wild with panic.

I start to run, but he grabs me. His hands reach for my chest, covering it with the tiny triangles, and then we race across the sand together. I reach down, grabbing my snorkeling stuff as I pass. I shove the flippers on in the water, taking off a layer of skin in the process. I don't bother to put my mask back on. I just paddle. Hard. Desperately. Jack rounds the corner of the island before me, and I hear him shout out.

I let myself hope as I push into view of the boat, but my stomach sinks as I see it pulling away. I keep paddling, my head in the air as I yell for it to stop. There are so many people on board, but everyone is looking ahead, eager to see the next thing. Only one is looking back. Fanny Pack Lady. With an ugly smile, she lifts her camera to her face and snaps a picture of us before turning away.

Chapter 22

I should've known better.

The words loop through my head again and again. A mantra. A reproach.

"Can you talk to me, please?" Jack sits next to me on the sand as I stare out at the sea. His rests his arms on his knees. "I need to know if you're freaking out."

"About what?" I don't look bother looking at him. "About the fact that we're going to die on a deserted island?"

"That tour runs every day, Ava. And I'm sure it's not the only one. Another group will probably be arriving any minute."

I don't respond. Jack could be right, but it doesn't matter. Two no-shows on my record? There are no other Northeast Air crew members in this country. The flight will have to be canceled. Because of us. Even if we're saved, I'm not going to have a job to go back to.

I should've known better.

"We'll make it back in time for our flight," Jack says quietly.

I scoff. Go ahead. Tell me it doesn't matter. *We're having an adventure! You worry too much, Ava. Everything will work out exactly as it's supposed to.* I know the speech. I've heard it a million times. The funny thing is it's not wrong. Everything probably does work out how it's supposed to. It just doesn't ever seem to work out how I wanted it to.

"They'll realize we're not on the boat," Jack says. "They'll come back."

He's either lying or fooling himself. It might've been true if we'd signed up for the tour like we were supposed to. But instead we snuck on board with a cash bribe like criminals. They probably assume we were using their boat to make a run for it.

My eyes follow a wave as I dig my toes down in the sand. Jack rests a warm hand on my knee. I swipe it off.

"Okay," he says. "You're mad."

Mad? No. I'm disappointed. Devastated even. I so badly wanted this to turn out differently. I don't think I even realized how much hope I'd let myself feel. I hid it behind reluctance, but it was there, little iridescent bubbles shimmering in the light of Jack's attention. I was irritable with him. I was angry. I was a competitive beast. I was all the worst parts of myself, and he liked me anyway. And *him*. Jack "Stupid Jacket" Stone. He was all the best parts of the people I've loved most. And I trusted him anyway. I let myself believe that, in the right person, those qualities might be able to add up to something different, something that wouldn't let me down.

"Can you just say something?" The words explode from his mouth like a volcanic eruption. "You're killing me here."

I turn to him slowly. "What, exactly, would you like me to say?"

"What would I like you to say?" He exhales his frustration. "Ideally, it would be something along the lines of 'We'll get through this, Jack. It sucks that it happened, but I don't blame you. It doesn't change the way I feel about you.' I don't want to hear it if you don't mean it, though. I'd prefer any of the jabs you've lobbed at me during the course of this trip. At least those make me laugh."

"I don't blame you." I watch as his eyes fill with hope.

Silly, stupid hope. Apparently none of us are immune.

"And . . ." He prompts me to say the rest, but I can't.

This does change the way I feel about him. Maybe if I hadn't already found myself here before—desert sand instead of beach, sure, but the rest of the details are almost identical. Knowing that without the person next to me I never would've ended up in this situation, with my job on the line. I made my rules for a reason. Yet here I am. Because of Jack. Because of my inability to stick to the boundaries I set for myself.

I shake my head and turn back to the water. It's too beautiful. All of this—the palm trees, the bright blue sky, the tittering monkeys at our backs—it's all too idyllic to be the setting for this scene. At least I was in a bathroom when everything with Alexander went to crap.

"So, just like that," Jack says, "it's over?"

"We've known each other for a few days, Jack. There's not much to end."

I feel the sand shift when he gets to his feet. Still, I'm surprised when he walks away. I hear his footsteps pad across the sand behind me, heading toward the trees. Apparently, he's decided the monkeys will be better company than me. I can't say I blame him.

After what feels like forever sitting by myself, I consider toeing the word *HELP* into the sand. Isn't that what you're supposed to do when you're stranded on a deserted island? Or is it *S.O.S.*? My stomach growls, and I stand up to go in search of some kind of stick. Clearly I'm going to have to learn to spear fish if I want to stay alive. I stick to the edge of the trees, looking for anything that might work. The thought of killing one of those gorgeous, colorful beings makes me feel physically ill.

I can't be so weak, though. I'm on my own. I'm a survivor. I will get off this island, and I will get back home. And when I do, these are skills I'll need to have. Without a job, my savings will run out quickly. I won't have money to go to the grocery store. I'll be the ridiculous girl fishing in the Chicago River.

It occurs to me for the first time that being stranded on a tropical island might actually be superior to the alternative awaiting me.

"Here." Jack tromps out of the trees and presses a bunch of small bananas in my hand. Half of them are bruised, but the other half are yellow and ripe.

"You picked these?"

"No." He avoids my eyes. "You were right. They were too high to reach. But there were several that had fallen. I ate a couple already. I think they're safe."

"Thank you."

He nods but doesn't respond. I wish he'd smile smugly and brag about his survival skills. Maybe it would make me more determined to spear my fish, the fire of competition burning through this terrible disappointment that has settled heavily on my chest.

He doesn't, though. He just runs his hand through his windswept hair, letting it spring wildly around his face. I resist the temptation to reach up and run my own fingers through it. Instead I walk toward the water. Sitting, I place the bananas in my lap and tear one off. It's hard to peel, but the fruit inside is white and fleshy. I take a bite, and the flavor explodes between my teeth. It's like eating a real cookie when all you've ever had is the sugar-free version. I want to swirl it around in my mouth and savor it, but I don't have the restraint. Before it clears my throat, I'm shoving another bite in my mouth.

I'm on my third banana when I spot the white dot of a boat on the horizon. For a moment, I'm certain it's an illusion. It's actually shimmering; it can't be real. It's headed straight for us, though. I call for Jack, but he's already running past me toward the water. His hands wave frantically, and his shouts burst through the air before being swallowed by the sea.

The boat doesn't speed up, but it doesn't turn away either. It keeps plodding our way until it stops in the same place our boat used to be parked. The words *Snorkel Time* are written across the side. About twenty pairs of curious eyes peer overboard at us. I can tell they're tourists by the Panama hats and mirrored sunglasses. Jack plunges in the water and swims to the ladder on the side of the boat. I follow after him.

He doesn't wait for an invitation to board, so neither do I. By the time I get to the top, Jack is already trying to talk the captain into driving us back. The other guys in Snorkel Time shirts are building piles of snorkel gear in the bow.

The captain seems friendly, helpful even—he offers to let us join the tour and says he'll take us back after—but he's unwilling to end everyone else's day early. It's understandable, but it still makes me want to cry. If we go with them, the captain estimates he can get us back around 2:00. It's close enough to make my stomach soar with hope, but the fact is we need to be dressed and in the lobby no later than 1:55. Anything later, and I might as well stay here and eat bananas.

"Can I use your phone?" Jack asks.

The captain's hand goes to his pocket like a shield.

"I will pay you twenty dollars to use your phone for two minutes." Jack is doing his blowfish thing again. Before my eyes, he's growing like the Hulk.

"You don't have to pay me," the captain says, "or try to scare me. I want to help you. Just be honest with me. Are you going to call out of country?"

"No. I promise." Jack reaches for my hand and unfolds my fingers so the number written in Sharpie across my palm faces up. "We're going to call this number."

WITH A STOMACH full of lead, I watch the Snorkel Time boat pull away. We're putting a lot of faith in Eddie and Celeste. Much more than I'm comfortable with. There's nothing about two wanderers who have settled here by chance that says, *We're the kind of people you should trust to keep you from being stranded overnight on an island.*

Jack made the decision to gamble on them rather than the safety of Snorkel Time. I don't know what I would've chosen if I'd been in his position. I have a secret suspicion I forced him to make the choice because I wanted to blame someone else if it didn't work out. The thought makes me feel icky. If it's true—maybe even if it's not—I don't think I've been entirely fair to him today.

I borrowed someone's sunscreen, but it was too little too late. I can feel the tightness in my skin. It's not sore yet, but it will be, and soon. I can't seem to make myself sit. Jack doesn't seem to be able to either. We pace the sand in different directions, taking care not to overlap paths. When one of us watches the sea too intently and veers toward the other, we swing apart like magnets gone wrong.

I've been counting out the seconds, trying to keep track of the minutes that pass. The boat left at 11:00. If I'm right, it's about 11:27. We're about an hour away from the hotel by boat, depending on whether a small boat goes faster or slower than a big boat. If Celeste and Eddie show up soon, we'll even have time to shower. *If.*

"I want to say something." Jack steps into my path, and I freeze, one foot in front of the other.

"Okay." I slide my foot back beneath me slowly.

"I don't know why you responded like this today, but I'm guessing it has something to do with your past and not being able to trust your parents to do what's best for you. I'd tell you that I'm not them—which I'm not—but I don't believe in talking someone into wanting to be with me. What I do believe in is honesty. So, for myself, I need to be honest and tell you that this—what we have—isn't a few days for me."

I open my mouth, but he holds up a hand, stopping me.

"Just let me get this out, please." His cheeks are already red with sunburn. Rather than make him look silly, it makes his eyes look impossibly blue. Mesmerizing.

"Okay," I murmur.

"Okay." He swipes his hand through his hair, and it sticks up in crazy tufts. "I know you remember that night in the bar as the night I tried to hurt you, but I remember it as the night I met someone who made my head spin. Every time I went to work after that, I looked for you. I'd see you laughing with other flight attendants and wish I could be the one to make you laugh like that.

"I asked people about you and found out that you're easy to fly with. You're kind to the passengers. You're not territorial. You open other flight attendants' cans for service and collect the trash in their section when you go out to do your own. You hold babies when single mothers are trying to deal with the bags, even though you know doing so could get you fired. You don't hang out with people off-hours, but they like you anyway. Actually, most of them seem to love you. *Of course* I'd end up with a crush on you. It was bound to happen.

"But the crazy thing was you were never nice to me. You weren't actively mean, but you were cold. The opposite of everything I'd heard. And then I saw you in the parking lot, and you were this tiny, seething ball of rage, and that was it for me. Just like that, in a moment, I was gone."

"But why?" The words fly out, even though Jack has made it clear it's not my turn to talk. I can't help myself. What he's saying makes no sense. "Are you some kind of masochist?"

"No, Ava," he says. "I'm not a *masochist*. But knowing you have that inside you yet choose to treat so many people with kindness anyway . . . it's admirable. Do you know how hard it is to find someone you actually admire? Not because they're pretty to look at—which, by the way, you are, beautiful, in fact—but because they make the world better just by being in it? I've flown with Gen before, and people act like she's crazy. They make jokes about her like she can't hear them. They treat her like the peroxide has fried her brain. Not you, though. You haven't made a single snide comment about her behind her back. I doubt you've even thought one."

"But it's not because I'm nice." I don't know why I can't just let him have this picture of me in his head. It seems lovely, and I like the idea of a fairy-tale me twirling around in someone's thoughts. But it doesn't seem fair to let him believe he's missing out on something when I'm not at all the person he believes me to be. "It's just because I'm scared. I worry, if I'm not easy enough to be around, I'll get left behind."

Jack studies my face for a moment before shaking his head. "I might believe that if you were one of those girls who goes around collecting a million friends. But from what I've gathered, you don't hang out with any of us outside of work. And I'm willing to bet you're not following passengers off the planes, trying to solicit declarations of allegiance from them. None of the people I'm referring to are staples in your life. So, what reason do you have for being so generous to them?"

I meet his eyes but don't respond. What am I supposed to say? *You're right? You* should *have a crush on me? Aside from my animosity toward you and my deranged determination to turn everything into a competition, I'm actually quite a catch?*

"I'd even guess," he says, "as much as you didn't like me and would've been thrilled to have me leave you behind, you still chose not to talk badly about me to any of our crew."

"Sure." I've got him now. "But you're probably underestimating how many bad things I let myself think."

The corner of his mouth curls up. "I'm guessing I have a pretty good idea."

I stare at his curved lips, pink from the sun. Tomorrow they will probably be peeling from sunburn, but today they look infinitely kissable. *Today.* That's what it always comes down to, isn't it? The choice to live life for today or the future. But what is the future, really? Does it even exist? I keep trying to reach it, but every time I wake up, it's today again.

Jack turns, and I catch the flash of his smile.

"They're here!" He runs toward the water, and it takes my

mind a moment to move past the thought of his lips to the reality of rescue.

Once it does, my heart soars. Eddie and Celeste have come through for us. I let Jack trust them, but I didn't allow myself to. *And I was wrong.* My feet catch on before the rest of me, jerking into motion, carrying me toward the sea. My hair streams behind me as I run across the sand and plunge into the salty sea. It welcomes me with its cold, invigorating me with relief. We're going to make it back. I'm going to keep my job. *Thank goodness.* After everything I've given up, it's all I have left.

I swim toward them, laughing at my own impatience. I hear a laugh at my side and realize Jack is cutting past me, his strokes strong and sure. I kick harder, not competing this time, just keeping up. Staying with him.

Eddie is grinning when we reach the edge of the boat, and he holds out a hand to help us in. "You know we were headed for the shore, don't you? We're here to rescue you."

"Thank you." I gasp the words as he pulls me up and over. And before he can help Jack in, I throw my arms around him, hugging him tightly. "Thank you so much."

I don't know how to tell them how much it means to me that they're the ones who proved most dependable. Two wanderers. Eddie must see it in my face, though, because he pats my head and says, "No problem, my strange, tiny iguana."

The boat wobbles beneath me as I cross to reach Celeste, and when Eddie pulls Jack over the edge, I squat and reach for the edge right before I fall. But then I'm up again, closing the distance and wrapping my arms around Celeste's bony frame. She smells like marijuana and orange juice. I never would've guessed it would be the smell of salvation.

"Thank you for coming." I squeeze her to me. "I would've lost my job."

"Is that all? Without jobs, you could've stayed here. Abercrombie panhandling topless would've guaranteed all the fish tacos you could eat."

"Who needs someone to buy them?" I wave the idea away. "I was just about to start spearing the fish myself."

Chapter 23

I keep sneaking looks at Jack on the ride back to the hotel. If he notices, he doesn't let on. He just stares at the waves. He looks like he's been created for this boat, this moment on the sea. His skin has been darkened by the sun, his hair swept by the wind. Long limbs, perfect for swimming. I can picture him living here, but I can also see him climbing mountains, conquering them with sure strides.

I don't need him.

I said it jokingly to Celeste, but it was true. I can spear my own fish. Well, not really. But I know I could learn. Haven't I spent most of my life fending for myself?

It suddenly seems like the silliest thing in the world that I was planning to marry Alexander for stability. That was the reason, after all, if I'm ready to be completely honest with myself. As much as I tried to convince myself it was also for companionship, deep down inside, I know that's not the truth. Alexander was always at work. Even when he wasn't, even when we were together, we were at his work functions. Side by side but separate. I was just his shadow, fading bit by bit as the day went on.

Even when we were at home, we weren't together. Not really. In order to be with someone, you have to be yourself. And I was never myself with Alexander. I was too quiet. Careful. Convinced I needed him more than he needed me.

But I didn't need Alexander.

And I don't need Jack; I *want* him.

I want to compete with him. I want to go on adventures with him. I want to say absurd things and hear him laugh. I want to say sweet things and have him kiss me. I want a weekend. And maybe forever. But forever doesn't have to be the goal because I'm fine. I'm here.

"I'm sorry." I say the words aloud, but they're whisked away by the wind before they reach him.

It's fine. I'll say them again when we get off this boat. I'll tell Jack I was wrong. I'll admit I blamed him for getting us stranded when I should've taken responsibility for myself. I'll confess to assigning him the sins of people who came before him, when he in no way deserved the blame. For now, I just reach for his hand.

He looks over, his brow lifting in surprise. His eycs drop to our hands, my fingers slipping through his. He doesn't pull me toward him, wrapping his arms around me like he did last night. But his palm squeezes mine, warm and firm against my skin.

RATHER THAN HAVE us jump off like he did last night, Eddie pulls up to the shore and parks the boat.

"Since we're here anyway"—he looks to Celeste—"lunch?"

She squeals and jumps up. "Fish dip!"

Eddie turns to us. "Do you have time to eat? It's just past one o'clock now."

"I know it sounds gross," Celeste says before I can answer, "but Belizean fish dip is the greatest stuff ever. It's, like, smoked or something. And you eat it with tortilla chips. It's amazing."

I lift a skeptical eyebrow. Fish in dip form?

"I wish I could," Jack says, "but I've got to shower and pack my stuff up."

"Same," I say. "But please charge your meals to room 105. Your drinks, too. It's the least I can do to say thank you for rescuing us."

"The least?" Celeste laughs. "I don't think you have a real understanding of how much this guy can drink."

"Please," Eddie says. "I'm the lightweight in this relationship."

Celeste lifts a hand to her mouth like she's telling me a secret. "He's not wrong."

I wish we had more time. I'm going to miss these two. Jack slips his hand around mine and starts toward the hotel.

"Charge everything to room 108 instead," he says, glancing back at Celeste and Eddie as they fall into step behind us. "Then I won't feel guilty about asking you to order an extra fish dip for me."

"You're going to try it?" I ask, enjoying the feel of walking hand in hand with him.

"When in Belize . . ." He grins. "I'll get myself together and drag my bags out so I can eat and head to the lobby straight from there. Do you want to order something? We can ask them to put it in a to-go box."

As tempting as it sounds, I don't want to be the person

stinking up the van with my food. It's right up there on the list of etiquette rules, just below not talking loudly on your phone.

"Nah. I'll grab something at the airport." I'll have to. I haven't iced my food bag in at least twenty-four hours. My frozen meals have undoubtedly gone bad.

"Oh! You know what we should do the next time you come?" Celeste skips up beside me. "The rock slides."

"You never take me to do the rock slides," Eddie whines.

"Because they kind of hurt my butt." Celeste looks at me reassuringly. "But not really. I mean, they do. But it's worth it for the experience. You're sliding down smooth rocks over all these mini-waterfalls—"

"But to our tiny little tadpole there," Eddie interrupts, "they'll probably be full-sized waterfalls. You know, because she's already mini."

Celeste tilts her head. "I wonder if they have one of those height things like you have to pass to go on roller coasters. One of those 'You must be this tall' signs. It's probably carved into a palm tree somewhere."

"By who?" Eddie asks. "Belize's manager?"

I'm so distracted by their conversation, I don't notice the group of people eating by the pool. Not, that is, until the moment Gen waves and jumps out of her seat.

"Ava!" Gen hops up and down with excitement. "Look what we found!"

I laugh at her enthusiasm, already thinking how much she'll like Eddie and Celeste. They can join her for lunch. If I shower quickly and leave the room with wet hair, maybe I'll even be able to spend a minute with them before we have to get to the lobby.

"It's your fiancé!" Gen grabs the arm of the man next to her, but he's already rising to his feet and turning around.

It all hits me in a single blow, strong enough to make me gasp. *Fiancé.* The sight of him. Alexander. Perfectly coifed but strikingly casual, in a white linen shirt and expensive aviators that hide the temperature of his eyes. They tilt toward my hand, still entwined with Jack's, and my stomach drops.

I pull my hand away. Or maybe Jack breaks free first.

Either way, I know it can't be good.

WE'RE IN MY hotel room. Alexander is sitting in the chair by the window, and I'm facing the mirror across the room from him, folding my newly washed hair into a wet braid down the side of my face and wondering how worried I should be that Jack walked away before I could explain anything to him. The look on his face as he backed away indicated *very.* On the bright side, at least he wasn't there to see Alexander follow me to my room.

"Can you just sit down and talk to me for a minute?" Alexander's face is tight with frustration. I'd have more sympathy for him, but it's 1:34, and I've already explained to him several times that I have to be in the lobby by 1:55 at the very latest. For someone who lives with rigid adherence to schedules, he doesn't seem able to summon any appreciation for mine.

Gen pops her head out of the bathroom, the wand of mascara still hovering in front of her eye. "No, she cannot sit down and talk. She needs to get ready."

They glare at each other. I can't believe they've been together since ten o'clock this morning without bloodshed occurring. Hopefully Gen was nicer to him when he showed up at our door. Now she's making no such effort. I can't decide if she's being mean to him because of my whispered "We're not together anymore" or because she doesn't like the way he's speaking to me. For me, it's definitely the latter.

"Well, I *needed* to be in the office today," Alexander says. "But I've flown all the way out here because my fiancée doesn't know how to answer her phone. I think a few minutes of face-to-face time is the least I could expect in return."

"I do know how to answer my phone." My voice comes out smaller than I want it to. All the calls I've missed in the past prick at my conscience, making me feel like I've done something wrong. "But there's nothing left to say. We broke up."

"We were engaged, Ava. That's not the kind of thing you end over the phone."

"Maybe not. But we did it anyway. There was no future for us, remember? You didn't want to be with a flight attendant." I'm not blaming him. It's my attempt to reassure him.

"What the hell is wrong with being a flight attendant?" Gen's outrage is palpable. "Everyone wants this job. The last time Northeast opened their website to applications, it crashed within three hours. Over ten thousand people had already applied."

"Gen," I say, "can you please go back in the bathroom?"

"Lawyers," she grumbles. "Now that's an easy job to get. I bet you just check your soul at the door and they welcome you in, slapping an 'Asshole' name tag on your fancy suit so people know what to call you while you're screwing them over."

"Gen!"

She sighs and disappears but leaves the door open so we can hear her when she says, "You know I'm right, though."

"I'm sorry." I turn to face Alexander, still holding my makeup bag like a tether to my choices. "This is all my fault. If

I'd been more honest with you about who I was, you would've broken up with me a long time ago. You deserve better."

"I don't want better." Alexander rises from the chair and crosses the room to stand in front of me. Gently he takes the makeup bag from my hands and sets it on the bed behind him. When he turns back to me, he strokes a hand down my cheek. In all the time I've known him, he's never caressed my face like that. It's something Jack would do, not Alexander. "I want to get married."

"But you don't want to get married to *me*." As certain as I am of the fact, my stomach roils with guilt. In realizing I never loved Alexander, I somehow convinced myself he didn't love me either. If I was wrong, I've moved on with a speed that can only be described as cruel.

"Of course I do." Alexander's voice takes on a patronizing quality. It's not the first time I've heard it from him, but it might be the first time I've ever allowed myself to acknowledge just how belittling it feels. "You're perfect for me."

"I'm not." Before I can expand—*I'm only perfect for you if I quit my job, and stop driving such an embarrassing car, and give up weekend travel opportunities in exchange for black-tie events, and don't dare to disrupt your expensive decorator's scheme with my thrift store picture frames*—Alexander raises his voice to speak over me.

"You *are*. You think you're not good enough, but you are. You deserve this, Ava. You deserve to be taken care of. You deserve to live a life where you don't have to get up in the middle of the night and go work on a dirty plane, serving sodas to ungrateful travelers. You deserve to have nice things, and to eat expensive meals, and to have a beautiful wedding at the Starlight. I can give you that life. You just have to let me."

"That's not the life I want!" The words burst out of me. Partly because I'm horrified that Alexander seems to have completely misread who I am as a person, but also because he's likely to speak over me again if I let him. "It never has been."

"Sure it is." His certainty reeks of arrogance.

"She's *telling you* it isn't." Gen pops out of the bathroom, pointing an eyeliner pencil at him. "You think you know better than her what she wants?"

I bite back the urge to argue the point. It's a waste of time, even if I did have any to spare. Alexander has no interest in understanding the difference between wanting to quit my job for stability's sake versus not liking the work itself. I could spend the next five hours talking, and he'd still believe I want a wedding at the Starlight because it's expensive, just like a new car must be better than my ancient VW bug that was the color of sunshine and smelled like freedom.

Ducking my head, I walk to the closet and pull my car keys from the tote bag. Once I'm back in front of Alexander, I lift my eyes to meet his.

"I've apologized for misleading you in this relationship," I say, "and I meant it. But I think the truth is we both chose what we saw in each other. You expected to be my savior. You wanted to believe I needed your money. Your apartment. Your car. And I expected you to be safe. I wanted you to love me and be my partner. But you never knew me well enough to love me, and I never needed your money." I press the keys into his hand. "We're not getting married, Alexander. There's nothing left to discuss."

"You know what?" His face freezes like an ice sculpture, and his fingers close around the keys. "Fine."

There's so much in that tiny word. The tacit permission, as

if I needed him to sign off on the end of the discussion. The sighed agreement, silently informing me, if I'd spent our relationship being as stubborn as I have the last couple of days, he never would've proposed in the first place.

I can't blame him. Still, I don't hate it when he walks out the door and Gen calls after him, "And just so you know: gel is supposed to be used sparingly!"

Chapter 24

I'm in the back of the plane during boarding, wondering why Gen, not Jack, is in the exit row. Or maybe I don't have to wonder. He's upset with me. He hasn't looked at me once since Gen declared Alexander my fiancé. He managed to avoid my gaze in the lobby, and he sat up front in the van. Like, up front, next to the driver. That's how desperate he was not to get stuck sitting beside me.

Now, apparently, he's at the front of the plane instead of standing in the exit row where he's supposed to be. My stomach twists. I should've told him about Alexander. And I should've made up with him while we were still on Eddie and Celeste's boat. The combination of the two events doubles the impact of each. Two fired bullets that have landed like a cannonball.

A mom and her daughter are slowing boarding down, and I stifle the urge to snap at them to keep it moving. It's not their fault I've managed to destroy things with the first guy I've ever been able to fully be myself around. The daughter is leading the line of passengers, one hand above her head, and her mom is holding it, allowing her to go at her own pace.

"Look at all the seats!" The mom's *Look at me being the best mom in the world* voice is absurdly high-pitched. She's what we call a Runway Mom. The aisle is her catwalk, and the people behind her are her unwilling audience to this travel version of *Sesame Street.* "We can pick any one we want. So many choices! What do you think, darling? Which is your favorite?"

The man behind them shoots me an annoyed look. He wants me to speed them up, but I'm not biting. If I do, he'll expect me to say something again mid-flight when the mom is walking her daughter up and down the aisle, pretending to explore. It's not that I don't want to. It's just that it's not my place. I'm not their show's director. Runway Mom is.

I reach for the interphone and make an announcement that everyone should sit in the first available seat they see. I don't have to worry about Runway Mom taking it personally because she's not listening any more than anyone else is. With a sigh, I flip open the drink cabinet. I'd really like a soda water with lime, but the limes got tossed back in the States, before the plane started for Belize. It's some international regulation that, like most of the others, makes no sense to me. I pop open a Sprite Zero instead. Turning to reach for a cup, I bounce off a body barreling toward the lavatory.

"Oops." The man grabs my shoulders and stops me from slamming against the counter. "My bad."

He has a nice smile, short salt-and-pepper hair, a sharp suit, and bare feet.

"Well," I say, wincing before lifting my eyes to his face, "you managed to get your shoes off quickly."

"Yeah." He at least has the wherewithal to look sheepish. "I left them at my seat. Just needed to hit the head."

"Good plan." I manage to keep the judgment out of my

tone, even though there is a lot of it to hold back. Considering the size of the lav and the inevitable turbulence, that floor has probably been peed on more than a porta-potty at Coachella. Not to worry, though. Every so often, the cleaning guys spread it around with a mop so it's more evenly distributed.

The man pushes helplessly at the door, and I only give a small sigh before turning the handle for him. He disappears inside, and I feel a twinge of guilt for making him feel self-conscious about his bare feet and inability to open a door. Why should I care if he wants to puddle-jump in urine? It's not like it affects me.

Jack's voice comes over the speaker. He's making the end-of-boarding announcement the A flight attendant is supposed to make. I want to call him on the interphone and give him a hard time for doing the wrong duties. But if I do, I'll just end up begging him to forgive me. I gulp my Sprite Zero straight from the can. It's warm, almost hot, and the carbonation makes my eyes water.

The aisle clears, and I move into it to start shutting bins. We're on the same plane we brought into Belize, and it still has the modified bins I can't reach. My stomach sinks, and my face heats with premeditated embarrassment. This is my job; I have to do it.

"Excuse me," I murmur to the lady in the aisle seat on the back row. With a sharp intake of breath, I put my foot on the edge beside her seat cushion and hoist myself up to snap the bin shut.

It's not the same as actually stepping in her seat, but it's pretty close. Close enough to be awkward for both of us. Never mind that I'm wearing a dress and the person seated behind me has probably caught a good view of cotton panties with baby pandas on them. I avoid all eye contact and move my unprofessional behavior to the seat across from her. Row by row, my own bouncy walk of shame.

I keep expecting Gen to catch on and come help, but she's still doing some bizarrely complicated briefing up at the exit row. Instead of settling for verbal affirmation that the passengers are willing to assist in an emergency evacuation, she seems to be making them prove they can open the door. One by one, they wiggle around each other to mime pulling the plastic cap off the handle and pulling it down. It's like a game of Twister no one volunteered to play. In spite of myself—and the fact that I've seat-jumped myself all the way up to row thirteen—I laugh at the absurdity.

I cover my mouth and try to suck it back in—laughing at the passengers is rude—but Jack peers into the aisle. He couldn't have heard me. Still, he catches me mid-smile, the mirth brimming out of me. I meet his eyes, and his face goes horribly blank. It's not a grimace. It's not the polite half smile I've seen him give overly chatty passengers. It's nothing. He could be looking through me. To him, I have ceased to exist.

It's like being hit by a wave of cold water. It knocks the breath out of me, sweeping away my amusement. Chastised, I turn and slump my way back to the galley. Before I've reached the end of the aisle, my back is straightening with resolve. Whether Jack likes it or not, he's about to be stuck with me. I'll have him hostage in our tiny galley. He'll have no choice but to hear me out. By the end, he'll have forgiven me, if only to make me shut up.

Brightened with resolve, I hurry back and double-check my galley. I'm reaching for the coffee pot when Gen fills the small space with the clomping sound of her heels.

"Guess what!" She does a little dance. "Jack swapped positions with me. I get to work back here with you!"

WE HIT TURBULENCE just as the plane crosses ten thousand feet. The first bump is like going over a pothole in the road. The second is more like the road has dropped out beneath us. My stomach plummets, then rises and plummets again. Normally, I love this feeling; it's like the ultimate roller coaster ride. Today, it's too much. My stomach doesn't need the highs and lows when it's already mimicking a Tilt-A-Whirl.

Because of the turbulence, service is delayed. I try to read, but I can't focus on the words. They swim on the page, rearranging themselves into frantic demands. *Hurry! You're running out of time! If you don't fix things on this flight, he'll be gone!* I don't know where Jack lives in Boulder. I don't even have his phone number. It's been months since I last ran into Gen in the airport, and she at least works in the same base as me. It could be years before I see Jack again.

I shudder at the thought and stand up to begin service. The sooner we finish, the sooner I can talk to Jack. Like good little flight attendants, Gen and Jack don't follow my lead. They stay seated until Captain Ballinger calls us to say it's safe to get up.

Even then, everything takes three times as long as it should. Gen talks about Pilot Paul instead of pouring her drinks. She tells me more details than I'd like to know about how fantastic the sex was, the unexpected streak of wildness he revealed. When she tells me she's planning to visit him in Wisconsin, I give in and let the ice melt in the drinks on my tray so I can listen, because I'm genuinely thrilled and want to hear all the details.

It's shocking to discover Gen grew up on a farm. Even more shocking to hear she misses the peacefulness of that life. I look at the sparkle in her eyes and the hopeful expression on her face, and it occurs to me that these two opposites might actually have a chance at something real. My eyes get watery at the thought.

The passengers ding call lights of annoyance from their seats, reminding us there's work to be done. I deliver my first tray of drinks quickly, but the second takes much longer because Gen steals my coffees. She sneaks a drink from the Dr Pepper I poured for the woman in row nineteen, and I have to throw it away and pour a new one. When she accidentally knocks my drink order sheet into the trash, I snap and grab her tray, dumping it over so all the poured drinks tumble into the trash.

Our eyes meet and widen in shock. I can't believe what I've just done. Never, in nine years of flying, have I behaved so aggressively. Never in my life, actually. Not until this week. It's Jack's doing; he's unleashed something inside me.

Before I can apologize, Gen bursts into laughter. She laughs so hard she bends over, holding her belly. I join her, embarrassedly at first, but then my laughter turns into something so wild it can only be categorized as a song of snorts. I can't breathe through it, and I don't care. I'm thrilled I dumped her tray. She deserved it. I'll help her pour a new one, but I won't say I'm sorry. *I'm not.*

I am sorry for how I've treated Jack, though. And I don't want to wait anymore. I want to clear things up. Now.

"I only have the back row left," I say. "Can you ask them what they ordered and take care of it for me?"

Gen snorts. "I have to pour my whole tray over, and you want me to do your section, too?"

"Yes," I say. "Please."

She shrugs. "Sure."

I squeal and say, "Thank you!" before hurrying past her and up the aisle. Because Jack hasn't had to work with someone intent on sabotaging all productivity, he's just finishing his section. He pretends not to see me coming and turns back toward his galley. I follow him up the aisle.

The lights are off in his galley, a subtle trick to remind passengers they can't stand up here. Still, the sunlight streams through the little round windows on the doors, leaving patterns across the floor. His tray has been cleaned, and the cans on his counter are organized in neat rows, just like mine always are.

"Hi," I say quietly.

He nods and leans against the counter, facing me.

I take a deep breath. "I owe you an apology."

"And, apparently, I owe you a congratulations." Jack doesn't say the words sarcastically. He doesn't even sound mad. He just sounds like he's speaking to a coworker. "When's the wedding?"

"There's no wedding. We only got engaged a few days ago, and then we broke up. Before I kissed you, for the record. It was over with Alexander before anything happened between you and me."

"Yeah?" He crosses his arms over his chest. "How long before?"

My stomach sinks. "We ended it the first night in Belize. That's why I was so rude to you at the pool. I'm sorry about that. And I'm sorry about the island. It wasn't your fault we got stranded. I shouldn't have acted like it was. That situation brought up some old issues, but I'm working through those."

"Glad to hear it." His polite dismissal is so much worse than anger. It says he doesn't need the details. He no longer cares.

"I should have told you I was engaged. But I wasn't trying to hide it from you." My voice rises with a frantic need to make him understand. "I was kind of hiding it from Gen because she was upset about a breakup, but really I was just keeping it to myself because I don't generally share personal things with coworkers. By the time you were involved, there was nothing to tell anymore. It was already over."

"Understood," he says. "Besides, technically speaking, you did tell me. I mean, nothing better conveys the enormity of ending a lifelong commitment than mentioning you don't think you're going to be able to 'work it out' with someone. Really, I can't imagine why Alexander felt the need to fly all the way to Belize in search of some clarity."

"Jack." I step into his space so he can feel the energy that's sparked between us since the moment we met. So he has no choice but to meet my gaze.

When he does, his eyes are shuttered. "It's fine, Ava. You're right. You've done nothing wrong. I'm sorry if I've made you feel like you have. I thought there was something between us, but there's not. Not a future, at least. I should've realized it when we got stranded, when *you* realized it. But I wasn't ready." His voice softens. "I am now."

I flinch beneath the blow of his words. "But I was wrong. There *is* something. Just give me a chance."

"I wish I could." He shrugs. Dismissive. Done. "But I already lived through one relationship destroyed by secrets. I don't have it in me to attempt another."

Chapter 25

When we land in Houston, I seriously consider making a run for it. A few years ago, between flights, a flight attendant grabbed a six-pack, popped the back door open, slid down the slide, and went fleeing across the tarmac. The idea of having to work our last flight to Chicago with Jack up front, actively not wanting me, makes that flight attendant's actions seem reasonable. Brilliant even. I, of course, would just stuff my pockets with minis. Beers seem much too unwieldy.

Instead I smile politely and help a woman shove her bag full of cement blocks into an overhead bin. On the way back to my galley, I accept emergency trash from a teenager. It's an empty pizza box that manages to smear marinara sauce all over my right hand. Even after the use of two sani-wipes, I keep catching whiffs of crushed tomatoes and garlic.

Because I'm a professional, I don't start crying until after I've completed service and collected trash. I'm in the back galley, sitting on the jump seat with Gen. It's so cold back here Gen has filled trash bags with hot water and we've got them balanced on our feet. I'm pretending to read.

The tears hit without warning, slipping down my cheeks

and plopping onto my Kindle. I try to wipe them off, and the stupid thing changes pages. Its incompetence makes me cry harder. I swipe at another puddle of tears, and the chapter changes. My shoulders shake with the force of my resulting silent wail, and Gen looks up from her magazine.

"Hey, little bunny," she says, leaning down so her face is in mine. "What's going on?"

"I just have something in my eye." I swipe at my cheeks, trying to get rid of the evidence.

"You do. It's called a tear, and you actually have quite a few of them. Is this about that fancy lawyer you were going to marry?"

I shake my head and am pretty sure I'm crying hard enough that some tears fly off my face like I'm a dog that just had a bath.

"Good," she says. "He made me feel like he was about to force me in a limo and whisk me away to a country club for an intervention on my lack of ladylikeness. What is it, then? Is it the guy who said 'A sirloin, medium rare' when you asked him if you could get him anything? Because I've heard that joke so many times it makes me want to sob, too."

I shake my head again and try to wipe away the tears, but they're quickly replaced by a new stream.

"Is it—"

"Jack." I cut her off with the truth because it's the only thing guaranteed to make her stop guessing. "I'm crying because I ruined things with Jack."

"Holy Mother of . . ." Gen trails off, mouth open like she's expecting me to throw a piece of popcorn in there. "You were holding hands with him when you walked up from the beach! How did I forget that?"

"You were too busy fighting with Alexander?"

"You kissed him, didn't you. You kissed Jack Stone! Tell me everything! Was it amazing? Soft or hard? The kissing, not his dick. I'm sure that was rock solid. Was there some touchy-feely? Sex? Or just a good, old-fashioned make-out?" Her face falls. "Oh, but wait. You said it's ruined. Do you want me to go talk to him?"

"No!" My hands jerk up, prepared to physically restrain her if necessary. I think I could do it. Gen is much bigger than me, but I have a terror-induced rush of adrenaline on my side.

"Are you sure?" Gen looks disappointed. "I want to help."

"Can you help me distract myself from my misery by figuring out what I'm going to do with my life?" I look at her hopefully.

"Where do we start?"

TO MY SURPRISE, Gen lets me get away with not telling her the details of what went down between Jack and me. Instead we focus on what's next. Mainly, my need for a place to live. We can't purchase internet while in the air because we'd have to use a credit card with one of our names to pay for it. Obviously, flight crew isn't allowed to be online. Rather than give up, Gen disappears into the cabin and comes back with a passenger's access code. They're multiuse, for people juggling several devices. Somehow, she has managed to talk a paying customer into sharing.

We spend the next half hour perusing rentals. I look at a few in Vegas because Gen wants me to, but I search in completely random cities, too. Austin. Seattle. Santa Fe. Even Denver.

My pride tells me I can't go there; Jack lives in Boulder, which is too close. It will look like I'm following him. But my practicality insists there are several reasons besides Jack to give Denver a try. There's a Northeast Air base there, for one. I've never been a commuter, and I don't particularly relish the idea of starting now. Then, of course, there's the plethora of hiking trails. There's also the cute room for rent I'm looking at. It's got a view of the mountains, a yard, and a potential roommate named Star, all for a price I can afford.

I bookmark it and a few others I'm interested in before the captain dings us for landing. During descent, the pictures run through my head. My heels begin to tap against the floor again, this time from excitement rather than anxiety. I have so many options. All the options in the world, really. For tonight, I'll have to stay in a hotel by the airport. They have shuttles, and several of them give us crew rates, some as low as fifty dollars per night.

I could do that for a couple of nights if I need to, but if I need more time, there are crash pads to consider. Flight attendants set them up near every base, houses with bunk beds in each of the rooms. Technically, they're for commuters, the idea being you'll only stay in them before and after your work trips when you land too late to get home or have to fly in the day before an early trip. You're not allowed to live in them. I could get one for a while, though, if I have to wait for the right rental to open up. I'd just have to double up on work trips to avoid crashing there too often. The extra income wouldn't hurt, and it would negate the need for the car, so I could wait to purchase one until I've settled somewhere.

By the time we land, I'm buzzing so much with the possibility of it all, I do the unthinkable. Instead of standing at the back of the aisle watching people jockey for a place in line like I'm supposed to, I hide in the back corner by the door of the plane and call the SleepyTime Hotel near the airport. The name alone tells me it's guaranteed to have flat pillows and a ridiculously ugly bedspread that will slip onto the floor at the merest touch. I love it already.

Three minutes later, I have a room booked, shuttle included for those of us who have just given our car keys away to our ex-fiancés. *Hello, world? It's me, Ava Greene, independent woman and professional wanderer.* I'm giddy with excitement.

I want to tell Jack. Even though he's mad at me, I have a feeling he'll appreciate my newfound lease on life. If this were a normal flight, he'd have to help straighten the plane after deplaning, forcing him to stay long enough that I could follow him to the parking lot. Since it's getting in late enough to be a terminator, meaning the plane is parking for the night, cleaners will come on and do the straightening for us. All I can do is hope he'll wait for me, despite all indications on his part to the contrary.

As if to illustrate how quickly this trip will be behind us, Gen pushes past the remaining few people trickling down the aisle.

"The last Vegas flight of the night is delayed! I might be able to make it!" She rips her bags from the overhead bin, and it falls onto the floor. Tilting it back up to a standing position with one hand and waving at me with the other, she yells, "Bye, bunny!"

"Wait!" I rip out my phone and wave it at her, not caring that the passengers can see my contraband. "Let's stay in touch."

"Really?" She stops, her mouth stretching into a pleased smile.

"Definitely." I hold out my phone for her to type in her number, but she backs down the aisle instead, calling the numbers out to me.

On the last digit, she runs into the man in the suit who used the bathroom during boarding. He's been held up by putting his shoes and socks back on.

"Don't even think about it." She wags a finger at him as she pushes past. "That number is for my friend." And then she's gone, pounding down the aisle, yelling "Move it!" at anyone unfortunate enough to be in her way.

I collect my own stuff and start up the aisle, checking the bins and under the seats to make sure no luggage has been left behind. By the time I get to the front, the plane is empty except for Captain Ballinger. Jack is gone.

I have a new friend and a new life to start, I remind myself. *I'm not sad. I'm excited.*

It's all true, but it's not enough to overcome my disappointment. I wanted Jack to change his mind. I hoped he would stay.

"Good night," I say to Captain Ballinger.

He nods without bothering to look up from his paperwork. I hurry up the jetway. At the top, the Ops agent is on his phone. He barely glances up long enough to wave me off.

The airport is winding down for the night. It's clear which airlines run red-eyes. Their gates are packed, while the others are empty except for passengers lying across multiple seats, trying to catch a nap. Most of the counters have gone dark, but the hot dog place is still open. People line up in front of it, desperate for any food they have left. It's like being in a mall at closing on Black Friday.

I pull out my phone and dial my mom as I walk. She'll love

weighing options with me, picking a new place to live as casually as one might pick a color of nail polish. Plus, I should probably let her know Alexander and I broke up.

Like her motherly instinct alerts her to the importance of my call, she answers on the first ring.

"Hi!" I chirp the word excitedly. "I'm so glad you answered!"

"Ava?" She laughs. "I was trying to video your father and must've hit the wrong button. Do you hear him?"

My enthusiasm deflates. She's answered my call by mistake. The phone fills with the sound of people like she's holding it up to a crowd, but I can't make out my dad's voice.

"I'll call you back when he's done," she says, putting the phone back to her ear. "He's singing! Isn't he the cutest? And to think I almost let him get away."

Her voice turns into a dial tone, and I keep the phone to my ear for a moment. Disappointment settles over me. I really wanted to talk to her. But it shouldn't come as a surprise that it wouldn't occur to her that I might need her. She doesn't need anyone, not when she has my father. *And to think I almost let him get away.*

Her words loop through my mind, making my brow furrow. *And to think I almost let him get away.* It's such a strange thing to say. Where would my dad have gone?

It hits me, and I can't believe I've let myself forget. I've heard their love story so many times I've stopped thinking of it as something that actually happened; it's just another anecdote to be pulled out around a campfire, something to entertain whoever they've happened to meet that day. But it's not just a story. It's a memory. Their memory.

My parents met at a bus stop in Reno. My mom was on her

way to San Francisco, and my dad was headed to Joshua Tree with a group of friends. They chatted over cheap cups of coffee and a shared piece of lemon pie. When they got to the last bite, my dad made her an offer: "Change your ticket and come with us. If you do, the last bite is yours." My mom set down her fork and pushed the plate toward him; she'd been dreaming of seeing the Bay Bridge since she was thirteen.

It wasn't until his bus started out of the lot that my mom realized what she might be giving up. She grabbed her backpack and started to run. My dad saw her through the window and yelled for the driver to stop. They changed the course of their lives that day. And they've never regretted it. I doubt they would've even if they hadn't ended up being soul mates. My parents aren't the kind of people who question their decisions. They pursue happiness at any risk. And they find it—always—in the little things and the big.

Whatever shortcomings they might have as parents, modeling a happy life has never been one of them.

My feet catch on before my head does. They start to pound against the floor in a run, propelling me forward. My bag buzzes behind me as my heart jumps to attention, banging in my chest like the beat of a drum. *Jack! Jack, Jack, Jack!* I don't care about the Bay Bridge. I don't care about my freedom, or adventure, or whatever name I'm supposed to put on it. I just want to live a happy life. I want the man with eyes the color of the sky and hair that reminds me of the wind. I want to see it all with him, do it all by his side. He may have given up on me, but I will not give up on him.

I run like my life depends on it, because I have a sneaking suspicion it actually might. I burst through the doors into the underground lot, but even when the cold hits my face, I don't slow. My trench coat flaps against my calves. My heels clack against the concrete like machine gunfire. I veer past the broken electronic walkways, up the slope, into the dark night air.

The parking lot shines from the streetlights, the parked cars gleaming beneath their glare. There are no lurkers this late. It's still and quiet except for the distant sound of a plane roaring into the air. I falter. Jack is gone. He must be gone. I would see him. I know he got a good spot. I take a few more hopeful steps, but it's pointless.

I've lost him.

Chapter 26

When I was a kid, my school had a science fair. The winner got to go to camp for the entire summer. It wasn't a subject I'd ever shown any natural aptitude for, but I'd never been to camp. I imagined it must be paradise. Eight whole weeks of roommates guaranteed to become your best friends. Scheduled activities. *Routine.*

Inspired by a stain on one of my mother's favorite tops (a strange, flowy thing that triangled out at her wrists like bell-bottoms for her arms), I came up with an idea. I'd test alternate stain removers. Not the ones in the store no one could afford, but the ones people were always suggesting on the road. Shampoo, soda water, hair spray, and baking soda. I got an old blanket and put dots of ketchup, mustard, and coffee on it. Then I tried to get rid of them.

I was delighted when I discovered hair spray was the clear winner. Hair spray was cheap. Portable. Everywhere. This would change people's lives! Brimming with confidence, I arrived at the science fair with my poster board chart under one arm and the bag containing my sample blanket on the other. I didn't even care that all the other students seemed to have family with them while I was all alone. It was better this way. Once I got to camp, I'd be the one impervious to homesickness. It would be my responsibility and privilege to console all those coddled, sheltered children.

It wasn't until Seth Errington assembled his dangling solar system next to me that I realized how amateurish my project seemed. His exhibit *moved on its own*. Mine was documented in purple marker. I'd been foolish to participate in something as beyond me as a science fair, much less to believe I could actually win. I'd missed too much school, was too far behind.

Long before the judges came around, I understood I wasn't headed to science camp. I hid my face by bending over the blanket. The red, yellow, and brown dots blurred together through my tears to form one ugly blight. For someone like me, science camp was as far away as Jupiter, the planet Seth Errington had decided to paint a deep crimson red.

Strangely, this is the memory that runs through my mind as I stand at the edge of the parking lot. I pant, winded from my run, and the night air hits my lungs like shards of glass. Sweat trickles down my face, stinging my skin. *Jack is Jupiter.* I shake away the ridiculous thought, but the thought takes advantage of my weakened state and springs back.

He *is*. Jack is Jupiter. He's still out there, orbiting, but I have no way to reach him. My best shot is to go back to work, ask around for his number, and pray someone happens to have it and is willing to give it to me. It's a crapshoot, though. There are over twelve thousand flight attendants at Northeast. Last year, the company swapped our manuals for iPads that could be updated online. Without the need for paper revisions, people don't bother going to the lounge anymore. Since it's always empty, I'll have to ask the flight attendants I pass in the airport.

I squint, seeing it play out in my mind. *Hi, coworker I flew with for three days two years ago. I know you probably don't remember me, but do you happen to know this very attractive flight attendant Jack Stone? I need his number. You see, I like him, and I'm pretty sure he likes me back. I mean, he told me he didn't want to be with me. And he didn't give me his number himself. But it's fine. He won't be mad if you pass along that personal information.*

No.

I'll be limited to asking the people I fly with, once I've spent enough time with them to convince them I'm not the type of woman who stalks men. So, new plan: there are two other flight attendants on each three-day trip. If I work a trip every week, I'll be able to ask eight people over the next month if they happen to have not only flown with Jack but also become good enough friends with him to get his contact info. I don't have any greater aptitude with numbers than I did with science, but even I understand those odds aren't encouraging.

One month. Two. I wrap my arms around myself, pulling my trench coat tighter. *How long do I have to hunt him down? How long before it's too late, before he moves on to someone new?*

I'm going to make myself sick if I keep standing here in the cold. I feel like Oliver Twist, shivering as I hold out my hands pathetically. I can't seem to make myself leave, though. I can't tear my eyes away from their hopeful scan of the parking lot. They slide back and forth, willing one of the hundreds of sets of brake lights to flare red, desperate to spot Jack's crooked smile through the windshield.

My body trembles from the wind that whips around my stockinged ankles. A particularly violent shudder knocks the last of my hope loose. My heart wrenches. *It's over.* Slowly I turn back toward the airport. I'll have to walk all the way back to Arrivals to catch my shuttle.

I hear footsteps as I near the hourly parking entrance. My stomach flips. I lift my head and see wide shoulders. My aerial stomach goes full gymnast, spinning and swooping with Olympic-level skill. The shadows clear from the man's face.

It's not Jack. It's Captain Ballinger. My stomach plummets, a heavy, match-ending fall from the high beam with no mats beneath. I force a polite, professional smile.

Have a good night, Captain Ballinger, is what I intend to say. Instead what comes out is, "Do you know Jack's number?"

My feet root into the ground, blocking his path. I cease to feel the cold. My eyes widen, and I can tell by the way Captain Ballinger's chin turtles into his neck that I must look as desperate as I feel.

He slows to a stop. "And you are?"

"Me?" Confusion peeks through my despair. "Um, I'm Ava?"

"Ava?"

I search his face, but there are no signs he's joking. "I'm the flight attendant who just worked with you for the last four days, Captain Ballinger."

His lips flatten, and his eyes flick toward my ears. "I see you took the feathers out in case you ran into a supervisor in base. I'd suggest next time you leave them at home."

"That was Gen, the other flight attendant." I wait for some evidence of embarrassment, but he merely shrugs as if to indicate we're all the same to him. "She's a foot taller than me? Her hair is blond instead of brown?"

His brow furrows like he's trying to determine why I'm still talking to him. "Fine. You were the one who almost missed the van. And?"

"I didn't miss it, though. I just . . ." I shake my head. *Stay on track, Ava!* "I know it's a long shot, but I need to get in touch with Jack. Is there any chance you know his number?"

"Do I . . ." A smile flickers across his face, disappearing again so quickly I wonder if I've imagined it. "Jack is the man who was working in back with you?"

My chest tightens as I nod.

"And you think I might have sought him out at some point during the last four days and inquired after his phone number?"

My shoulders droop. "I was hoping . . . maybe . . ." *In case of emergency?* It's too silly to say aloud. There are protocols set up for special situations like that. He'd call Scheduling, and they'd reach out to whoever needs to be contacted.

"Shockingly, I did not." He tips his captain's hat. "Now, if you'll excuse me."

I nod and slump out of his way. I don't know why I feel so let down. I was clearly grasping at straws with Captain Ballinger. They say grief comes in stages, though. This must be what denial feels like.

I need to move on to the burying-your-sorrows-in-junk-food stage. I should stop for provisions while I'm still at the airport. If I load my stomach down with carbs, maybe it will abandon its Olympic aspirations and calm down. Nothing I passed on my way out sounds good, though. I could walk over to terminal A. I think there's a Hanson News that stays open late. They have all sorts of packaged snacks. And the pizza place might still be open. To show its displeasure at my desire to thwart its activity, my stomach turns. It's pointless anyway.

I'm too miserable to eat anything, much less a slice of greasy pizza.

Something tickles at my mind, and my head jerks up.

Pizza.

Jack said something about eating pizza after every trip. I squeeze my eyes shut and try to think. *When?* He said it when he was irritating me with all those questions, back when I didn't want to admit I liked him and didn't feel compelled to listen to half of what he said. My fingernails press into my palms. This is what karma feels like, isn't it? I'm going to miss my last chance with him because I was such a jerk in the beginning. *Fine.* I was a jerk in the middle, too. I've been a jerk practically the whole time I've known him.

Firenzo's!

Jack goes to Firenzo's, a by-the-slice pizza joint near the airport. I reach for my phone, but my fingers are frozen. They fumble impotently at the slick sides. I grit my teeth and focus, gripping it tightly and wrenching it out of my coat pocket. A quick map search tells me Firenzo's is only eleven minutes away. Headlights wash over me as Captain Ballinger's car heads toward the exit. My eyes narrow. I've seen Jack eat. He inhales his food like a python, and pizza by the slice is already cooked. He could be in and out of that place in ten minutes.

I grab the handle of my roller bag and run toward Captain Ballinger's car. But like a maniac, I run *right at it.* I am the deer in the road, the foolish animal playing chicken with a metal beast five times its size. Professionalism has taken a backseat. Actually, it's in my rearview mirror, a tiny speck in the distance. I lift my free hand above my head as I run, waving it frantically.

For a moment, Captain Ballinger shows no signs of stopping. He actually seems to speed up the tiniest bit. Our eyes meet, and I see it—how shocked he is by my behavior, how appalled. I can only imagine he spots the complete lack of caring or survival instinct in me because he gives in, slamming on the brakes at the last possible minute. His car screeches to a halt mere inches from my knees.

"Are you out of your mind?" His question gains volume the farther down his window rolls. Once it's fully open, he leans out. "Are you entirely insane?"

"I'm so sorry," I say, scurrying to his side of the car. "But I need you. You have to help me. Please."

"What's wrong?" There's a shift in his tone. He sounds almost concerned. "Is there someone out here? Do you feel unsafe?"

He's looking at me so intently I lose my words. It's the first time since we met that I feel like Captain Ballinger actually sees me as a real person standing in front of him. "Um . . ."

"I am your captain," he says. "If you're in danger, it's my duty to protect you."

I blink in the face of such self-perceived responsibility.

"Well . . ." Every part of me yearns to take advantage of this chink in his armor. I *am* in danger . . . of losing Jack. Unfortunately, I'm acutely aware Captain Ballinger wouldn't care if I died loveless and alone with an army of roaches using my body as a jungle gym. He is obligated to me only as far as our trip reaches. This parking lot is probably at the farthermost edge of the border.

Impatience tightens his features. I'm losing him.

"I'm scared." I flinch in the wake of my blatant manipulation. It's not a lie, though. I *am* scared. I'm terrified this opportunity will pass and I'll lose Jack for good. "Can you get me out of here, please? I just need a ride down the road."

"You want to get in my car?" Out of his mouth, it sounds more like *You want to spray-paint neon flowers all over my car?*

"Yes," I say. "Please."

"But I'm a stranger." He frowns his disapproval. "You don't know me."

"I just spent four days with you."

His frown deepens, and my back stiffens. We're wasting time, and he's not going to help me. Car rides are beyond a captain's duty, apparently. Never mind that he's not just a captain, that he's also supposed to be human.

"I *should* know you," I say. "You and I traveled together. We went to another country. The last few days have changed my life. I got engaged. I went on adventures. I got stranded—twice. I fell for someone. I blew up my entire life, ending things with my fiancé and losing my car and my home. To you, I don't even exist. But there are real, living people on the other side of that cockpit door, and I'm one of them. And I'm standing here, asking you for a simple favor, so pop your trunk, unlock your doors, and *give me a freaking ride*!"

Captain Ballinger's eyes widen in response to my outburst, and I meet them with wide eyes of my own. My hands are on my waist and my heart is pounding. It's Gen's overturned tray all over again. I'm out of control, and I know I should apologize.

But I don't want to.

Instead I tilt my chin toward the trunk. Captain Ballinger leans forward, breaking our gaze. The trunk pops open with a satisfying click. I nod at him and wheel my bag past, waiting until he can't see me before allowing my smile to stretch across my face. *I'm going to find Jack!*

Unsurprisingly, Captain Ballinger's trunk is pristine and empty aside from his own roller bag. I slide mine in beside it, set my tote and food bag on top, and scurry to the passenger seat. The inside of the car is fantastically warm. It smells new, like fresh upholstery.

"Thank you," I say, settling in and reaching for the seat belt. "I really appreciate it. Do you know where Firenzo's is?"

"The pizza place?"

"Yes." I know from my quick search on my phone there's only one nearby. "The one that sells by the slice."

"It's on my way home." His voice lowers to a mutter. "Not that you'd care if it were out of the way."

"What was that?" My words are sharper than they have any right to be.

"Nothing."

Once again, I find myself holding in my smile. Captain Ballinger isn't as impervious to other people as he pretends to be. He might even be a bit of a softie. The car coasts out of the lot, its engine a gentle purr.

"So," I say as we turn out of the airport, "what's your story? You clearly live around here. Are you married? Kids?"

"I'd prefer to keep my personal life personal." His gaze remains locked on the road in front of us, his hands in the ten-and-two position on the wheel. "And before you're tempted to chastise me again, I'd like to remind you I'm currently in the process of doing you a favor."

Nope. Not a softie.

"Understood," I say. "Do you want to hear the reason we're going to Firenzo's?"

"Not particularly."

"Music, then?"

Captain Ballinger clicks a button on his steering wheel, and music fills the car. To my surprise, it's not some classical, instrumental piece I've never heard. It's the soppy, soaring melody of "My Endless Love." I wait for him to change it, but instead he turns it up. Streetlights illuminate the interior of the car in brief flashes as we pass. The heat blasting from the vents thaws my icy skin. I pull up Firenzo's on my phone and start the directions, muting the voice so Captain Ballinger doesn't take offense. I just need to make sure we don't accidentally deviate from the course.

Nine minutes. My hands wring together anxiously. I glance at the speedometer on the other side of the dashboard. Naturally we're going the exact speed limit.

"So, Captain Ballinger," I say, "the thing is, the person I'm meeting isn't necessarily going to stay at Firenzo's to wait for me. Do you think you could speed up just—"

"No." He cuts me off. "And what do you mean, they're not going to stay?"

"Nothing. It's fine. He'll be there."

He will be there. And it is fine. Jack left, what? Ten minutes before us? We'll catch him. We have to. To distract myself, I begin to hum along to the song.

I'm expecting Captain Ballinger to stop me, but to my shock, he begins to sing along with my humming. His voice is deep and out of tune. My eyes flick anxiously from the windshield to the window beside me and back again. Nerves wreak havoc in the pit of my stomach. To bury them, I begin to sing with him.

My voice is much higher-pitched but equally out of tune. The song swells, and we both get louder. By the time it ends, we're belting out the words like opera singers. I sneak a peek at Captain Ballinger, but his gaze doesn't falter from its locked position on the road. Somehow, his expression is as professionally detached as always.

"That's 'My Endless Love' going out to Jessica from Mason," says a female voice on the radio. I recognize it immediately as Layla Day, the host of the show I was listening to when I battled for the parking spot with Jack. "While it was playing, we got a call from Jessica, the recipient of Mason's endless love. Jessica, are you on the line?"

"I'm here, Layla," a young voice says.

"Welcome, Jessica. And might I ask, why are you calling me right now instead of Mason?"

"I just couldn't decide if I should forgive him or not, and I thought maybe you could help."

"What has Mason done to upset you?"

"He forgot our anniversary," Jessica says. "Our six-week anniversary! Can you believe it? That's a big one."

I groan, but Captain Ballinger doesn't acknowledge her silliness.

"Well, Jessica, let me ask you something." Layla's voice is warm and comforting, completely lacking condescension. "Excepting that particular day, does Mason make you feel special? These last six weeks, has he made you feel cared for? Or does he often make you feel forgotten?"

"Oh," Jessica says, "he's usually wonderful! He makes me feel so loved."

"Then I think you have your answer. Relationships aren't made up of a single day. They're a collection of moments and feelings. If you care for Mason, and he cares for you, do you really want to fight over a mistake that was made in a single moment?"

Captain Ballinger sighs.

"It's your car," I say. "You can change the station if you want."

"Are you kidding?" He sounds appalled. "Why would I change the station? That woman is brilliant. She always gives the most insightful advice."

If I weren't so anxious, I'd have to hold in a laugh. "Well, she has been giving it out for an eternity. I used to listen to this show when I was a teenager, hoping against hope someone would call in about me. Teenage narcissism at its most intense. Layla is qualified, too. Did you know she's been married forever? If I remember correctly, she married her college boyfriend."

"It was her high school sweetheart, actually," he says. "And they have seven children. Layla does the show from her basement so she doesn't have to leave them."

My eyebrows shoot up, but I manage to restrain myself from teasing him about his extensive knowledge about a loveline host. "That's sweet."

"Shh. Jessica wants to dedicate a song to Mason."

This time I do laugh, but Captain Ballinger is too intent on the radio to notice. "I Will Always Love You" by Whitney Houston comes on. I look back down at the map in my lap. *Four minutes.* Two hundred and forty seconds until I find out if I've lost Jack, possibly forever. I sing along with Whitney, our voices so high-pitched I wonder if we're actually yodeling. Amazingly, Captain Ballinger sings with me instead of shoving me out of the moving vehicle.

We're at full intensity in both volume and passion when the captain turns left into a parking lot. A red-and-white-checkered sign has the word *Firenzo's* written across it in black lettering. Windows glowing with yellowed light line the front, the tops of red vinyl booths peeping through. There are only two cars in the lot. One of them is old and brown and looks like it has seen the world.

The last time I saw it was when I was willing to smash into it to get a parking spot.

"He's here!" I reach for the door handle, pulling it before the car has slowed to a stop.

"Whoa!" Captain Ballinger slams on his brakes as the car beeps its warning. Cold air rushes in.

"I'm sorry. But thank you. Thank you, thank you, thank you!" If he were anyone else, I'd reach over and hug him. Instead I say, "May Layla Day bless you always!"

I jump out and run to his trunk. I'm tugging my bags out when he appears beside me.

"Do you need me to wait?" He takes my tote from my hands and slides it over the handle of my roller. "It doesn't sound like this is a guaranteed ride."

"It will be fine." I'm not being overly optimistic, just practical. I didn't have the time to wait for a taxi to bring me here, but if Jack turns me down, I'll have all the time in the world. I'll just have one take me back to the hotel. "Thank you, though. It means a lot that you'd offer."

"Well"—Captain Ballinger offers me a sheepish smile—"I know you now."

I tilt my head. I still know nothing about his life, nor does he know anything about mine. But we've sung together, albeit badly, so I guess that counts for something. I hug him before he can stop me, squeezing him for the briefest moment before letting him go.

"Wish me luck," I say, stepping back.

He grimaces. "I don't believe in luck."

"Of course you don't." I grin and turn away, dragging my bags behind me. My breath catches in my throat as I scan the windows. Nerves flutter in my stomach. I don't see Jack, but he's in there. He has to be.

I push open the heavy, dark green door and am greeted by a warm blast of air and the mouthwatering aroma of garlic and oregano. A man behind the counter calls out a greeting, but I'm already scanning the room, desperately searching for Jack. The booths are empty, save for one. There, in the corner, a man sits with his back to me. His dark head is bent so that I can't see if his hair is windswept from the cold night air.

My breath catches, and I start toward him. He looks up at the sound of my heels clicking against the floor. His head turns, and my heart skips a beat at the familiar face. It's Jack. Jupiter Jack. Jack Stone. Surprise flashes across his face, and he tosses the napkin in his hand on the empty plate in front of him.

"Hi." I feel light-headed, and it suddenly occurs to me how unstable I must seem. Is this stalking? Am I a stalker now?

Jack's face turns unreadable. "What are you doing here?"

"You told me this place had the best pizza." I slide into the seat across from him, scooting over the long tear in the vinyl. "I wanted to try it."

"Okay." His eyes don't quite meet mine. They focus on a spot just to the left of my ear, and I stare at them, trying to decipher the weather behind the cloudy blue. "Well, I'd invite you to join me, but I've just finished up."

"I'm lying." I exhale loudly. "I don't want pizza. I want you."

"What?"

"I raced here so I could catch you. I was worried I'd never see you again."

"Ava." He shakes his head, and my heart cracks.

"I know. You told me how you felt. That you didn't want to be with me." I lean forward, forcing him to look at me. "But you also told me there's something between us. How was I supposed to know which speech to listen to?"

A smile tugs at the corner of his mouth, but it doesn't travel up to his eyes. "It's generally understood that the most recent words are the best indicator of the current situation."

"But that was just a moment. A single moment against all the other moments when you wanted this. I messed up, Jack, but is what I did really so unforgivable?"

"No." His voice softens. "It's not."

"Then give me another chance." My voice cracks. "Please."

"I'm sorry." To his credit, Jack does actually look sorry. His mouth is tight, and his head droops. "It's not you. It's me. I just . . . can't. The secrets . . ." He shakes his head and stands up, collecting his trash with intense concentration. When he has nothing left to collect, he turns slowly and meets my eyes. "As much as I wish I could, I can't begin something with you when I'm already wondering what else I don't know. It's not fair to either of us."

"But . . ."

"It was a hell of a layover, though, wasn't it?" He offers a sad smile. "I know I'll never forget it."

I stay seated as he walks away. I couldn't move if I wanted to. I feel like he's knocked the wind out of me. *Breathe in. Breathe out.* Tears collect in the corners of my eyes, but I blink them back. I've cried enough. I did everything I could. I tried my hardest. I pull my phone out to order a ride, but I can't concentrate. I tilt my head back against the booth and stare up at the ceiling. There's a brown watermark in the shape of a caterpillar.

"Ava?"

I whirl at the sound of his voice and almost hit my chin against the back of the booth. Hope blooms in my chest.

He looks at me questioningly. "Your car isn't outside."

The hope withers. "I know. I gave the keys back to Alexander."

"Then how did you get here?"

"Captain Ballinger brought me." I note the skepticism that appears on Jack's face and can't resist rubbing it in. "Unlike some people, he seemed excited for the opportunity to spend more time with me."

Jack lifts an eyebrow. "Really?"

"No," I admit. "But he did turn out to be a pretty cool guy. He didn't leave me stranded in a parking lot, at least. And he's got an impressive memory for old love-song lyrics."

We share a brief smile, but when Jack's fades, I can tell he won't prolong the conversation by asking for details.

"Do you need a ride somewhere?" he asks, proving me right.

"No, thanks."

"Come on, Ava." His voice turns coaxing. "I can't leave you here with no car. Just let me drop you off somewhere."

He looks so earnest, so impossibly kind, that I feel a spark of anger. If he's determined to leave me, why won't he just go? Conveniently ignoring the fact that he did, in fact, try to go, and I managed to chase him here, I allow myself to dive deeper into this new narrative. Jack Stone is the worst, trying to rub in my face what a nice guy he is. He just wants to make sure I know what I've lost.

"Ugh." I groan the word and roll my eyes.

Jack's head tilts back in surprise. "Did you just *ugh* me? For trying to give you a ride?"

"I *get it*," I say. "You want to rub in how wonderful you are. But you're not perfect, you know."

His mouth curls. "Oh, trust me. I'm aware."

I stand up, facing him, and put my hands on my hips. "And you were the one who lied."

"Me? What did I lie about?"

"You told me you know me." I huff out my annoyance. "You insisted it, in fact. But you didn't know me. If you did, you'd know I'm not the kind of person who lies or keeps secrets. The Alexander situation? That wasn't a secret. It wasn't even an omission. It was me trying to become someone else. Nothing about that belonged in our world because, with you, I was content to be myself.

"I showed you exactly who I am," I say. "I'm a woman who asks strangers for a ride to see the bioluminescence. I'm prone to wander out into the world without knowing where I'm going, and while I'm gone, I often forget to answer the phone and tell people I'm okay. I am territorial about my food. And, apparently, I've recently become something of a live wire. Those are the things you should count against me, not some inherited hang-up from your ex-girlfriend."

His chin tilts up. "An inherited hang-up?"

"That's how I see it. My shortcomings are real, but I'm fully capable and willing to have an honest relationship."

"Just not one where you share your food." He takes a step toward me, and my stomach leaps to attention.

"We weren't made to share food, Jack. Eve gave Adam a bite of her apple, and God punished them both."

"I'm not sure you read that story right."

"Another thing to add to my list of shortcomings," I say. "When do we get to talk about yours?"

"I think we've already begun. Apparently, I tend to project inherited hang-ups on potential girlfriends."

"Yeah, well, sometimes it's an understandable mistake." I shrug. "You know, like if you find out she's neglected to tell you about the years she spent in prison. Or she's hiding a secret fiancé."

A smile tugs at Jack's mouth. He takes another step forward, so close we're almost touching. "So, is it just the fiancé I'm supposed to overlook, or do you also have a history of crime you need to confess to?"

I try to think of something clever to say, but his sudden proximity sends all my energy toward the effort of breathing. "Just the fiancé."

"You're saying it could be worse then." Jack murmurs the words, and his gaze drops to my lips. Like some kind of Pavlovian response that only happens with him, my tongue slips a line across them. "I guess it's possible I've overreacted."

I tilt my head up, and our eyes meet. "Is it too late to fix it?"

"I hope not." His hand slips around the back of my neck, and he pulls me to him.

For a moment, our mouths hover a breath apart. I can smell him, cedar and leather and the salty sea air, and I yearn to snort him like a drug and feel him course through my veins. The thought makes me laugh—it feels like the kind of thing Gen would think, not me—and Jack pulls back at the sound. But I'm too quick. I tug him toward me and crush my mouth against his.

Then all thoughts of laughter fade. There's nothing funny about the heat of his tongue slipping against mine or the way our bodies press together. It's just intensity and reassurance and a deep sense of relief.

A polite cough from behind the counter breaks us apart.

Jack glances over his shoulder and calls out, "Sorry, Sal," before dropping his forehead lightly against mine. "We should go."

"Where?"

"Where do you want to go?"

"Hiking."

"It's kind of dark for that."

"We've got a long drive to get there."

Jack grins. "Then we better get started."

My eyes catch on his mouth. "I did book a hotel room ten minutes from here."

"Really?" He meets my eyes, and his darken in a way that makes my skin tingle.

I nod, but I can feel the reluctance that tightens the movement. It has surfaced from nowhere, surprising and baffling me. The road calls, but I'd gladly give it up to explore the six feet of tanned skin in front of me.

It's not Jack that's giving me pause; it's the place.

Chicago belongs to the person I thought I wanted to become. It belongs to Alexander. It's my past, not my future. And I don't want to stay here another minute.

"We could stay somewhere else, though." I search his face for disappointment, only to discover him studying mine. "Some motel in a little town with a blinking neon sign out front."

He's silent for a moment.

Slowly he nods. "The kind of place you'd find on the road, instead of by the same airport we've driven to a million times before?"

Warmth blooms in my chest. "Exactly."

"We haven't had much sleep, though." He slips his hand

through mine and tugs me toward the door. "We'd better stop for gas station cherry pies to keep our energy up."

My heart soars, and I laugh, tossing off a wave at Sal before the door swings closed behind me. The cold air hits my skin, but it's undaunting. Jack opens the passenger door and waves me in, closing it gently behind me. The backseat is full of all the things he's packed for his final drive to Colorado. It smells like old French fries, but I love it. I squirm in the seat, overwhelmed with the excitement of our impending adventure.

The door to the backseat on the other side of the car opens, and Jack slides my bag on top of a pile of boxes. He has to use his shoulder to shove it all the way in, but it settles into place with a defeated creak. I clap enthusiastically, and Jack bows before swinging the door shut. He climbs in next to me and fires up the engine.

I reach for the radio and scan the stations to find *In Love with Layla* as he turns out of the parking lot. We don't talk about directions or try to figure out exactly where we're going because it doesn't matter. We're just *going*. If this were a romantic comedy, we'd be headed into the sunset. But it's not. It's the story of us, two wanderers, brought together by fate. Where else would we be than here, in the dark, sharing the road with the other misfits of the world?

Epilogue

They insisted it was going to rain today, but it hasn't. The sky is belligerently blue, sunlight burning off any clouds that try to form. It stretches out like a promise above us, a sign that things don't always happen like you think they're going to. Thank goodness, because the tents were ordered too late. The ceremony is already in progress, and they're not scheduled to arrive until tomorrow at noon.

The cool spring breeze catches at the bottom of my yellow thrift-store dress and sends it swirling around my knees. In front of us, a hundred matching wooden chairs are lined in rows across the grass, filled with a wild, eclectic mix of people. A girl named Emmy catches my eye and waves excitedly. Her hair is newly dyed purple, but her smile is as contagious as ever. We met at work a few months after the layover that changed my life, and even though we live in different cities, we've managed to become good friends. I wriggle my fingers back at her in a sneaky wave before I direct all my attention toward the wildflower-lined aisle.

An electric guitar cuts through the fresh Wisconsin air, and Gen steps into view, causing everyone to erupt into applause. I whoop aloud, clapping so hard my hands sting. It's impossible not to. She's wearing a fuchsia wedding dress that's split into a crop top and a bottom that resembles a tutu, no shoes, and movie-star sunglasses. At our cheers, she raises her arms into a victory V above her head and sashays down the aisle, stopping to high-five people in different rows. Across from me, Jack lets out a piercing whistle and slaps Pilot Paul on the back.

Paul steps forward like he can't wait, like he's going to run down the aisle to meet her halfway. He looks like a man who has just won the lottery. Somehow, though, he manages to restrain himself. He lets Gen come to him. And with a complete lack of restraint of her own, she wraps her arms around him and kisses him passionately.

Arm in arm, they turn toward the Elvis impersonator officiating the wedding. I look to Jack, wondering if he, too, is thinking of the Pen Plan. I know we could never take credit for something as perfect and destined as this union, but still. I love our part in Gen and Pilot Paul's story.

Jack's eyes meet mine, and even from here, I can tell that his have taken on the color of the sky. His shoulders are military-straight under the white linen shirt, but his thick dark hair flutters in the breeze. He's so handsome it makes my chest squeeze. His mouth stretches into his full, crooked smile, and it occurs to me, not for the first time, that I will love this man for the rest of my life.

"THEY LOOK SO happy together." Emmy gazes wistfully at Gen and Paul.

We're at the reception, which is outdoors and still tentless. Thankfully, the weather has held. The sun is beginning its slow descent, burning streaks of orange through the sky, but it's still bright enough out to highlight the grassy field that stretches out beyond the party. A slow song is playing, and Gen's head is resting on Paul's shoulder as they sway from side to side. They both look exhausted but deeply content. It's been a long and wonderful day.

"You should've seen them planning the destinations for their road trip," I say. "They were so happy about discovering the World's Largest Can of Spinach that I had to take their car keys away so they wouldn't skip the wedding and start their honeymoon early."

I fork a bite of neon-orange wedding cake into my mouth, and my lips pucker at the taste. It's kind of like sherbet but different. Sweeter, maybe? Or tarter? I keep telling myself I don't like it, but this is my second piece, so it's possible I do. I wish Jack were here. He'd take it away and make me dance. And then, once we'd worked up an appetite, he'd get two more pieces for each of us and make me race him to see who could finish first. By the end, I wouldn't care what it tasted like.

Jack snuck out after the ceremony, though. He left with a whispered "I didn't think it was possible to upstage the bride, but the whole time Elvis was speaking, I couldn't tear my eyes away from you in that dress."

It's strange not being able to swap smiles with him when Gen's niece makes me laugh with her robotic dance moves or someone's purse-dog leaps on the table to nab a leftover bread roll. I'm not used to being without him. Despite living together in our one-bedroom apartment in Boulder, we can't seem to resist trading into each other's work trips so we can be on the road together, too. The opportunity to explore other cities on the company's dime is too good. Not to mention the appeal of room service and lazy layovers in bed.

Sometimes we even manage to score overnights in Portland to see his dad, or we'll catch my parents wherever they happen to be. Jack is great at keeping them on a military-tight schedule. And it turns out R.J. is much more open to dinner when it involves him stealing food from my plate.

The alarm on my phone beeps, and my stomach flutters.

"Can you excuse me for a minute?" At Emmy's nod, I put my cake down on a nearby table and make my way hesitantly toward the band.

They're on a stage that's only about a foot off the ground, but it's still intimidating. I'm not the maid of honor, so I didn't expect to make a speech, but Gen asked me to. I did remind her that, without uniform bridesmaids' dresses, everyone would just assume I've gotten drunk and wandered up to the mic, but she only laughed and said, "Perfect. That's exactly who I'd want to speak for me on my special day."

I wave at the singer, and he squints at me through heavily lined eyes. His long black hair falls into his face as he bends forward to croon the final note, and then he curls a finger my way. The nail on it is painted black. I glance down at my phone before I go up. I'm right on time, but I look to the sky nervously anyway. *It's out of my hands now.* I can only do my part and trust that the rest will work out.

I take the mic, and it's heavier than I expected. The revelers are already turning my way. I shift from one foot to the other and lift the mic to my mouth. There's a hint of chill in the air now that the sun is going down, but I've started to sweat.

"Hi," I say weakly.

A few friendly faces call out "Hi" in return. Gen is one of them. She turns and leans her back into Paul, and he wraps his arms around her waist.

"I just wanted to say that I'm so happy for the two of you." The speech I've prepared flees my mind, and my stomach sinks. I blink at the crowd before lifting my eyes to the sky again. I want to hear the buzz so badly that, at first, I think I'm imagining it. But there it is, distant but unmistakable. Jack's face flashes through my mind, and a thrill goes through me. I stand a little straighter, and my voice strengthens. I don't need a speech. I just need to speak from my heart.

"Gen and Paul, I've been lucky enough to get to know both of you so much better over the last year, and you have become two of my favorite people." I clear my throat. "Gen, you have this amazing ability to live life to its fullest. You approach the world with an excitement that's contagious. And Paul, you are one of the kindest people I've ever come across. Your heart is so big. But the best thing about you both is your optimism. You have this way of always looking for the best in life. You expect it. And you find it. Every day, you manage to find it. And now you've found each other."

The buzzing grows louder, filling the sky, and a smile breaks across my face as I look up and spot the little green-and-white Cessna headed our way. Some people look up, but Gen and Paul are focused on me.

"This has been the best wedding I've ever been to," I say. "Because it's such a perfect representation of each of you. But one thing is missing. Gen, you told me on the jump seat once that your wedding would be full of glitter. Well . . ."

I wave up toward the sky just as Jack dips the plane toward us. With perfect timing, biodegradable glitter begins to float down from the sky. It shimmers in the sunset, otherworldly. There's a moment of shocked silence before the crowd erupts.

People begin to cheer. Paul lifts Gen in the air and spins her around. The band starts back up, and the singer pulls the mic from my hand, but I barely notice. I don't move from the stage because I can hardly breathe with how well it's turned out, how magical.

I wish Jack could be here to see the shiny flakes dancing down, but they all will have settled by the time he returns. He won't care. He'll just swing an arm around my waist and most likely tease me by pretending this was his idea instead of mine. I care that he's missing it, though. It's the best representation I've ever seen of what it feels like having him in my life. Because this isn't the first time Jack Stone has made my world shimmer with magic.

He's managed to do it every day since we took to the road together.

Acknowledgments

They say, "Write what you know." I thought that meant flying but quickly came to realize it meant love. Isaac Waldon, I love you. You are my best friend and my partner in crime, and the day I met you is the day my world took on a brighter hue. Thank you for making my life feel like a never-ending adventure. And thank you for plotting every one of my story ideas. If I were a better person (and you weren't already crushing me in height, fitness, and scholarly pursuits), I'd totally give you the coauthor credit you deserve.

I spent hours upon hours writing in hotel rooms and jotting down notes on napkins in the back of the plane. It was a hobby that traveled well. But I'm not sure I ever allowed myself to believe it might one day turn into an actual book, on shelves, to be read by other people. Thank you to my agent, Claire Friedman, for first giving me hope, then delivering on such an incredible dream. You have been my champion, my writing partner, and most importantly, you have become my friend. Now please, stop setting buildings on fire. It's dangerous, and you know I feel left out when you do fun things without me.

Thanks to my editor, Margo Lipschultz, and her assistant,

Patricja Okuniewska, for their endless support, enthusiasm, and determination to shape this book into the best possible version of itself. Thanks to everyone at Putnam for gifting me with their talent and hard work. I feel so lucky to be part of such a dynamic team.

Thanks to Amanda Lomax, Tina Quigley, Keri Francisco, Autumn Christensen, and Christina Babcock for starting this journey with me and being willing to slog through the books that didn't make it. Your insights guided me in my future efforts, but it was your enthusiasm and unwarranted praise that gave me the strength to keep going. I will forever be grateful to have found you guys. You are my people.

Thank you to Jane and Bob Anastario for being the best parents a girl could ever ask for. And to Staci Smith, Missi LeGrand, and Carey Page for being the best sisters. I love you.

Thank you to the people who have popped up along the way and become a huge part of my writing journey. Shaylin Ghandi, you're the greatest. Katy Sweet, your hair looks nice today. Susan Waters, I always enjoy the laughs, but it's your suggested ending to this book that's earned my eternal gratitude. The Ladies' Literary Salon (sorry, Josh and Tae, but I'll never be able to call it anything else—blame Betsy's husband), thanks for letting me ramble endlessly during the querying/submission days and for inspiring me with your own submissions.

Thanks to the Staley family for getting me through more than one bout of writer's block. And thanks to Jamie and Dana in particular, just for being great. I hope we can stay friends forever, but if Jamie continues to surpass me in Isaac's affections, we probably won't.

Writing is a lonely endeavor. Thank you to all the friends who made it feel less so.

Discussion Questions

1. When we first meet our heroine, Ava, what is her stance on her career and relationship? Could you relate to her reasoning for wanting to change the trajectory of her life?

2. What is Ava's relationship with her parents like? How does her childhood influence the decisions she makes as an adult? Similarly, discuss how Jack's relationship with his father is portrayed in the book.

3. What turns Ava off from Jack initially? How does he develop as the hero of the story the more we learn about him and his past? How did your opinion of him change?

4. Discuss the differences between Jack and Alexander. Why is Alexander not the right choice for Ava, and how does she come to realize that?

5. In addition to Ava and Jack, *The Layover* has many memorable secondary characters, including Gen, Pilot Paul, R.J., Captain Ballinger, and Celeste and Eddie. Who were some of your favorites, and how do they contribute to Ava's journey?

6. Like Ava, author Lacie Waldon is a veteran flight attendant. Did you discover anything new or surprising about how flight attendants operate from *The Layover*? How did your perceptions of the airline industry change?

7. As referenced in the title, *The Layover*'s characters get stranded in Belize for twenty-four hours. What does Ava's time there ultimately teach her about what she wants out of life? How does the trip affect Jack and Ava's relationship?

8. At first, Ava thinks she wants to live a safe, structured life, but how does her journey teach her that unpredictability could be a good thing? Are you a wanderer at heart like Ava is, or do you prefer stability?

9. What is your dream layover, and why?

Lacie Waldon is a writer with her head in the clouds—literally. A flight attendant based in Washington, D.C., Waldon spends her days writing from the jump seat and searching the world for new stories. *The Layover* is her debut novel.

VISIT LACIE WALDON ONLINE

laciewaldon.com
LacieWaldon